D0282875

DEATH GRIP

DEATH GRIP

Elaine Viets

This first world edition published 2020
in Great Britain and 2021 in the USA by
SEVERN HOUSE PUBLISHERS LTD of
Eardley House, 4 Uxbridge Street, London W8 7SY.
Trade paperback edition first published
in Great Britain and the USA 2021 by
SEVERN HOUSE PUBLISHERS LTD.

British Library Cataloguing in Publication Data
A CIP catalogue record for this title is available from the British Library.

ISBN-13: 978-0-7278-9018-4 (cased)
ISBN-13: 978-1-78029-755-2 (trade paper)
ISBN-13: 978-1-4483-0493-6 (e-book)

All Severn House titles are printed on acid-free paper.

Typeset by Palimpsest Book Production Ltd.,
Falkirk, Stirlingshire, Scotland.
Printed and bound in Great Britain by
TJ Books Limited, Padstow, Cornwall.

For my Don, with love and thanks.

ACKNOWLEDGMENTS

Chouteau County, Missouri, guards its secrets. The local robber barons hang onto their money, their grudges, their sins and scandals. When some of those buried secrets are accidentally unearthed in *Death Grip*, Angela Richman tries to bring a killer to justice.

Investigating a murder is difficult and intricate work, and I wanted to show that. Special thanks to Dr Sharon L. Plotkin, certified crime scene investigator and professor at the Miami Dade College School of Justice, who read my crime scenes for accuracy. Detective R.C. White, Fort Lauderdale Police Department (retired) and licensed private eye, provided hours of advice and help. Thank you to death investigator Krysten Addison and Harold R. Messler, retired manager-criminalistics, St. Louis Police Laboratory. Gregg E. Brickman, author of *Imperfect Escape*, helped me kill off my characters. These experts helped me strive for accuracy, but all mistakes are mine.

Many other people helped with *Death Grip*. Most important is my husband, Don Crinklaw, my first reader and best critiquer.

Thanks also to my agent, Joshua Bilmes, president of JABberwocky Literary Agency, and the entire JABberwocky team. Joshua reads my novels and gives me detailed suggestions to improve them.

Thanks to the Severn House staff, especially editor Sara Porter, whose deft editing was helpful, as well as copyeditor Loma Halden. Cover designer Piers Tilbury perfectly captured my book.

Sarah E.C. Byrne made a generous donation to charity to have her name in this novel. She's a lawyer from Canberra, Australia, and a crime fiction aficionada.

I'm grateful to Judge Bill Hopkins, Will Graham, Alan Portman, and Joanna Campbell Slan – author of *Ruff Justice*; Jinny Gender, Alison McMahan, Dana Cameron, author of the Emma Fielding archaeology mysteries; and Marcia Talley, author of *Tangled Roots*. Special thanks to the many librarians, including those at the Broward County library and St. Louis and St. Louis County, who answered my questions, no matter how ridiculous they sounded. I could not survive without the help and encouragement of librarians. There are more people who helped, but they need to be anonymous.

Please enjoy Angela Richman's latest adventure. Email me at eviets@aol.com

ONE

If it hadn't rained for six days that spring, we might never have found the bodies. Chouteau County guarded its secrets. The local robber barons hung onto their money, their grudges, their sins and scandals.

But outsider Liz Loconto hiked deep into the woods that ran between the mansions, where almost no one went. Maybe she believed our woods would somehow be better.

When Liz first saw the hand sticking out of the washout in the creek, she thought it was a twig. When she looked closer and saw the arm bones, she figured it was an old Halloween decoration. But then Liz edged closer, lost her balance and slid down the muddy creek bed. That's when she realized the bony hand was real – and attached to a body. A dead body.

Liz was still screaming when she called 911 on her cell phone. And that's how I wound up trudging through the Missouri woods. I'm Angela Richman, Chouteau County, Missouri, death investigator. I work for the medical examiner's office, and I'm in charge of the bodies at the crime scene. Chouteau County is about thirty miles west of St. Louis, and Chouteau Forest is its biggest town. We're an exclusive pocket of white privilege.

I was lucky that Detective Jace Budewitz caught this case – he's one of the best on the Chouteau Forest force. I was on call that April afternoon and he gave me the news about six-thirty. Jace is a Chicago transplant, used to the toughest neighborhoods in that city. He's starting to learn that the Forest isn't all that different – we simply have better-dressed thugs.

'It's a bad scene, Angela,' he said. 'A hiker has found one body, but we have some indications there may be more. I've brought in the cadaver dogs.'

'Are we getting Nitpicker?' I asked. Sarah 'Nitpicker' Byrne was the Forest's top CSI tech. It would take days to retrieve the body and the evidence.

'She's on her way,' he said. 'Nitpicker's extra careful, so no evidence will be lost.'

'I'll get my things,' I said. 'Where are you?'

Jace gave me the closest intersection, then said, 'It's way back in the woods. I'm surprised the witness stumbled on the victim. I'll have a uniform waiting to take you back. Wear your oldest clothes and boots – it's muddy. And you'll need to wear protection. The decedent is badly decomposed.'

I made sure I had a jumpsuit with a hood, as well as gloves, goggles and a face mask. I could get tuberculosis and other diseases from contact with a decomposing body. Then I threw on jeans, boots, and an old chambray shirt, pulled my long, dark hair into a practical ponytail, and slapped on some mosquito repellent. I knew I'd need it. I'd had other cases in the deep woods. Chouteau County was a densely wooded area studded with nineteenth-century mansions. The richest residences were guarded by gates and security, but a network of paths – mostly used by local teenagers – threaded through the woods behind their estates.

Ten minutes later, I found the intersection Jace gave me, off a remote part of Gravois Road. Police cars and other official vehicles were strewn about like abandoned toys. Mike, the uniform, waved at me. He was about twenty-five, with an open, smiling face and short blond hair. I brushed away his offer of help with my DI kit – a black rolling suitcase – and we followed a deer trail through the muddy woods, with me half-carrying, half-rolling the suitcase.

It was a glorious spring day. The new leaves were a tender green, and I saw patches of purple – flowering redbud trees – and clouds of white dogwoods. A perfect day for a walk in the woods. Except I knew the grim end to this hike.

By this time, Mike was puffing a bit as he worked his way up the trail, which made me feel a little better. I was out of breath, too. At forty-one, I was glad I could keep up with him. The trail was narrow, and the slippery mud made dragging my DI case difficult.

I smelled the site before I saw it. As we topped a hill, the odor of decomposition hit me like a wall. Mike slashed Vicks VapoRub under his nose to block the odor, then offered the jar to me. I waved it away. 'Thanks, Mike, but my sniffer will short out quickly.'

'Wish mine would,' he said.

I didn't want to embarrass Mike by saying that Vicks was rarely used, especially by veteran homicide staff. He'd catch on soon enough.

We kept walking on the deer path. The scene started along a branch of Chouteau Forest Creek, about twenty-five feet from where the body was found. 'Is this the same path the killer took?' I asked, as I unzipped my DI case for my iPad.

'Don't know yet,' Mike said.

I saw three canopy tents set up in a little clearing for shade – and to block the view of any TV helicopters. Rick, a solemn-faced uniform at the entrance to the scene, was in charge of the crime scene log.

'Hi, Rick. Angela Richman, Death Investigator. Looks like my time in is 6:58 a.m.'

Rick noted my arrival in the log.

As I started to write the time on my iPad, I said, 'What's our case number?' He gave it to me.

Now we were in the thick of the investigation, I could see a small landslide at a bend in Chouteau Forest Creek, exposing the red clay soil. Under one canopy was a partially decomposed body, lying on a rock-strewn bier of red-brown clay.

Jace – Detective Budewitz – was directing the search of the area, plus the cadaver dog handlers and their animals. He waved at me.

'How's it going?' I asked. Jace is six-two, with a perpetual boyish face. He wiped the sweat from his forehead, which was rapidly getting higher.

'One body so far,' he said. 'I suspect there are at least two more buried here.' He pointed at a thick clump of weeds and saplings about ten feet away. 'I'll bet my next paycheck that's a body dump. The body fed that thick overgrowth. Same for the spot over there, to the west of it.

'I've got uniforms searching the creek bed in case any bones or evidence washed downstream. We may have gotten lucky there. I think the creek wall collapsed after last night's heavy rain. The arm looks intact, but we're missing some finger bones. The searchers have come up with nothing so far.'

'Any idea who the victim is?' I asked.

A dog handler shouted, 'Detective! Over here! I think we may have another one.'

'Damn!' Jace looked sick. He wiped his sweating forehead with his hands and smeared mud across it. 'Sorry, Angela, can't talk now.'

By that time, Nitpicker had arrived, suited up in a white disposable coverall. She was a short, muscular woman in her thirties, who loved changing her hair color. Today it was the same lime green as the spring leaves. She kneeled down to survey the exposed parts of the body.

'Time to suit up, Angela,' she said.

I opened my suitcase and pulled on my hooded suit, then added the goggles and face mask.

I knew we were all looking at long days. Bodies located in the woods would be worked through the night until the scene was cleared. We could not leave the decedents in the ground and come back. We would have to stay there, suited up, sweating, swatting mosquitoes, barely sleeping, working slowly and meticulously to document every step.

When we got closer to the body, we could see the creek cave-in had exposed part of the face, along with the arm. 'What can you tell me about this decedent?' I asked.

Nitpicker brushed her already sweaty green hair out of her eyes. 'This one appears to be a female, possibly in her early twenties. I'll know more as we go on.'

Four hours later, I was finally able to do the formal body inspection. Nitpicker still thought the decedent was female, probably blonde, possibly in her early twenties.

'This was no drifter,' she said. 'She has good teeth.'

Once I got past the 'Oh, my God!' reflex I always have when I see a badly decomposed decedent, I could see that the dead woman's skin was too decomposed to tell her race. She was supine, lying on her back. Mud blocked her eyes, and her lips were pulled back in a horrible rictus. I could see those straight teeth, now clogged with mud. She'd had good dental work, and that would help identify her.

'Let me show you what I found around the victim's neck,' Nitpicker said. She crawled toward the body's head and pointed at the neck with her trowel. I leaned in closer, and wished I hadn't.

The odor was overwhelming, even through the face mask, and I fought not to gag. So much for my nose shorting out.

'See?' she said.

I mastered my rebellious stomach and peered closer. 'It looks like muddy string. Green string.'

'I think it's jute garden string,' Nitpicker said. 'My mom uses it to tie back her tomatoes.'

'Do you think the victim was garroted with it?'

'That would be my guess, but the ME will have to say for sure.'

The string would stay on the victim's neck until the medical examiner removed it. I would photograph it – especially the knot. Knots could tell us a lot about her killer.

I took out my point-and-shoot camera and photographed the body – wide shots and close-ups, then more close-ups of those teeth. Then I put on multiple pairs of gloves. I placed the dead woman's hands in paper bags secured with evidence tape in case there was any evidence under her nails.

I didn't see any visible open wounds, but the decomposition could be hiding them.

Nitpicker pointed to the decedent's running shoes. 'Looks like the victim tied her shoes herself. I hope the bastard didn't make her walk here. We'll have her shoe soles analyzed for traces of earth materials besides this sticky clay.' The victim's running shoes also got the paper bag and evidence tape treatment.

'She's wearing a green T-shirt,' I said, 'with the Chouteau Forest High logo.'

Nitpicker lowered her voice and said, 'I hope this doesn't leak to the press, but I think the decedent may be Terri Gibbons, the Forest High track star.'

'What? That can't be,' I said. 'Terri went missing eight months ago. This body hasn't been in the ground that long.' Terri Gibbons was the pride of Chouteau Forest High, the local answer to East St. Louis's track and field star, Jackie Joyner-Kersee.

At the time of her disappearance, Terri had two track and field scholarships, including one to UCLA. Last August, Terri went out for a run, telling her mother she'd be back by dinnertime. When she didn't turn up by nine o'clock, her frantic mother called the police. Terri's disappearance made the national news.

I felt a crushing weight in my chest. So much promise lost.

The police said Terri was universally liked, did not have a steady boyfriend, drink or use drugs.

'I knew she probably wasn't alive,' I said. 'But I'd hoped she'd cracked under the pressure and taken a bus to Florida.'

'I think we all hoped that,' Nitpicker said. 'At least her poor mother will know what happened to her daughter and have someone to bury.'

'Closed casket,' I said, looking at the young woman's nightmare face.

'I hope her mother doesn't insist on seeing her body,' Nitpicker said.

'Jace and I will try to talk her out of it,' I said. 'Terri disappeared in August. There's no way this body has been in the ground eight months.'

'That's my guess, too,' Nitpicker said. 'That means someone had been holding her for at least six months or so.'

'Holding.' A polite word for torture, maybe worse.

Someone local. Who knew the secret ways of the Forest.

TWO

Nitpicker and I worked in silence. As so often happens in Missouri, the pleasant spring day turned blast-furnace hot, and we wilted in the humidity. My hair was dripping with sweat. Flies buzzed everywhere – in my eyes, ears, even my mouth. The insects tormented me inside my hood. The mosquitos were particularly vicious after the heavy rains. No matter how much mosquito repellent I slathered on, the nasty creatures always found a spot I'd missed.

As I worked, I tried to persuade myself that this wasn't the body of Terri Gibbons, the lost track star. I asked Nitpicker, 'Do you really think this is Terri? Anyone could wear a Chouteau Forest High shirt.'

'We can't be sure until the ME confirms it with DNA or dental work,' Nitpicker said, 'but last time I checked there were no other missing persons' reports for someone this age around here.'

'Maybe she's a sex worker from St. Louis,' I said.

Nitpicker quickly dashed my last hope. 'And some kink put her in a Chouteau Forest High shirt because it turned him on? I doubt it. Her dental work is too good for her to be a drifter or a hooker.'

She was right, and I knew it. As I worked, I thought about the twisted freak who'd killed Terri. That's who she was in my mind now, even though she hadn't been officially identified. I wanted to put a human face on this horror show. I'd seen Terri's photo, and she'd been a strong, smiling young woman with determined brown eyes and the long, lean muscles of a runner.

I swatted a mosquito on my ear, and continued my routine for Terri's death investigation. I opened the 'Information to be Developed for Unidentified Persons' form on my iPad. The body was face-up in a shallow grave, about three feet deep, her head pointing to the east, away from the creek.

I measured her body. She was about five feet six inches tall, and I estimated her weight at maybe 125 pounds. I wasn't sure of her race – decomposed bodies darken – but if it really was Terri, she was Caucasian. Her mud-streaked hair appeared to be natural – medium blonde with hints of darker tones. In other words, dirty blonde. I couldn't tell her eye color – I wasn't sure if they were still there.

The flesh had sagged, the abdominal cavity had caved, most of the internal organs were gone, and there had been extensive maggot activity. I gathered samples of all the insects, including the flies and beetles. I had to note all the insect life on her body. Awful as they were, they were Nature's clean-up squad.

The advanced decomposition hid any marks, deformities or scars, including surgical scars. I wouldn't be able to make out any tattoos or body piercings. It was impossible to determine if there were holes for pierced earrings on her lobes. Her left hand and lower arm (the ulna and radius) had been exposed by the creek cave-in and were skeletonized. Two fingers were missing, the phalanges and metacarpals for her ring and little fingers. The eight remaining fingers had the remains of pale blue polish. The decedent wore no rings or other jewelry.

I noted the green string around the victim's neck that Nitpicker had pointed out, and photographed it again, taking special care to document the knot. The ME would cut the string during the autopsy and leave the knot intact. It was an odd knot, not a square or granny knot. My guess – and I shuddered at the thought – was that it was some sort of slip knot used to control the victim. There may have been bruising on Terri's neck, but the advanced decomp made it hard to tell.

The victim's muddy shirt had a pocket, and I found something inside.

'Hey, Nitpicker, look at this!' I used tweezers to extract a bit of vegetation from the shirt pocket. 'It looks like some kind of flower, but I'm not sure what variety.' The flower was brown and wilted, but appeared to have five petals and was sort of funnel-shaped. I put the dead flower gently in a paper envelope I kept in my DI kit. It would be sent to a botanist later.

'Do you think the killer put that flower in the victim's pocket?' I asked.

'Maybe,' Nitpicker said. 'But killers usually put flowers on top of the body or in the victim's hands, as if staging a funeral, and I haven't found any. Maybe the victim hid it in her shirt to help us find who killed her.'

I felt a flash of pity. What had Terri's last days been like, knowing she was going to die and perhaps leaving clues for the people who might find her? I shook off those thoughts. Wallowing in the awful details of her death wouldn't help. Documenting what I found would.

'I swear we'll get justice for you, Terri,' I said, then realized I'd spoken my words out loud. Fortunately, Nitpicker didn't seem to notice my melodramatic pronouncement. Red with embarrassment, I went back to work.

I noted that Terri's clothes were muddy but intact. She wore matching green gym shorts and white socks, and it looked like she'd put her clothes on herself – nothing was inside-out or back-ward. There were no tags or identification.

When I examined her right arm, I saw that a rectangle of skin appeared to be missing. The missing patch was four inches long and two inches wide – a neat cut two inches above her wrist. 'What do you think this is?' I asked Nitpicker.

She examined the wound. 'My guess is the cut was made after her death, possibly to remove a distinguishing birthmark or tattoo.'

Jace came over and I showed him the missing patch of skin.

'Her description mentions that she had a blue butterfly tattoo on her right arm, near her wrist,' he said.

I spent more long hours securing the evidence. At last, that task was finished. Now it was growing dark. Long black shadows reached for us like dead fingers, and the air was suddenly chilly. Nitpicker and I were finished. We were both sweaty and mud-smeared, and we stank. The dogs had found another body, bringing the total to three, counting Terri.

Who would murder Terri? I wondered, as I packed up my gear. Why had her killer buried two more women deep in the Forest woods? Those were older burials. Although an outsider – a curious hiker – had discovered the first body, I was pretty sure a Forest resident had created this remote burial site. While the Forest paths were mostly used by teenagers, plenty of grown-ups remembered where they used to hook up or get hammered.

But this hidden glen was no kids' party place. The uniforms had found little evidence for that. No downed tree trunks or big rocks for comfortable seating, no signs of youthful partying – beer cans, used condoms, or joints. In my mind, I could see the killer here, leaning against a big tree, contemplating his crimes, enjoying owning these victims. Savoring the knowledge that no one else in the whole world knew where these victims were.

A chill wind dried the sweat on me and I shivered, but not entirely from the cold. I wanted out of here. The night woods felt like they were closing in. The dusk was still and stifling.

'I'm ready to call the pick-up service,' I said. Chouteau County had a contractor to move bodies to the morgue. 'Are you going to work the other two bodies, Nitpicker?'

'No, those are older burials. They seem to be mostly skeletons.'

Climate and the environment affected the rate of decomposition. Here, it took about a year for a body to decompose into a skeleton in these conditions, so the decedents had been here a while.

Nitpicker was packing away her tools. 'We're going to have to bring in a forensic anthropologist from City University – Dana Murdoch.'

'I know her. She's good.'

'The best,' Nitpicker said. 'But you won't be doing the body inspection on those two decedents.'

I felt relieved, until Jace came over and reminded me that my work wasn't done. 'We're going to have to inform Terri's mother that we need her daughter's dental records,' he said. 'We'd better get there before that poor woman finds out through the Forest rumor mill.'

That was my job – the worst part of it – to inform the victim's family. Some jurisdictions assign this task to another investigator, but not the Forest.

'Didn't you ask for Terri's records after she was missing for a while?' That was standard procedure in a missing person's investigation.

'We did,' he said, 'two months after Terri went missing. The case was getting a lot of attention, what with her being a track star and everything. Her mother refused to give them to me. I tried to be tactful, too. I asked about Terri's physical health and mental health, and who her doctors were. Her mother said Terri was fit mentally and physically, and she was elated over her sports success. No indication that she was cracking under the pressure. I asked her mother if she'd sign a healthcare release form, "in the unlikely event we need any records."

'Terri's mother saw through me. She said it wasn't necessary, because in her heart she knew her daughter was alive.'

'Back then, Terri probably was alive,' I said.

'You know, Doc Stone is a stickler for the HIPAA privacy regulations,' Jace said. 'He won't release the dental records unless he has permission from the next of kin. That's Terri's mother. The father's long gone.'

'Couldn't Doc Stone look at the morgue X-rays?' I asked. I really didn't want to do this.

'We'd still need Terri's dental records,' he said.

There was no way out of my unpleasant duty.

'I'll go with you,' Jace said. I could have hugged him, except no one would want me near them in my current state.

I looked down at my muddy jumpsuit and said, 'Give me time to shower and change into something decent.'

'I should change, too,' he said, brushing mud off the knees of his pants. 'Terri's mother, Lillian, lives on Duchesne Circle. I'll meet you at the entrance to her street in an hour.'

I pulled off my jumpsuit and bagged it in the contaminated

trash at the site, then looked around at the suddenly cold forest. I hurried down the deer trail to my car.

On the drive home, I was pleased that Jace had volunteered to go with me to break the news to Terri's mother. This was always an emotional time, and I didn't like to go alone. Ordinarily polite people reacted unpredictably to the news that they'd lost a loved one.

Three months ago, when I told a mother that her only son had died of an opioid overdose, she screamed, 'Liar!' and tried to hit me. Jace stepped between us just before she raked her sharp red nails across my face. Eventually, he calmed her down. She was a fifty-six-year-old assistant bank manager. After several cups of tea and an ocean of tears, she said, 'I don't know what came over me. I'm so sorry.'

I knew she was, but I also knew I had to be careful.

Jace and I had an even worse task. Usually, I came with absolute news, telling someone the son, daughter, husband or wife they loved was dead. But this mission was even more delicate.

We weren't sure that Terri Gibbons was dead. In effect, I'd be saying, 'Sorry, your daughter may be dead. Can we have her dental records?'

That was far worse. When Jace and I would be asking Terri's mother, Lillian Gibbons, for her daughter's dental records, we were giving that poor woman sorrow and uncertainty at the same time. Lillian was smart enough to know what that request meant. We were really breaking the news of her daughter's death to her. Maybe.

I headed home, threw my clothes into the laundry, showered, and longed to fall into bed, but that luxury was denied to me right now. I was a widow – my husband had died young of a heart attack – and I missed his love, his comfort, and most of all, his conversation.

Today I was alone, and the bearer of bad news. Even worse, I had some idea of how my news would affect that poor woman: she'd be wounded to the depths of her soul.

THREE

'She's dead, isn't she?'

Terri's mother opened the door, took one look at Jace and me, and said the words in a flat voice. We didn't even have to introduce ourselves. Lillian Gibbons had been expecting this news, and her face was ravaged by grief. She was about fifty years old, and under different circumstances might have been attractive. Her hair was a smart brown bob, and she wore a gray sweatshirt and straight-legged jeans. But all the color left her face when she saw us on her doorstep.

I found her complete lack of emotion frightening. I was afraid she'd suddenly break and lash out in a violent storm.

We stood on the doorstep of her ranch house in the working part of Chouteau Forest, with the sneery nickname of Toonerville. I caught a glimpse of a green-painted hall, the wall covered with photographs of a young woman in sports clothes. Terri, I presumed.

'We're not sure, Mrs Gibbons,' Jace said, his voice quiet and cautious, the way he'd approach a possibly dangerous person. 'We need your help.'

'We've found someone who could be your daughter,' I said, 'but we need to confirm it.'

'Why can't I identify her body?' she asked, in that same dangerously flat voice.

'Uh, the body has been buried,' Jace said. 'For a while.'

You couldn't possibly recognize the daughter you love, I thought, damn the killer's shriveled soul.

'But her body's been found,' Lillian said, her voice insistent. 'Why can't I look at her?'

'Because, uh, the person we found doesn't resemble what she looked like in life,' I said. In fact, she doesn't even look human, I thought.

Lillian began screaming. 'I would know my own daughter! No matter what she looked like now!'

I flinched, but stood firm. 'I'm sorry, Mrs Gibbons, but you don't want to see this person, whether or not she's your daughter.'

Jace gently took her arm and steered her inside. 'The best way to help us confirm this is Terri is to sign the papers allowing Dr Stone to release your daughter's dental records, so we can compare them to this person's. Then we'll know for sure.'

I softly closed the door and followed Jace into the kitchen at the end of the hall. It was a good choice. The room had the comforting smell of cinnamon and coffee. Blue-checked curtains gave it a homey look. We sat down at a polished pine table with a blue bowl of fruit as a centerpiece. The short walk and Jace's soothing tone gave Mrs Gibbons time to recover.

Now she was weeping openly. 'I knew my baby was dead,' Mrs Gibbons said.

Jace handed her a fresh, white handkerchief and she wiped her streaming eyes.

'Thank you,' she said. 'I know the day she died, too. It was February twelfth at twelve-seventeen at night. I felt it. I felt it in my soul. Something stabbed my heart and I blacked out for a few minutes. I was in bed, and when I came to, I knew then that my Terri was dead.

'I guess you think I'm crazy.' She looked at me, a challenge in her voice.

'No, I don't doubt you,' I said. 'I never question the connection between a mother and child. She's part of you.' Besides, the time-line was eerily right for Terri's death, judging by the condition of her body.

'We were connected, the two of us,' Mrs Gibbons said. 'Her father took off when she was just a baby, and from then on, it was Terri and me. I went to every practice, and took a part-time job to get her the coaching she needed. I was so proud when she got those scholarships. That's why, when she didn't come home that night, I knew something was wrong. I knew she was in trouble.'

She started crying again. When her tears stopped, I asked, 'May I make you some coffee?'

'I'd like that,' she said, sniffling. 'But you don't need to make it. The coffee in the pot is still fresh. If you would pour me a cup, I'd appreciate it. I take mine black. Pour some for yourselves, too. The cups are in the cabinet next to the stove.'

While I went to get the coffee, Jace introduced us formally. I brought three mugs of coffee over to the table and we sipped the fragrant coffee.

Mrs Gibbons broke the silence. 'Ever since I knew she was dead, I've been praying that my girl would be found, so I could bring her home. I want her to be with her grandparents. She loved them so much. They were our support system.'

She sounded almost as if Terri would be living with them, but I guessed that was her way of coping with the dreadful news.

She took a deep breath, then said, 'I'll sign those papers now. How long will it take to make the identification?'

'Not long,' Jace said. 'I've called Dr Stone and alerted him. He's on standby. As soon as he gets permission from you, he'll compare the X-rays and give us his decision.' Jace didn't add that my friend, Dr Katie Kelly Stern, assistant county medical examiner, had stayed late at the morgue to X-ray the body. She'd already emailed those X-rays to Dr Stone.

'Do you have a scanner?' he asked.

'No,' she said. 'Would a fax machine work?'

'That will work fine,' Jace said.

'I have one in . . . in . . .' Mrs Gibbons stopped, gulped back more tears, and finally said, 'in Terri's room.'

She signed the paperwork and we followed her to Terri's room. It was painted a dramatic dark blue cut with bold slashes of red. The walls were decorated with posters of women track stars. I recognized Olympians Allyson Felix and Sanya Richards-Ross. I hadn't the heart to ask Mrs Gibbons about her daughter's Olympic aspirations. Like the rest of the house, Terri's room was scrupulously clean. Three tall bookcases were crowded with trophies and packed with books.

Across from the bed was a desk with a fax machine and a phone charger. 'The police took my daughter's laptop and cell phone,' Mrs Gibbons said. She showed us how to work the fax machine, and we faxed the signed permission paper to Dr Stone. Jace stepped outside to phone Katie and Dr Stone.

'Do you have someone to stay with you this evening, Mrs Gibbons?' I asked. 'Someone you can call so you won't be alone?'

'Yes, my cousin, Bobbie Kramer. I'll call her now. Even though she's my cousin, Terri always called her Aunt Bobbie. My phone's in my room.'

She left to make her call and I studied the books on Terri's shelves: fat, worn history and math textbooks, and five shelves of novels, including the Harry Potter series, the Vampire Diaries, and saddest of all, *The Fault in Our Stars* by John Green. That touching novel was about trying to live your life to the fullest when your time is limited. Did Terri sense that her time was limited, just like her mother believed she knew when the young woman had died?

Mrs Gibbons came back and announced, 'Bobbie is on her way. She works in downtown St. Louis, and she should be here in about forty minutes, if the traffic's not too bad.'

'I'll stay with you until she arrives,' I said, and saw the gratitude on the woman's face. I quickly switched the subject. 'Your daughter's quite a reader.'

'Yes, she is.' Mrs Gibbons smiled, eager to brag about her daughter, then the smile slipped from her face. 'I mean, she was. From the time she learned how to read, we had a monthly book date, where we'd go to a bookstore and she'd pick out a new book. If she hadn't won the track scholarships, she could have had an academic scholarship. She's that smart.'

Mrs Gibbons looked ready to cry again, then stopped herself. 'The police detective, Budewitz, is a kind man,' she said.

'Yes, he is,' I said. 'He's the best.'

'Would you like to go sit in the kitchen?' she asked.

I followed her back there. After we sat down, she said, 'I have a question. Did my daughter – I mean – did the dead girl suffer?'

'No!' I said.

My mind flashed on the green string with the slip knot around the dead woman's decomposing neck, proof that I was lying. I didn't care. It was the only comfort I could give that poor woman. Let her believe that Terri died quickly and painlessly. Parents who knew how their children really died tortured themselves for the rest of their lives. Mrs Gibbons was in enough pain.

I was relieved when Jace returned and said, 'We should have an answer for you in less than an hour, Mrs Gibbons.'

'Thank you,' she said. 'It will be good to know one way or the other. Would you like some cinnamon coffee cake? I baked it today.'

'That sounds good,' I said. Jace agreed, and she cut us two generous slices. I'd missed lunch and dinner and was surprisingly hungry, but I hoped wolfing down the cake would be seen as a compliment. Jace quickly demolished his cake, too.

'Where was Terri – uh, the body – found?' Mrs Gibbons asked.

'In Chouteau County, deep in the woods off Gravois Road,' Jace said. 'A hiker found them.'

'Them? Then there was more than one person?' she said.

'We believe there were three,' he said. 'They haven't been identified yet.'

'But if all the . . . dead . . . are deep in the woods, they must have been killed by someone local,' Mrs Gibbons said.

'We don't know yet,' Jace said.

We heard a car pull into the drive, and Mrs Gibbons said, 'That must be my cousin, Bobbie.'

She hurried to the front room, and we heard both women weeping. Jace's cell phone rang, and he stepped into the living room to take the call. Mrs Gibbons and Bobbie hurried into the kitchen. Bobbie was about sixty, with short gray hair and eyes red from crying. Her black business suit and blue blouse had a tired, end-of-the-day look. After she sat down, I poured her a cup of coffee, and introduced myself.

Jace appeared at the door, and I could tell by his face that he had news. So could Mrs Gibbons. She looked at him and said, 'What is it?'

'I'm sorry, Mrs Gibbons,' Jace said, 'but the body has been identified as your daughter, Terri Gibbons.'

Bobbie let out an unearthly shriek, and fainted dead away. She fell face-forward on the kitchen table, knocking over her coffee.

'Bobbie!' cried Mrs Gibbons, and began working on reviving her cousin, while Jace and I mopped up the spilled coffee with paper towels. Smelling salts finally brought the woman around.

'I'm very sorry,' Bobbie said. 'I skipped lunch.'

'No need to apologize,' Mrs Gibbons said. 'You were Terri's favorite aunt. Let me fix you some dinner.'

Jace and I left Mrs Gibbons, who was ministering to her distraught cousin.

FOUR

It was almost nine o'clock when I left Terri's mother. Jace walked me to my car and I waved goodbye. I nearly fell into the driver's seat, feeling like my strings had been cut. The horrors of the day – the death investigation of the young woman and the terrible grief of Terri's mother – had drained me. There was no cure for the unbearable heartache this killer had unleashed. I rolled down my driver's side window, hoping the blast of chill air would revive me, then checked my cell phone messages.

The first was a text from Katie, the assistant ME: *Be at my office at nine a.m. I've found something.*

The only thing she'd text me about was Terri Gibbons's autopsy. The carefully worded message told me Katie had found an important clue. Did I miss something during my DI examination? Or did we have some hope of catching the evil creature who killed Terri? I'd have to wait until tomorrow.

I also had a voice message. I smiled when I heard his voice, warm enough to chase away the evening chill. 'Hey, Angela, it's Chris. How about dinner tonight? I miss you.'

I could picture Officer Christopher Ferretti, the Chouteau Forest force's newest hire: six feet four, close-cut blond hair lightly touched with gray, kind blue eyes, big shoulders and muscular arms. He smelled like starch and Old Spice.

What more could a woman want?

I wanted what I could no longer have – Donegan, my late husband. He'd died suddenly of a heart attack two years ago. I liked Chris, but I still loved Donegan, and I kept the police officer at arm's length. Like I was doing now, when I returned his call.

'Sorry, Chris,' I said. 'I'm too tired to go out. I had to inform a poor mother that her daughter was dead.'

'That's rough,' he said. 'You could use comfort. Want to come over? We could order pizza. Or I could come to your place and bring one.'

And then what? I wondered, but I knew the answer. I was too skittish to see him. And he was being so damn understanding.

'Thanks,' I lied. 'I'd rather be alone tonight.'

Chris wouldn't take no for an answer. 'How about dinner tomorrow night?' he said. 'Someplace nice.'

'Deal,' I said, mostly to get him off the phone.

'Pick you up at seven o'clock?'

'See you then.'

I mustered the energy to drive home, and parked my black Charger in the garage. A bone-white spring moon shone on my two-story house, bleaching the stone walls tombstone white. The dark windows looked like dead eyes.

My home had been a guesthouse on the Du Pres estate until crafty Old Reggie Du Pres sold it to my parents. My mom and dad had worked for the man who ruled Chouteau Forest, and I inherited the house when they died. Donegan and I had been so happy here. It was hard to go home to an empty house.

I opened the front door and flipped on the light, wishing I'd summoned the energy to see Chris tonight. But that would lead to complications I wasn't ready to tackle.

I'd fix myself dinner after I dumped my stuff upstairs, but my bed looked so inviting I laid down for just a moment . . .

And woke up at seven the next morning, still wearing my black suit. I threw my wrinkled, slept-in clothes in the laundry basket, showered, dressed, and revived myself with toast, eggs and strong black coffee.

By then it was eight a.m., a sun-gilded spring day, and I was anxious to hear what Katie had to say. I picked up two coffees at Chouteau Has Beans, the local coffeehouse. Ten minutes later, I was at the county morgue in the back of the sprawling Sisters of Sorrow Hospital. I parked my car far enough away to avoid the funeral home vans and desperate smokers huddling by the hospital Dumpsters.

I keyed in the access code at 8:14, and was hit with the morgue's sharp disinfectant smell covering the faint sweet odor of decomp. And the sadness. That had its own special smell, and I thought it seeped into the walls. But that could be my imagination.

I was early, but I knew my friend Katie would be there. Sure enough, she was shoe-horned behind her desk in her office, a closet-sized cubby with barely enough room for a file cabinet and a wire contraption that passed as a chair. One wall was decorated with a fall woodland scene. The grinning plastic skull pasted into the leaves on the ground gave me the willies today. It was too close to what I'd seen yesterday.

'I brought you coffee,' I said, and handed her the steaming cup.

Katie smiled. 'Bless you, my child. The office brew can strip paint.'

At first glance, Katie seemed plain. She had neat, short brown hair, sensible shoes and a brown suit under her lab coat. But then you saw the intelligence that flashed in her brown eyes, and she was transformed. Katie had snared Montgomery Bryant, the Forest's most eligible bachelor. I knew he called her his 'nut-brown maid' and she'd slice me with a scalpel if I ever revealed that.

'Why so early?' she asked, and gulped down half her coffee. 'Damn, I needed that.'

'I'm here for Terri Gibbons's autopsy report,' I said. 'I assume that's why you texted me.'

'You'll have to wait until Jace shows up. And speaking of cops, how are things going with that hunky cop of yours, Chris Ferretti?'

I bristled at her comment. 'He's not mine, and we're having dinner tonight.'

'And?' she said, drinking the rest of her coffee.

'And that's it,' I said.

Katie tossed her empty cup in the trash. 'What the fuck, Angela? You're living like a freakin' nun.'

'That's my business,' I said. I felt the anger rise up inside me.

'I know you loved Donegan, but it's been two years since you buried him. Hell, you didn't crawl into the coffin with him. He loved you, too. What would he want?'

Furious tears filled my eyes. 'What would Donegan want? He'd want to be alive, that's what he'd want!'

With that, Jace knocked on Katie's office door. He immediately detected the fraught atmosphere. 'Morning, ladies. Everything OK?'

'Fine,' Katie said, giving him a false smile. 'We were just talking about dinner.'

Jace left that alone, though he had to know by my angry face that Katie was lying. I was comforted by Jace's friendly, boyish manner. Unlike some cops, he was faithful to his wife, and that made him easy company.

'Tell us what you found out about Terri,' he said.

'She had probably been kept alive for several months before her death,' Katie said, 'and she was well fed.'

'Kept alive? Somewhere here in the Forest?' I asked.

'I can't tell,' Katie said. 'She was strangled. The hyoid bone in her neck was broken. There may have been bruising around her neck, but the decomp was pretty far advanced.

'Angela noted the green string around the victim's neck. I confirmed it's common jute garden string, used to tie plant stems. I believe the victim was garroted with the garden twine.

'I've sent it to the lab for further examination, but the knot in the twine looks like a taut line hitch. It's a slide that can tighten or loosen the loop around the victim's neck, so it could have been used to control her – do something the killer didn't like, and he'd choke her.'

Katie was a farm girl, and knew her knots. I was pretty sure the lab would back up her conclusions.

'The bastard,' I said.

'Was she raped?' Jace asked.

'I didn't find any semen or DNA on the victim,' Katie said. 'She was too badly decomposed.'

'What about the flower I found in her shirt pocket?' I asked.

'City University's botany department is taking a look at it.'

'What flower?' Jace asked.

'I found a flower in her shirt pocket. I wondered if she was sending us a message.'

'If so, she sent us another message,' Katie said. 'Look at these photos. I found this under the inner sole in Terri's right shoe.'

So it wasn't something I'd overlooked, I thought, and felt relieved. I couldn't remove any of the decedent's clothing.

The photos showed a flat bit of aluminum foil. Katie had photographed it inside the shoe, then removed it with tweezers and photographed it again.

'That foil looks like it was torn off a gum wrapper,' I said.

'That's what I think,' Katie said. 'I'm having it tested.'

The message was on a scrap of paper, and it appeared to have been scratched with a ballpoint that was almost out of ink.

Jace and I stared at the message in shocked silence. It said, *Briggs Bellerive drugged me and locked me in his house. If you find this, he's killed me.*

'Who's Briggs Bellerive?' Jace asked. He was new to the Forest and its ways.

'A problem,' Katie said.

'A big problem,' I said, echoing her.

FIVE

'At the risk of sounding like a giant owl,' Jace said, 'who the hell is Briggs Bellerive? Damn, I hate the secrets in this place.'

Jace had my sympathy. I wasn't a Forest insider by any means, but I grew up here and I knew how it worked. It was a frustrating place for an outsider like Jace. All the old families had something to hide, and one way or another, those of us who served them helped with the cover-ups.

'He's the Forest's most eligible bachelor,' I said. 'He always has Desiree Gale, an international model and TV personality, on his arm.'

'I've seen her,' Jace said. 'Tall, blonde, tight dresses.'

'The bandage dress she wore on TV yesterday was more like a tourniquet,' I said. 'Briggs is a square-jawed hunk. He's in his early thirties – thirty-one, I think. He and Desiree go everywhere together in his vintage E-Type Jaguar or on his private jet.'

'He's also richer than God,' Katie said.

'And connected,' I added.

'Connected how?' Jace said. 'And to what?'

'To everything and everybody who's anybody,' I said. 'His mother was a judge and his father a US senator. They're both dead now, but they did a lot of favors for the Forest – and people here have long memories.'

Jace was pacing Katie's tiny office, taking up all the room and most of the oxygen. Katie stayed behind her desk and I retreated to the uncomfortable wire chair, which poked me in the back and creaked when I moved. It was like sitting on a pile of hangers. I'd drunk my coffee and poured myself a cup of the office paint stripper. It was so bitter I used it mainly to keep my hands warm in the sub-zero air-conditioning.

'So this Briggs guy flies off in his private jet with his hot babe to have dinner in London or Paris,' Jace said.

'Not exactly,' I said. 'He goes to London for his suits and shoes, but he prefers dinners at his home. He likes to cook for his friends.'

'He's also a gardener,' Katie said. 'He grows prize nasturtiums.'

'You can eat them,' I said.

'Why would I want to eat flowers?' Jace said.

I shrugged. 'Beats me. You won't find me munching marigolds.'

'Briggs is in the papers all the time,' Katie said. 'Puff pieces by the *Forest Gazette* and the St. Louis papers featuring his house decorated for Christmas, or his latest dinner party.'

'With recipes,' I said. 'He's also a big donor to the local charities. He gave a new hospital wing to SOS in honor of his parents. And he agreed to cook dinner for six at his home for a charity auction. It sold for six thousand dollars.'

Jace whistled.

'I was one of the guests,' I said. 'I went with my friend, Mario.' Mario is my gay hairstylist. He was between boyfriends at the time.

'Did you eat flowers?' he asked.

'We did,' I said. 'We had a salad with nasturtium seed pods, which were pickled and used like capers. It was pretty good. We also had nasturtium mayonnaise with our broiled lobster. I liked them both but I couldn't bring myself to eat the nasturtium garnish.'

'Sounds odd, but foodies eat lots of weird things now,' Jace said. 'What's that fizzy fermented tea that's so popular?'

'Kombucha,' Katie said. 'Supposed to be good for your gut.'

'OK, I get it,' Jace said. 'The guy's a rich foodie. But what's wrong with me going over to his place for a little talk?'

'You're going to accuse Mr Perfect of murdering three women and burying their bodies in the woods?' I said.

'Give me some credit,' Jace said. 'I'll just talk to him and get a feel for what he's like.'

'He's smart,' Katie said. 'If even one of your questions makes him uncomfortable, he'll lawyer up – and his lawyer will complain to the police chief, who will shut down your investigation.'

'He's got enough money to get the police to back off?' Jace said.

'You're talking about the CEO of Bellerive Industries,' I said. Finally. A light dawned in Jace's eyes. He whistled. 'They make that tranquilizer, Calmatay.'

'Right. Half the world is tranqued on Calmatay,' Katie said.

'And Briggs knows lawyers,' I said. 'He wasn't always perfect. About fifteen years ago, he killed his best friend, and it took the best New York suits to get him out of that scrape.'

'Killed him? How?' Jace asked.

'Strangled him,' I said.

Jace frowned. 'Even more reason for me to talk to this bird now.'

'But you won't find any record of that murder,' I said. 'It was covered up, and since Briggs and the boy he killed were juveniles, the file was sealed. Briggs's best friend, Craig Wendell, heir to a shoe fortune, died in Briggs's bedroom the summer before their senior year in high school.

'Briggs claimed the boy's death was accidental – his story was that he and Craig were just "goofing around in his room" and he accidentally strangled his friend with his belt.'

Katie snorted. 'Any rookie detective could see through that explanation. It takes considerable pressure to strangle a strong young man, and Craig's neck was broken. The detective who caught the case believed that Wendell had died during sex, and this was a case of erotic asphyxiation.'

'In other words, this Briggs dude gets off on strangling people during sex,' Jace said. 'Just like he did to that young woman, Terri Gibbons.'

'We *think* that's how Terri was killed,' Katie said. 'We don't know for sure.'

'If Briggs killed another rich kid, why didn't the dead boy's family go after him?' Jace asked.

'Because both families wanted to hush up the scandal,' Katie said, 'and neither wanted their sons to be labeled gay.'

'You're kidding,' Jace said. 'This was like, what – 2005? Kids experiment all the time with sex. Does anyone even care if their kid's gay any more?'

'They do in the Forest,' Katie said. 'Even in 2005. Don't you have a son? What if you found out he was gay?'

'Joey's only seven and currently has a crush on Olivia, a little blonde in his class. But if he comes out as gay later, he's still my son, no matter what. His mother and I will do our best to make sure he's happy.'

I shook my head. 'That attitude will never do, Jace. In the Forest, children are supposed to make their parents look good, take over the family business, marry a suitable spouse and produce an heir. Parents here do everything they can to cover up what they consider "deviant behavior." They will marry off a lesbian daughter or gay son to a willing partner. The chosen husband or wife gets big bucks for the wedding, and once they produce an heir, they're even richer. Everyone turns a blind eye if they step out. Some of these marriages of convenience work very well.'

Jace shook his head. 'This place is a whole 'nother world.'

'Amen to that,' Katie said. 'It's also a whole 'nother century. The Forest is trapped in the nineteenth century. When Craig Wendell died, his family was embarrassed that he might have had a gay fling with Briggs, and helped cover up his cause of death. He'd broken the code: Forest sons are expected to carry on the family name, not have affairs with other men.'

'Jeez,' Jace said. I tossed my coffee cup in the trash. It was cold as well as bitter.

'And good old Evarts Evans, the ever-cooperative Chouteau Forest chief medical examiner, declared that Craig's death was an accidental strangling,' Katie said. 'His report made no mention of erotic asphyxiation or the semen he found in the dead boy's anus.'

'How do you know this?' Jace asked.

'I knew the assistant ME back then,' she said. 'He listened to Evarts rationalize what he did. Evarts decreed that it was better "for the sake of the grieving family" to hide the true cause of death. The detective in charge of the case agreed. They both patted themselves on the back for their kindness. The assistant ME had no say in the matter.'

'Poor Craig was quickly buried, along with the scandal,' I said.

'The family didn't even want a memorial plaque at his high school. The embarrassing story never made the media. Briggs was sent off to boarding school in England. That's about the time Calmatay was released, and hailed as the savior of the human race.'

'At least the nervous ones,' Katie said.

'Briggs did well in Britain,' I said, 'and graduated from the London School of Economics. He came back home to become CEO of his parents' chemical company, and he's good at his job. He's a favorite extra man at fundraisers and parties and a fixture on the charity circuit. He's often seen with the beautiful model, Desiree Gale, but since there's no diamond on her finger, the Forest matchmakers still have hopes that some local woman will snag him.'

'And that's the man you're trying to bring down,' Katie said.

'Good luck,' I said. 'You'll need it.'

Jace looked angry. 'If Briggs killed those poor young women and left them to rot in the woods, I'll make sure he goes to jail – I don't care how connected he is. He stole Terri Gibbons's brilliant future, and broke her mother's heart.'

I flashed back to our visit when we broke the news to her mother, and the way the light died in that woman's eyes.

'You know this Briggs person, Angela?' Jace said.

'I wouldn't say—'

He interrupted my protest with, 'At least you've been to dinner at his house. Would you come with me when I talk to him? It will seem friendlier. He may drop his guard and let something slip.'

'Sure. I have to work tomorrow, but I'll be glad to go with you.'

'I guess I should ask what happened to the detective who caught the case?' Jace said. 'Did they fire him? Might as well know what they'll do to me.'

'Nothing so crude,' Katie said. 'He took early retirement. Bought a house in Sarasota.'

'I don't want any house in Florida,' Jace said. 'It's too damn hot there. Besides, what's the worst he can do to me? I've walked a beat in a Chicago winter.'

'Just make sure you don't end up like his friend, Craig,' Katie said. 'Six feet under.'

SIX

When Katie finished, I tried to slip out of her office with Jace, but my friend called me back. I reluctantly returned for what I knew would be another lecture.

'So, about your date tonight,' she said.

'It's dinner,' I said. 'That's all.'

'You know Chris is seeing that cute little nurse in the ER, the one with the pixie haircut.'

'So? He's free to see whoever he wants.'

'You need to stake your claim,' she said.

I tried to tamp down my anger. 'Stake a claim? What is he, a gold mine? You're my best friend, Katie, but you have no business interfering in my love life.'

'There's nothing to interfere with,' Katie said. 'Since Donegan died two years ago, you've locked yourself away. You're too young.'

'I'm forty-one,' I said, 'and I'll live my life the way I want. Take care of your own love life. Everything OK with you and Monty?'

Hah. I could see by her stricken face that I'd hit a nerve.

'What's wrong? Does he want some space?'

'Worse,' she said, her voice flat. 'He wants to get married.'

'What's wrong with that?'

'I don't want to.'

'Why not? Is there someone else?'

'Of course not.'

'Is there anything about him that you don't like?'

'He drops his socks on the floor instead of putting them in the clothes basket.'

'Seriously?'

'Seriously. It's really annoying.'

'You've snagged the most eligible bachelor in the Forest. He's at your house – or you're at his – six nights a week. Might as well tie the knot.'

'And then what? He dies and I turn into the walking dead, like—'

'Like me,' I interrupted. 'You're afraid, Katie Kelly Stern. Well, I'll tell you this. Donegan's death may have knocked me for a loop, but every minute I had with him was worth it. Worth it!'

I escaped out her door, heart pounding, blood electric with anger. The nerve of Katie, telling me how I should live my life! I settled into my car, took a couple of deep breaths, then checked my cell phone. One message from Jace: 'Got the warrant. I'll stop by your house at eight a.m. tomorrow to brief you.' Good. I was looking forward to a showdown.

It was after two o'clock. Time to get ready for my date, I mean, dinner with Chris. I saw my hair in the rearview mirror. I looked like I'd stuck my finger in a light socket. I called Mario's salon, Killer Cuts, and he agreed to fit me in at three-thirty.

While Mario fussed over my hair, he plied me with shots of Cuban coffee and guava pastries made by his latest boyfriend, Carlos. Where that man managed to get tropical fruit in the middle of Missouri was beyond me, but I hoped Carlos was a keeper.

The three Cuban coffees – thimbles of the thick, sweet beverage – were like rocket fuel, and I rattled on. When Mario found out I was going out to dinner tonight, he did my make-up, too, then made me promise to wear my little black dress and high heels. It cost him another guava pastry, but I finally agreed.

I heard Chris's red Mustang pull into my drive at 6:59 p.m., and he was knocking on my door at 7 p.m.

'You look amazing,' he said when I answered the door.

'You look good, too,' I said. He looked better than good. Chris was about my age. He worked out, and his navy sport coat and blue shirt didn't hide his narrow waist and big shoulders. He smelled good, too – Old Spice and coffee.

'Want to come in for a drink?' I asked.

'Later,' he said. 'I don't want to be late for our reservation. Is dinner at Solange OK?' I liked his boyish uncertainty.

'Perfect,' I said. Classy, I thought, and expensive for a cop.

His car gleamed and I wondered if he'd shined it up for our dinner.

SEVEN

I went to bed with two men that night, one dead and one alive. Chris's warm, real kiss still burned on my lips, and I wrestled with the memory of my dead husband's kisses. The night seemed endless. I watched my bedside clock tick off one o'clock, then two and three and four, thinking about both men. I finally fell asleep about five in the morning, and woke up at 7:42 a.m.

I had eighteen minutes to dress before Detective Jace Budewitz showed up for our strategy meeting to bring down Terri's killer. I washed my face, trying to ignore my puffy, red-rimmed eyes, then ran a brush through my hair, threw on my black DI pantsuit and ran downstairs to plug in the coffee maker and defrost a cinnamon pound cake.

Jace arrived promptly at eight, just as I was putting plates and mugs on my kitchen table. The homicide detective was one of those annoyingly cheerful morning people, but I forgave him.

He breezed into my home with a sunny smile and his news. 'I got a warrant from Judge Ludlow, but it was touch and go. I had to work hard to convince him that we would find something. Kitchen smells nice. Is that pound cake?'

I cut him a thick piece and poured his coffee, then left the thermal pot on the table.

'When we get there, I'm going to ask the suspect questions quite politely and hope he denies ever knowing the girl or denies she was anywhere near his property. That will make things a little tighter when we find something that proves she was there. I want to give this suspect enough rope to hang himself with his denials. Then I'll flip the warrant out after the polite conversation ends.

'The warrant says we can search Briggs's house' – he reached into his pocket and opened an official-looking document and started reading – '"and anywhere or anything thereon at number two Olympia Circle, where there might be stored, to include, but not limited to, the entirety of the house and any outbuildings, vehicles, sheds, storage containers located at the location sought to be searched.'"

'Holy cow. I hope you're bringing a lot of folks for the search. Briggs has a huge estate.'

'We can do it,' he said. 'He's just another rich guy.'

Briggs wasn't, but Jace would have to find that out himself. 'Do you think we can find something?' I took a small sip of my hot black coffee.

'We better.' Jace gulped down half his mug and poured himself more. 'Ludlow didn't let me forget that Briggs is a big deal in this town.'

'He is,' I said.

'In fact, the judge said he'd had dinner at his house several times. May I have more of that pound cake?'

'Help yourself. Does Briggs know we're coming?'

'Oh, yeah. I had to go through six secretaries and assistants to talk to him. His office manager is a dragon.' Jace cut a slice that was nearly one-third of the pound cake and slathered it with butter.

'Bernice?' I laughed. 'That's her job. She's one tough lady. How did Briggs react when you called and said you had a search warrant?'

'I didn't tell him. Not yet, anyway. I just said I wanted to talk with him.'

'What are you looking for?'

'I'm hoping Terri left her jewelry stuffed under the basement sink, or in the toilet tank or something.'

'Was Terri wearing a class ring? She's the right age,' I said.

'No, that was in her jewelry box. Her mother said she always wore a gold necklace, a gift from her grandmother, a birth stone necklace with a purple stone. An amethyst. Her birthday is in February. Was.'

We had a moment of sad silence for the promising young woman who would have no more birthdays.

'If Terri was locked up but not tied up,' Jace said, 'she could have hidden her cell phone under a loose board. That was never found.'

'If she had a cell phone, Jace, she could have called 911.'

'Right. I need more coffee.' He poured yet another cup. 'She could have scrawled a message somewhere using her blood or bar soap. I'm hoping she did that.'

'We already have that message she wrote and slipped into her shoe,' I said. 'Katie says it was written on the inside of a gum wrapper. She says it was clove gum – Beeman's brand. That's pretty unusual.'

'Not really. You can buy Beeman's clove gum on Amazon. But we should be on the lookout for any gum chewers. If we can't find a message, then the warrant says we can look for hair – she may have left hair behind as a clue.'

'If she was smart enough to leave us a message in her shoe, that's a possibility,' I said. Jace finished his cake and helped himself to another giant slice, lavishly buttered. I poured myself more coffee, still hoping to wake up.

'There's also DNA and fingerprints, as well as evidence relating to the cause of death.' Jace used his fork to illustrate each point.

'Katie believes she was strangled with common garden string,' I said.

'Right, but maybe we can find the roll he used in a garden shed. The search warrant covers everything from his house to all the outbuildings.' Jace helped himself to the last of the cake.

'What's my role? I've only had dinner once at his house,' I said. 'I'm hardly a family friend.'

'But you know him,' Jace said. 'You're not one of those people, but you can talk to them. That's why I need you along. You can make small talk with him. He can tell you about his prize hollyhocks.'

'Nasturtiums,' I said. The word sounded odd, like something that belonged in an English drawing room comedy.

'Whatever. Talk to him about his flowers. And he likes fancy food. I'm a meat and potatoes man. Get him to relax. That's a good way for him to let something slip.'

I didn't think it was going to be that easy. There were three people buried in the woods, and two of their bodies were skeletonized. That meant Briggs had been getting away with this for years. Socially, he was sophisticated, smooth and polished. He had money and power on his side. We wanted to accuse him of murdering three women. We wanted to destroy this clever man with his own words.

'I hate to bust your bubble, Jace, but what if the cops searching his place come up empty-handed?'

Jace looked surprised. 'Then . . . uh, hm . . . I'll continue interviewing the victim's friends, reexamine her cell phone bills, see if I can get anything from that.'

In other words, Jace had no plan if this didn't work. He was betting all his meager political capital on this move.

He checked the time on his cell phone. 'Shall we saddle up and ride?'

Jace stood up, abandoning the rest of his cake. I took a last slurp of coffee, and we set off on our quest.

EIGHT

'Wow! Is that a house or a federal courthouse?' Jace said.

'It's quite a house, even by Forest standards,' I said. 'You really can't see it from the road. It's tucked away behind a couple of acres of woods.'

'Looks like Tara on steroids,' Jace said. 'You know, that movie, *Gone With the Wind*?'

I shifted uneasily in the passenger seat of his car. Jace was overawed. Despite my warnings – and the judge's – Jace was only now beginning to appreciate the Bellerive family's power and money. He was driving slower than usual, taking in the sights: the spring green trees parted to reveal smooth velvety grass crowned by the gleaming white showplace. The mansion was a white neoclassical house with four massive Corinthian columns.

'I bet Briggs's mother, the judge, felt right at home here,' I said. 'You almost expect to have "Equal Justice Under the Law" carved on the pediment.'

'The what?'

'That triangular thing above the four columns,' I said. I wished he'd snap out of this and be his usual street-smart Chicago self.

The marble steps leading to the double front door were wide enough for a platoon of lawyers. Clay pots the size of kettledrums lined the steps, rioting with colorful flowers. Nasturtiums, I assumed.

It had taken us nearly ten minutes to get this far. There was a long delay at the wrought-iron gate while the beige-uniformed guard called the house. He was no retiree, either. Bellerive's crewcut guard was young and fit and looked to be ex-military. Security here was serious.

Finally, the guard waved us through the gates. Jace drove up the long, curving drive at a crawl, and we parked alongside the house next to a six-car garage.

An anonymous twenty-something brunette in a plain charcoal suit and white blouse met us and took us to the side entrance. 'I'm Emily,' she said. 'One of Mr Bellerive's assistants. I'll take you to him. He's in the library.'

We went in through the kitchen, which I was relieved to see was clean but outdated, then down a dark hall with a cheap brown runner and beige walls. This was definitely the servants' entrance, but at least it brought Jace to his senses by the time Emily opened the double doors to the library.

What a room. It must have been forty feet long with twelve-foot ceilings. Three walls were lined from floor to ceiling with cherry-wood bookcases. I inhaled the perfume of old books, leather, and lemon polish. A long library table was piled with books and magazines, as well as a crystal bowl of salmon-pink nasturtiums.

Briggs was drinking coffee and reading a newspaper in a brown leather wing chair near the French doors. He stood when we entered the room. He was handsomer than in his newspaper photos, but shorter than I remembered – an inch or two shorter than my six feet. He was wearing a rather battered sport coat, well-worn but good quality. Up close, Briggs was pretty-boy handsome, with long, girlish eyelashes and a slightly weak chin. He shook both our hands, and his hands were soft and manicured.

'Angela,' he said. 'Good to see you again.' His smile revealed perfect white teeth.

He turned to Jace. 'How may I help you, Officer?'

'It's detective, Mr Bellerive,' Jace corrected him. Good, he was snapping out of it. 'Chouteau Forest Crimes Against Persons.'

Briggs raised one eyebrow. 'What kind of crime, Detective? Rape, murder, assault with a deadly weapon?' He sounded playful.

Jace did not. 'Do you know this young woman?' He showed Briggs a photo of Terri.

'I've seen her picture in the newspapers,' he said. 'She's a runner, right? And she ran off somewhere last fall?' Briggs was treating this as a joke. I could see Jace's jaw tighten. He was getting ticked off.

'Did Terri ever come here? Eat flowers for dinner?'

Oh, dear. Jace was losing his cool.

'I assure you, Officer, we don't have any lotus-eaters here. Do you know Homer?' He waved his hand at the bookcase to his left. 'We have several translations, unless you prefer to read it in Greek.'

He was mocking Jace now, flaunting his money and his education.

'However, I do like to cook with my nasturtiums, so I guess that does make me a flower eater. Angela can tell you about those. You've eaten them, haven't you, my dear?'

'Yes,' I said, my voice flat. I didn't want to be baited into responding.

'You came to dinner here with that Cuban gentleman, what was his name?'

'Mario,' I said. 'Mario Garcia. He owns Killer Cuts. He came to the US with nothing and built a successful business.'

'Admirable,' he said, dismissing me and Mario. 'What did I make for your dinner? Oh, yes, I remember, Caribbean lobster – I find Maine lobster too bland – with nasturtium mayonnaise. I make the mayonnaise from scratch, you know, and add chopped nasturtium leaves and pickled nasturtium seed pods in place of capers. What did you think of it, Angela?'

'It was interesting,' I said, my standard noncommittal answer.

'I detect a lack of enthusiasm. You must try my veal loin with nasturtiums,' he said. 'It has a marvelous peppery flavor.'

'Mr Bellerive,' Jace said, 'I'm not here to discuss recipes. I want to know if you knew Terri Gibbons?'

'No. I don't associate with high school girls, Officer.'

'Detective,' corrected Jace.

'Detective, then. I prefer adult women.'

'Was Terri Gibbons on your property for any reason? Did she

ask to run on your grounds? Was she here for some kind of special event?'

'I can assure you that Terri Gibbons, to my knowledge, has never set her fleet foot on these grounds. May I ask what this is about?'

'Terri Gibbons was found dead.'

'Oh, that's too bad,' Briggs said, as if he'd heard someone's cat had died. 'But what does that have to do with me?'

'Your name was found in her effects.'

'My name?' Briggs laughed. 'Young girls often get crushes on so-called older men. They see me in the newspapers or on TV and try to email me. After all, I'm rich and single and some of them are looking for a sugar daddy. You've heard of the sugar baby phenomenon, haven't you? Where attractive young women accommodate older men in exchange for money for college, nice clothes and exotic trips? There are even sugar baby websites. My secretary, Bernice, fends off those women for me. She gets dozens of letters and emails every month from pretty women propositioning me. She's very protective and turns them down politely. I'll have her check and see if there are any from this young woman – what was her name again?'

'Terri. Gibbons.'

Briggs picked up the phone extension on the wall and said, 'Bernice, did I get any letters or emails from a young woman named Terri Gibbons? Thank you. I'll wait.'

Briggs paced while Jace and I sat on the edge of our seats. After about four minutes, Briggs said, 'Nothing? You're sure?' Briggs winced, as if the secretary had scolded him. 'Of course. Thank you, Bernice.'

He hung up the phone and said, 'There you have it. Bernice says there was no contact with this young person at all – no phone calls, no emails, no letters. Bernice is a bit of a battleax, but nobody is more thorough. So I guess we're finished here, Officer.'

I wanted to wipe that smirk off Briggs's face. This time, Jace didn't bother correcting him about his title, but I could tell the detective had had enough. His neck and ears were red.

'No, we're not finished,' Jace said. He stood up and handed Briggs the search warrant. 'Read this.'

As Briggs read it in his wing chair, the smirk disappeared. 'Hey,' he said. 'I thought we were just having a friendly talk.'

'We were,' Jace said. 'Now playtime's over. We have a search warrant for this address.' He held up his cell phone. 'I'm making the call. Tell your guard at the gate to let my officers in.'

'Not until I clear this with my lawyer,' Briggs said. His surface politeness had vanished, along with his smile. His eyes were hard and dark.

'Feel free,' Jace said. 'You can fax him the whole thing. But I'm making my call now, too. And if my officers don't get through, you *and* your guard will be arrested.'

NINE

'Well, Angela, since my home is overrun with gendarmes, shall I show you my flowers?'

'I'd be delighted,' I said. And I was. That's why I was here – to see if he'd reveal anything about Terri's death.

He gave me his best smile, but I didn't trust it. I'd seen how he'd reacted when Jace had flipped out that warrant. His genial smile had vanished, replaced by a hard mouth and mean eyes.

At first, Briggs sputtered like an old car. Then he called his lawyer, Claude X. Obert, and ordered his assistant to fax the warrant to him. Obert said that the warrant was valid and the police had the right to search the entire Bellerive estate. Claude volunteered to monitor the search – although I don't think this was charity. He got at least seven hundred dollars an hour. Briggs told Claude to go ahead.

Meanwhile, Jace made his phone call and a platoon of police showed up at the Bellerive front gate. Jace met them there. There was a mild kerfuffle when the gate guard tried to stop the police from entering.

'We have a search warrant for this address and we'll break down this gate if we have to,' Jace said. 'Step aside or you will be arrested.'

The guard defied Jace long enough to phone Briggs, who gave

his approval – not that Briggs had any choice. I was proud of Jace.
It took guts to buck the Bellerives and their minions. Especially
since Jace wasn't connected in the Forest. People as powerful as
the Bellerives could get Jace fired with a phone call.

Jace unleashed a small army to search the estate, and he'd
organized the huge group into teams. They brought flattened
boxes, packing tape, evidence bags (plastic and paper), envelopes,
evidence tamper-proof sealing tape and more.

They were already taking video and still photographs of the
gate. They had to video and photograph the search from start to
finish. Jace would have to be able to establish where his teams
were and what that area looked like both before and after the
search. Did the police trash the place? Break anything? Crack that
Ming vase on the mantel? Videos and photos answered those
questions.

The searchers also had to document what they found and where
they found it, and how that area related to the other parts of the
estate.

The microphone on the video recorder was muted. Most detectives learned that from bitter experience. Cops were an irreverent
bunch, and used offbeat humor to get through bad scenes. Too
often during a video recording, there was what was politely called
background 'noise' from careless officers or detectives. Comments
like these were heard at a murder scene: 'The SOB deserved it'
and 'Would ya look at the size of those fake tits?' They did not
sit well with the prosecutor, much less the defense attorney.

Ten minutes after the search started, Claude X. Obert roared
up in his sleek black Mercedes. The lawyer had a lean, predatory
look and a suit only the wealthy could afford. It fit like a second
skin.

Claude advised (although it sounded like a command to me)
that Briggs stay out of the way during the search. That's when
Briggs decided to be my tour guide. He'd recovered enough to
return to his affable host mode.

Back in the library, he offered me a drink. 'Would you like
coffee, tea, or something more interesting, Angela?'

I asked for hot tea, and a uniformed maid brought it into the
library, along with a plate of 'fingerprint' butter cookies surrounded
by pink nasturtiums. The fingerprint depression was filled with a

citrusy apricot jam. Briggs poured himself a scotch, and the two of us crunched cookies for a bit.

'I gather you didn't like my nasturtium mayonnaise, Angela,' he said.

'I can't bring myself to eat flowers. They're so pretty.'

'But tender Bibb lettuce isn't? Or curly leaved Romaine?' He popped a pink nasturtium in his mouth and chewed it.

'OK, you've got a point,' I said, and took a polite sip of tea. 'But I still can't eat flowers.' I reached for another cookie.

'Really? You're eating them now.'

'Where?' I looked at my tea, as if nasturtiums were lurking in the cup.

'The cookies,' he said. 'They're made with nasturtium flowers. There are more flowers in the jam.' He was laughing. 'Admit it now. They're good with a cup of tea.'

'They are,' I agreed. 'As long as I don't know I'm eating flowers.'

'Come, come, Angela, it's not like the horrible things they put in hot dogs. You're not eating ground-up pig lips. Just gently snipped nasturtiums. And I personally inspected them for bugs and slugs.'

That did it. I put my nasturtium cookie back on my plate.

'Are you single, Angela?' The way Briggs studied my ringless left hand gave me the creeps. Or maybe it was because I knew he was a killer.

'Widowed,' I said. 'But I'm seeing someone.' And that's all I'm doing, I thought. Looking at the guy. Just keep away from me. OK?

'Let me know if you change your mind,' he said and positively leered.

I put my teacup on the tray. 'You were going to show me your flowers.'

'Right,' he said. 'Let's go.'

I followed him out into an enormous hall that could have been a hotel lobby – three crystal chandeliers, a black-and-white marble floor, lots of gold-framed mirrors (to make the place look even bigger?), and Louis the something-or-other chairs and settees scattered about.

We went through the polished black double front doors. From the vast marble porch, the pots of nasturtiums were a river of color running down the stairs. The spring breeze stirred them slightly and we were treated to a sweet perfume.

'These yellow ones are Peach Melba,' he said, 'and the trailing ones are Salmon Baby.'

'Pretty,' I said.

'Useful, too. During World War Two, when there was a shortage of pepper, people ground up the seeds and used them as a pepper substitute. Gum?'

'Excuse me?'

'Would you like a stick of gum?' He handed me a stick of Beeman's clove gum.

I was momentarily stunned. I recovered enough to say, 'Thank you' and stashed the gum in my pocket. Another link to Terri's death. And a reminder to be careful around this man, no matter how much he tried to charm me.

We followed a stone path around the house to the back, where Briggs showed me his 'kitchen garden' – a vegetable patch.

'I grow heirloom tomatoes, two kinds of potatoes – Irish Cobbler and Red Norland – asparagus and winter squash. I love to cook with them.'

'Speaking of cooking, I was surprised you had such a—' I paused. What was the polite word? Outdated? Antiquated? 'Vintage kitchen.'

'Vintage? Oh, Emily took you through the servant's entrance. That's their kitchen. Let me show you mine.'

He led me to an addition on the other side of the kitchen garden, and showed off his kitchen, rattling off terms designed to impress: a Sub-Zero refrigerator and freezer. A Viking gas range that operates with higher-than-usual BTUs, which 'allows for larger, hotter flames.' Three ovens, plus a convection oven. Warming drawers. A pot filler over the stove. Three sinks. Two dishwashers.

My head was spinning by the time we were back outside on the stone path. It was soothing to look at the massive beds of spring flowers – buttery yellow daffodils and fiery red tulips. Missouri was heavenly in the spring.

The path passed a two-story stone building with a white gingerbread porch.

'That looks like my home on the Du Pres estate,' I said. 'It used to be a guesthouse.'

'I'm not surprised they look alike,' Briggs said. 'Our guesthouse was constructed by the same architect who designed the one on the Du Pres estate. Both were built in the 1920s. As a boy, this was my "playhouse." Now it's useful for stashing unwanted guests and relatives.'

And captive young women? I wondered.

Inside, the two-story guesthouse's expensive, casual furniture had the look of a decorator's touch. No castoffs here.

By this time, the police had finished searching the main house and were starting on the guesthouse. Claude followed them inside, and stood around with his arms crossed. It was one o'clock, and the lawyer was at least twenty-one hundred bucks richer.

Jace motioned me to speak to him. I followed him past the flower beds, out of Briggs's earshot. 'This guesthouse is as big as my home,' Jace said. 'I'm hoping we'll find something here.'

I told him Briggs had given me a stick of gum, and Jace said, 'You're doing good. Keep getting him to show you things. See if you can tour those woods behind the house.'

That's the last thing I wanted to do, but I said, 'OK, just keep your ears open in case I need help.'

Back with Briggs, I pasted a smile on my face and tried to keep it there. 'You have a really big garage,' I said.

'It can hold six cars,' he said. 'Do you like cars?'

'Love them,' I said, and that was the truth.

The garage was painted white, inside and out, and the gray concrete floor was shiny. This was a showplace, not a hangout for mechanics to tinker with cars. In the first bay was a new Ford F-150 pick-up truck – the body didn't have a ding or a dent. Next to it was an old but well-cared-for gray Toyota, then a snappy BMW convertible. Next to that was a big black Mercedes. The fifth vehicle was under a gray cover.

'What's that?' I asked.

Briggs lifted the cover reverently. 'That's my 1962 E-Type Jaguar,' he said.

We both admired the sculpted silver body. 'It's a collectible,' he said. 'But one I can drive.'

'Is there a sixth car?' I asked.

'No,' he said. The garage floor was so clean, I couldn't tell if he was lying or not. But he did answer awfully quickly.

When we left the garage, I saw a cloud of pink flowers in the woods that Jace had wanted me to search. 'Are those pink dogwood?' I asked, pointing in that direction. 'Can we go see them? I love dogwood.'

'You can see them from here,' Briggs said.

'But I like to look at them up close,' I said. 'You know the legend of the dogwood, don't you? That its wood made the cross Christ was crucified on?'

'Not possible,' he said. 'The tree is too small to be a cross.' His voice was drained of its smooth affability. He sounded annoyed.

'That's it,' I said. 'The legend says the tree was distraught when it found out it had been used to crucify Christ, and Christ made it a promise: the dogwood would never again grow large enough to be used that way. Now it has cross-shaped blossoms with "blood stains" – the brown marks on the petals. Dogwood only bloom a short time each year. I have to see them.'

'Angela!' Briggs shouted. 'Come back here.'

But I didn't. I kept running toward the pink dogwood trees. They were gorgeous. And behind their lacy pink curtain was a new Range Rover. No wonder Briggs didn't want me looking at the dogwoods.

'Jace!' I yelled. 'Jace, come here!'

Both Jace and Briggs came running, followed by the lawyer. Briggs looked angry, and the lawyer showed no emotion at all. But he must have been worried, or he wouldn't be in these muddy woods, wearing his fancy shoes.

'What is it, Angela?' Jace asked.

'A green Range Rover, abandoned behind those trees,' I said.

'It's mine,' Briggs said. 'So what?'

'Why isn't it in your garage?' Jace said.

'I'm having the vehicle hauled away for scrap.'

'Your Range Rover looks almost new,' Jace says. 'There's not a mark on it. Why scrap it?'

The lawyer interrupted: 'Briggs, you don't need to answer that question.'

'Yes, I do,' Briggs said. 'I've got nothing to hide.'

When someone said that they usually had plenty to hide. My heart was pounding as Briggs kept talking. Did he use this car to transport the dead women? Was he going to talk himself into a jail cell?

'My stupid housekeeper ruined it! A freaking Range Rover! When the warm weather started this March, I wanted a barbecue. Three weeks ago, the stupid woman picked up two hundred pounds of meat and then left for the weekend. Said she had to visit her sick mother. The idiot left the meat in the Range Rover and when she came back Sunday it was rotted! Rotted – I can't get the stink out. I had to throw out all that meat and buy more.'

'What happened to the housekeeper?' I asked.

'She was fired,' Briggs said. 'Without references. I deducted the cost of the meat from her severance pay and sent her packing.'

'What's this housekeeper's name, sir?' asked Jace.

'Rosanna,' Briggs said. 'Rosanna McKim.'

'Where does she live?' Jace wrote this down in the notepad he kept in his pocket.

'Somewhere in Toonerville.' Again, the Forest elite's derisory nickname for the working section of town was used.

'Where?' Jace insisted.

'I don't know exactly. My assistant has her address.'

'Where did she buy the meat?'

'The Forest Specialty Meat and Fish Mart.'

'Would you open the vehicle, please?' Jace asked.

Briggs opened the driver's side door, and the unmistakable odor of death poured out. The lawyer looked sick to his stomach, and even I felt a little green.

'We'll have to tow this vehicle to the station for examination,' Jace said.

The lawyer opened his mouth, but Jace cut him off before he could say anything. 'We have that right and you know it, Mr Obert.'

Briggs retreated inside the mansion with his lawyer. All the way to the house, the lawyer tried to scrape the mud off his shoes on the stone path.

By the time the tow truck arrived and carted off the Range Rover, the search was concluded.

As we were leaving, Briggs presented me with a colorful bouquet of nasturtiums, tulips, daffodils and even pink dogwood.

'For you, Angela,' he said, trying again to charm me. 'They are as lovely as you are.'

'Thank you,' I said. I managed to take the huge bouquet without touching him.

I climbed into Jace's car. I was weary, and wanted out of there.

TEN

As we drove out of the Bellerive estate, Jace was positively gleeful. The detective was ready to break out the champagne. He listed the prizes from this search.

'We've got a number of small things to tie him to the victim, like that green jute gardening string. I've got a ball that looks like the same kind that garroted the victims. We've got the clove gum, so we can tie that to him. I noticed that Briggs has a brand-new wheelbarrow. That made me suspicious. Someone who's been gardening that long should have an old battered one.

'But best of all, we have the death car!' He slapped the steering wheel in celebration. 'That's thanks to you. There's no doubt what's causing that stink.'

'Briggs says his housekeeper let two hundred pounds of meat rot in there,' I reminded him. 'Her name is Rosanna McKim. I think I went to school with her older sister, Diana McKim. I didn't want to interrupt your interrogation to ask him.'

'I'm glad you didn't say anything. I had a rhythm going there and that would have put me off. I know this Briggs is guilty, Angela. You know it, too. When I told him that Terri's body had been found, he never asked me where, like an innocent person would.'

Maybe, but I was worried. I wondered if Briggs was slyly taunting us with the gum, the flowers, and the car, but I wasn't going to say anything to bust Jace's bubble. Let him celebrate for now.

Once we were on the main road, I said to Jace, 'Pull over. I want to dump these flowers.'

'Why?' he said. 'They didn't do anything. It's not their fault they were grown by Briggs.'

'They give me the creeps.' I couldn't suppress a shudder just looking at them. Every time I saw them, I pictured the dead Terri with that wilted flower in her pocket.

'There are nasturtiums in that bouquet, right? The same kind that were in Terri's pocket. We can test their DNA. Plants have DNA just like people.'

'Will the CFPD pay for a plant DNA test?' I asked.

'I doubt it, but I have a professor friend in the biology department at City University,' Jace said. 'I knew him when I worked on the Chicago force and he'll do it for free.'

'They're all yours.' I turned around and placed the bouquet in his backseat. I was relieved to be rid of it.

Soon we were back at my home. 'Thanks, Angela,' he said, as he pulled into my driveway. 'You were a big help.'

'Just don't tell anyone,' I said. 'I'm not supposed to be investigating cases.'

'Deal,' he said.

I waved goodbye. As I was unlocking my front door, my work cell phone rang. Damn. I could tell by the ringtone it was Detective Ray Greiman. I hated working with him.

'Angela,' he said. 'We've got a vehicular fatality, right off I-55.'

I got the exact address and said, 'I'll be there in ten minutes.'

I made it in eight, never mind that the traffic was backed up at the scene. I drove on the shoulder of the road until I got to the knot of official vehicles. I saw Greiman near the wreckage of a black Beemer that had slammed into a towering oak. The car's glossy front end was trashed. The Forest homicide detective looked camera-ready in his sharp navy suit and starched white shirt. Badge bunnies loved his dark good looks.

Greiman was talking to a fluffy brunette in her late twenties wearing red high heels and summery white dress, spattered with blood. Was she an accident survivor? I pulled my DI case out of the car trunk, and rolled it over to the scene. Greiman had guided the brunette to his car, wrapped her trembling body in a blanket, and helped her sit in the passenger seat. Her long, dark mane hid her face.

As I got closer, I could hear her crying. 'I don't know what happened,' she said, her words nearly drowned by her tears. 'One minute we were on the road and the next Dr Bob hit the tree. Do you think he had some kind of seizure?'

Greiman looked up. 'Oh, hi, Angela, you finally made it.'

I didn't take the bait. He was always trying to rile me. I vowed he wouldn't succeed today.

The brunette was sniffling into a tissue and dabbing at her eye make-up, which was running down her cheeks. She had doll-like features and blue eyes. An ugly bruise was coming out on her forehead.

I pulled Greiman away from the woman long enough to get the case number and the accident facts.

'The victim is Dr Robert Beningham Scott,' he said.

'The big-deal plastic surgeon?' I asked. Dr Bob, as he was known in the Forest, was the leading local doctor for breast implants and assorted nips and tucks. Rumor had it that Dr Bob enjoyed test-driving his clients' newly improved chests and gave 'special injections' in hotels.

'Couldn't you tell by the size of her tits?' he asked.

'I was looking at her face,' I said. 'I heard her say she thought the doctor might have had a seizure.'

Greiman sniggered. 'Only if she grabbed his cock with cold hands. He died with his junk out.'

'Oh.'

'This case is gonna be trouble,' Greiman said. 'He's a married society doc and she's someone else's trophy wife.' Greiman didn't mention the woman's name. She was just a brunette who 'belonged' to another rich guy.

'What's her name?' I asked.

'Melissa DeMille.'

'Is she married to Joe DeMille, the hedge funder?'

'Retired hedge funder,' Greiman said. 'Melissa is his fourth wife. They've been married six months.'

'And she was the only passenger?'

He nodded. I'd talk to her later.

'She says they were coming back from a business lunch at Solange,' he said.

Odd, I thought. That restaurant was off Gravois and they both lived in the Forest. They wouldn't need to take the highway to go to Solange or their homes.

'How fast was the car going when it hit the tree?' I asked.

'She says it was going forty, the exit ramp speed. I'm guessing it was going at least seventy miles an hour from the way that car hit the tree. This is one of the newer BMWs. I think it has a "black box" or EDR, Event Data Recorder, on board. If not, we'll have to get an accident reconstructionist.'

Greiman had pronounced Dr Bob dead at 3:46 p.m. In Missouri, a quirky law allows any adult at the scene to pronounce someone dead.

I opened my iPad to the Vehicular-Related Death form and put on four pairs of nitrile gloves. I would pull them off during the exam so I wouldn't cross-contaminate the body. The doctor was in the driver's seat, and he wasn't wearing his seatbelt. His head had hit the windshield, which was spider-webbed with cracks. The windshield was drenched in blood.

The doctor had been a handsome man with a thick mane of graying hair, now bathed in blood. He wore a charcoal three-piece sharkskin suit, light blue shirt, and rep tie, and yes, the suit pants were unzipped and his private parts were in his lap – exposed but attached, thank goodness. Still, the Scott family jewels looked like butcher shop rejects.

I brought out my point-and-shoot camera and began photo-graphing the victim. Greiman came running over, eyes wild. 'Angela! Stop! You aren't going to photograph him the way he is?'

'Yes, of course. That's my job.'

'Aren't you going to zip him up?'

'No, I can't interfere with the body.'

'That's disrespectful.'

'That's the way he died,' I said.

Greiman sneered at me. 'You can sound all high-and-mighty, but what about his poor wife?'

I knew Greiman didn't give two shakes about Dr Bob's wife – he was worried about offending the local bigwigs, including Melissa's hedge fund husband, Joe DeMille.

'It's up to the medical examiner whether he wants to mention this in his autopsy report, but I'm not interfering with a death scene.' I tried not to sound too sanctimonious.

'By the way, are you going to charge Melissa DeMille with causing this accident?'

Greiman looked at me like I had two heads. 'No, it would be

tough to prove she caused it,' he said. 'Unless she starts babbling and says she was blowing him, or he has bite marks on his dick – and he doesn't – or she chomped it off and we have her DNA on the stump – again, negative – I can't charge her. Even then, I don't see a criminal case. After all,' he said, his voice growing increasingly righteous, 'the doctor could have pulled over to pee on the side of the road and forgotten to repackage things.'

'Really? With an attractive young woman in the car?' I said. 'He just *forgot*?'

'Or maybe he took things out and tried to get her to play and she declined,' Greiman said.

'So the doctor ran into a tree and killed himself?'

'Just do your job, Angela, and I'll do mine.' He turned on his Fendi-clad heel and left.

For once, Greiman made sense. I went back to work. I bent down to check the victim's shoes to see if there was the imprint of the gas pedal on the sole – usually a sign of suicide. But Dr Bob had had his foot on the brake pedal when he'd hit that tree. Along with the coppery odor of blood, the decedent smelled strongly of alcohol. I noted that odor and mentioned that the doctor may have been drinking. The ME would check his blood alcohol level.

Next, I answered the form's road condition questions. The accident occurred on a concrete highway exit ramp, and the vehicle was southbound. The roadway was dry, there was no debris, and there was no rising or setting sun to blind the driver. The form had no boxes to check for the fatal distraction the doctor had probably encountered.

The vehicle was a black 2020 BMW M4 with a red leather interior. It could seat five. I noted the license plate number. The airbag, which might have saved him, was disabled. There were no attempts to resuscitate him at the scene.

After I'd photographed the decedent, and the police tech had photographed him and videoed him inside the car – all of him, just the way he was – I began the body actualization. I spread out a sterile white sheet from the ME's office.

Greiman was busy 'comforting' Melissa, the surviving passenger, but Mike, a patrol officer, helped me move the decedent's body onto the sheet face up.

I measured his height at six feet and estimated his weight at two-hundred-ten pounds.

Now I could see Dr Bob's injuries more clearly.

I started with his head. He had a six-inch cut on his forehead – so deep I could see the yellow-white frontal bone – and his nose appeared broken. From the angle of his neck, it also seemed to be broken. Head and facial wounds bleed a lot, and it was hard to see his features – and his hands.

The doctor had put his hands out in front of him when the car hit the tree, and they were badly fractured: three metacarpals on the left hand and two on the right had what looked like compound fractures – the delicate bones stuck up through the skin. If the doctor had survived, I wondered if he'd ever have been able to operate again. Two nails on his left hand were broken. The decedent had surgeon's hands, long, slender and well-cared-for. There was no dirt or skin under his nails, but both hands were bloody. Because of the damaged condition of his hands, I protected them with paper bags secured with evidence tape.

On his right arm, he wore a Cartier tank watch with a brown leather band. He did not wear a wedding ring or any other jewelry. His blood-soaked clothing had been beautiful. His shirt cuffs were monogrammed and his handsome charcoal suit was a Tom Ford, the same designer who dressed Daniel Craig in the James Bond movies. He had a black alligator card case in his pocket. I left it there for the ME to examine.

Dr Bob's suit was torn at the knees, and both patellas had two-inch 'cut-like defects.' I couldn't say he had cuts on his kneecaps. If this case went to court, and those marks were something besides accident-related cuts, the lawyers could tear me apart. I suspected both legs were fractured, but the ME would determine that when the body was X-rayed.

His black socks were extra-long and appeared to be silk, and his shiny black lace-ups were bespoke. There were no injuries to his feet.

'Mike, can you help me turn him?' I asked the patrolman, and he obligingly helped me roll the heavy body over. 'Whoa?' he said. 'What's this? Looks like it fell out of his back pocket.'

I picked up the white paper. It was a receipt for the Parkside Hotel, an elegant St. Louis boutique hotel. It was dated today at

2:25 p.m. That explained why the doctor was driving off an I-55 exit ramp – he and Melissa had been at a hotel in the city.

I showed the bill to Mike. 'Wow! Eighteen hundred dollars. That's more than I make in a week.'

'The good doctor treated his lady well,' I said. 'He paid nine hundred dollars for the suite, and the rest for an in-room lunch of caviar, chicken and a magnum of Roederer Cristal champagne. I don't know if 2008 was a good year, but at seven hundred dollars it was definitely a good price.' Mike whistled at the champagne price. I photographed the receipt front and back, then bagged it. It would go with the body. I found nothing unusual on the back of the body, except a thirty-seven-inch patch of blood on the shirt collar and suit jacket.

Now it was time to interview Melissa DeMille, the accident survivor, and see what lies she would feed me about her lunch with Dr Bob.

ELEVEN

Melissa DeMille told me she was twenty-six, but she looked even younger. Greiman had given her a white hand-kerchief, and she'd wiped the tear-smeared make-up off her face. Now she was weeping even harder. I couldn't tell if it was for the dead doctor or for herself.

'When did you first encounter the deceased today?' I asked. I was writing down her answers on my iPad.

'I drove to the restaurant – Solange – for a lunch meeting,' she said, through her tears. 'I'm co-chair of the Forest Holiday Ball, and I wanted to discuss a sponsorship with Dr Bob. He's so generous.'

'What did you have for lunch?' I asked.

'I had the lemon sole and he had the porterhouse. We had Caesar salads mixed at our table.'

Lie number one, I thought. No, two lies. They'd had lunch in St. Louis, not at Solange.

Melissa delicately wiped her tear-stained eyes, and the sun

caught her diamond ring and nearly blinded me. The rock was the size of an almond and her wedding band glittered with square diamonds.

'Dr Bob agreed to a Premier sponsorship – that's twenty-five thousand dollars,' she said. 'He signed the donor form. Do you think I can collect it from his estate?'

I had a hard time hiding my shock. Under that pretty exterior was a heart as cold as an arctic winter.

'You'll have to ask his wife,' I said, mostly to see her reaction.

Melissa gave an unladylike snort. 'She didn't deserve a good man like Dr Bob. They had an open marriage. He couldn't divorce her because she'd take everything he's worked for.'

Lies three and four, courtesy of Dr Bob. I'd bet my next paycheck Dr Bob didn't have an open marriage or a greedy wife. Why did women still fall for those shopworn lines?

'What happened after he signed the donor form?' I asked.

'He was taking me home when we had this terrible accident.'

Her blue eyes were clear and untroubled and she delivered yet another lie without blinking.

'Melissa,' I said. 'You told me you live on DuBarry Circle, seven miles west of here. Solange is on Gravois, ten miles west. Your home is three miles straight down Gravois. Why would Dr Bob go ten miles out of his way and take the highway?'

'I don't know,' she said. 'I wasn't driving.'

OK, time for some truth. 'Melissa,' I said. 'We found a receipt on Dr Bob for an in-room meal at a fancy hotel in St. Louis.'

'Yes.' She was wide-eyed, but not particularly innocent.

'Why were you two having lunch at the Parkside Hotel?'

'Oh, that,' Melissa said. 'He was checking my implants, but he didn't want to examine them in his office. That's so clinical. It's better if he can see them under natural circumstances.'

Right. I wondered if Melissa's insurance would cover the eighteen-hundred-dollar hotel bill.

'Was Dr Bob drinking?' I asked.

'No,' she said.

'Are you sure?' I said.

'Well, maybe just a little. My stitches had healed so well, he thought we should celebrate with champagne. It was good, too.

Cristal. I got the implants because Joey – he's my husband – wanted me to get them. I'd wanted a D-cup, but Dr Bob told me that a C-cup would look more natural. And he was right.' She lifted her generous chest for me to admire.

'And your husband? Which did he like: C or D?' OK, I shouldn't have, but I couldn't resist.

'Joey wanted a D-cup, too, but Dr Bob talked to him. He explained that a C-cup would look classier and more ladylike. Joey wants me to be a society lady. That's why I'm co-chairing the ball this year. It helps to get on the important charity committees.'

'So Dr Bob had champagne for lunch, and then he was driving you home.'

'Well, not home, exactly,' she said. 'He was taking me back to Solange, where I'd left my car. We'd had a drink there before our meeting in St. Louis.' At first, Melissa had said they were driving back from a business lunch at Solange. Now she said they were driving back to Solange.

'So how many drinks did Dr Bob have at Solange?' I asked. 'One – what? Scotch, bourbon?'

'Martini,' she said. 'Solange makes the best martinis. I like to suck his olives.'

I prayed for the strength not to turn this interview into a dirty joke. I reminded myself that I was a professional and the decedent was a man – a flawed one, maybe, but who wasn't?

'So Dr Bob had one martini at Solange?'

'Two,' she said. 'He drank most of mine, too. Then we went to the Parkside for the examination.'

'What happened to your car?'

'I left it at Solange. We were driving back to get it. At the Parkside, we also had some champagne.'

'How much?' I knew a magnum held about fifty ounces of champagne, or ten five-ounce glasses.

'I just had a glass,' she said. 'Dr Bob drank most of the bottle.' She saw me typing that on my iPad and said, 'But he wasn't drunk. Not really. Dr Bob could hold his liquor. When we left the hotel, he walked just fine. He didn't slur his words or anything. And he didn't drive too fast on the highway, either.'

I suspected the doctor had driven at a drunk's pace, just below the speed limit.

'We had a nice talk on the way home, and then he looked at his watch and said, "Jesus, I'm late!" He turned off the highway and *BAM!* – he hit the tree and was dead. It was terrible.'

'How fast was he going?'

'The speed limit,' she said. 'Forty-five.'

'Really?'

'Maybe a little faster. I wasn't paying attention.' She burst into torrents of tears. I doubted I would get more information out of her.

Now came the difficult part of my job – informing the decedent's wife. It would be doubly difficult because Dr Bob had died under embarrassing circumstances. Usually the detective who caught the case went with me, but Greiman refused. 'I have to take Melissa back to her car at Solange,' he said. 'She's too shaky to drive after the accident.'

Pretty little Melissa was clinging to him like kudzu. He helped her into the front seat of his patrol car.

'You can go with that new guy you're banging – Chris Ferretti. I gave him a call. He'll be here shortly,' Greiman said.

I started to tell him that Chris and I had just had one dinner date, but I bit back my words. There was no point trying to change his mind. He hopped into his unmarked car and drove off with Melissa.

By the time the morgue van had arrived for Dr Bob and I'd signed the conveyance paperwork, Chris was there, looking fresh and handsome in his uniform.

'Detective Greiman radioed me and said you needed an escort to inform the next of kin,' he said. I could smell his spicy aftershave.

'Thanks. Greiman took the accident survivor back to her car.'

'Let me guess,' he said. 'She's young and pretty.'

'You're catching on,' I said. 'I'm glad for the company. This is one of the downsides of the job.'

'You never know how the next of kin are going to react,' he said. 'In Chicago, a grieving father whipped out his gun and tried to shoot the minister who told him his only son had died in a drive-by.'

'Wow. I've never had anyone react like that. Mostly, they try to hit me. I'm not expecting Samantha Scott, the late doctor's wife, to attack me, but you never know.'

I gave Chris the address – number two Laurent Lane – and he followed me. Dr Bob had lived in a massive white stone Romanesque revival mansion bristling with arches and pillars and stained glass. We climbed the white stone steps and I rang the doorbell.

A thin blonde woman in her early forties answered the door. She saw the two of us – me in my DI black suit and Chris in the CHPD uniform, and rage transformed her delicately boned face into an angry mask.

'He's dead, isn't he? Let me guess – he was drinking and driving and he had some slut with him. Did he kill her? Tell me he did. Please tell me he did!'

Chris was too stunned to answer. I gently took the new widow's hand and led her inside to her living room. The main foyer was an impressive display of nineteenth-century oak woodwork, which glowed in the slanting afternoon sun. We crossed an Oriental rug the size of a pocket park, and I sat her down on an antique velvet sofa.

'Mrs Scott, I'm sorry to inform you that your husband did die in a car accident, and it appears that he had been drinking. The medical examiner will be able to confirm that.'

'Who was the slut he had with him?' she asked, her voice hard. 'Is she dead, too?' Her blue eyes were narrowed, and framed by deep crow's feet, and her chest was flat as a tabletop. She definitely didn't use her husband's services.

'Uh, he was accompanied by Mrs Melissa DeMille. She was unharmed.'

'He did her tits! Let me guess – he'd been examining them at some hotel.'

I didn't reply.

'Hah! She wants to break into society. I'll make sure this is the last major event she co-chairs. And I don't care how many tables her husband buys – she'll never be allowed in society! She'll be shunned by everyone!'

While Samantha Scott was pronouncing the fate of her husband's paramour, I pulled my iPad out of my purse.

Chris said, 'Mrs Scott, may I make you some coffee or tea?'

'Tea, please. It's in the kitchen. First cabinet.'

'Mrs Scott, I'm the death investigator on your husband's accident,' I said. 'I have a few questions for my files.'

Samantha Scott was nibbling the polish on her French manicure. She had the hands of a chronic nail biter – her nails were gnawed well below the rounded tops of her fingers, and her cuticles were ragged. The manicurist did their best to make her nails look almost normal, but it was a hopeless task.

'Go ahead,' she said. 'I'll answer them.'

Samantha Scott said the doctor's health was nearly perfect. 'He got a clean bill of health this December and he takes no medications. He's not allergic to anything, either. He started drinking heavily about a year ago. Bob's staff enabled him: they scheduled his most difficult operations first thing in the morning, and none after lunch, when he usually had too much to drink. I prayed that he wouldn't botch those procedures and we'd lose everything in a malpractice suit. In fact, I even made an anonymous complaint to the hospital's Impaired Physicians Committee. They did nothing. My husband was a big moneymaker for SOS.'

I continued with my list. 'Did he have any hospitalizations?' I asked.

'None,' she said.

'Any mental illnesses?'

'None, unless you count humping everything in a skirt.' With that, her anger dissolved into tears, and she pounded on a velvet couch pillow.

'I still love the two-timing bastard,' she said. 'And I hate myself for being so weak.'

Chris came in with a mug of hot green tea. Samantha sipped some and thanked him.

When Samantha was calmer, I said, 'Mrs Scott, is there someone you'd like to stay with you?'

'My sister, Vanessa. I'll call her now.'

She went into another room to make the call, then came back and said, 'She'll be here in ten minutes.'

She sat in silence, sipping her tea, until we heard a car in the gravel drive. Samantha looked out the window and said, 'That's her. You can leave. I'll be OK.'

She paused, then said, 'I hated myself for loving that tomcat, but I did. Now the spell is broken. I'm free.'

TWELVE

As soon as her sister arrived, Samantha couldn't wait to get rid of us. Vanessa jumped out of her white Mercedes coupe, and ran up the stone steps. She was a younger, leaner version of Samantha, with long dark hair.

'Sam, darling!' she cried, and folded the new widow into her arms. Samantha cried on her sister's shoulder. Vanessa hugged her tightly, then guided her to the sofa and turned to Chris and me.

'You can go now,' she said and showed us the door, in case we didn't get the point.

We did. I stashed my iPad back in my purse, and nodded at Chris. He was ready to go. After we walked out the door, Vanessa slammed the door behind us – and locked it.

We'd been given the bum's rush. Chris and I found ourselves standing in Samantha's driveway.

'Do you feel as dazed as I do?' Chris said.

'Yes, that was unreal.'

'I'm off work now. Would you like to grab a coffee at the new shop, Supreme Bean?'

'I'd be delighted,' I said, and this time I didn't hesitate. I wanted to be with Chris. No reservations.

I was angry at our high-handed treatment by the two sisters, and needed to shake off my anger. I knew people did strange things when shocked by grief. Talking it out over coffee with Chris would help me relax after a trying emotional scene.

We climbed into our cars and met again at the coffee shop, about a mile away. The lot was crowded and we were lucky to snag two parking spaces. Supreme Bean was a small white Victorian cottage trimmed with gingerbread. Inside, the walls were lined with bookshelves. The shop was crowded with twenty-something customers. Some lounged on the Oriental rugs or stretched out on the comfortable sofas. Others sat at tables and chairs. All were chatting, drinking coffee and studying their smart phones. A few even read magazines and fat school textbooks.

A blackboard announced the specials: oatmeal raisin cookies and avocado toast on seven-grain bread. Homemade desserts and snacks were displayed behind the counter. We were greeted by the smiling owner, Trey, a thirty-something guy in jeans with his dark hair done up in a man bun.

Chris and I both settled for dark, rich Colombian coffee in thick brown mugs and a couple of oatmeal raisin cookies. We spotted an empty table by the window. Chris chose the seat where he faced the door. I smiled when he did that: cops were only comfortable when they could watch the entrance.

Once we settled in, Chris said, 'That woman had the strangest reaction. Talk about a love-hate relationship with her husband.' He was careful not to mention Samantha's name or her dead husband's. I did the same. This was a smart move in a public space, where eavesdropping was a popular sport.

'Poor woman,' I said. 'He must have humiliated her daily. At least she gets his money. Even though that's cold comfort.' I crunched my cookie and wrapped my hands around my coffee cup for its warmth. I still felt cold after my encounter with Samantha and Vanessa.

'She's an attractive woman,' Chris said. 'I hope she finds the right man.'

'If that's what she wants,' I said. 'After that marriage, she may prefer to live without one. At least she has her sister to take care of her.'

Chris asked how the investigation into the 'young women' was going, and in the sketchiest terms, I told him we were waiting for the results of the items we'd gotten from the search.

From there, Chris talked about the searches and crime scenes he'd known in his job. 'Nobody in my family was ever a cop,' he said. 'My mom thinks the murders I encounter are like the ones on TV. You know, where the dead victim is artistically arranged in a perfectly clean home.'

'The decedent is blonde, of course,' I said.

'And beautiful,' he said.

'Her living room has expensive Italian furniture,' I said, 'and an all-white carpet. A few decorative drops of blood are splashed about to add pops of color to the scene.'

He laughed, and said, 'I don't tell Mom anything that would change her image. She worries enough.'

I was happy for this chance to get to know Chris. When we went to dinner at Solange, I'd still been keeping him at arm's length. Our conversation had been more impersonal. Not today.

'Is your father still alive?' I sipped my coffee. The temperature was just right.

'No, he died two years ago and Mom died a year later. I understand you're a widow.'

'Yes,' I said. I let it go at that. I didn't want to bring Donegan into this.

'And a couple of years ago you had your own brush with death – six strokes and brain surgery?'

Another subject I liked to avoid. 'Yes, but I'm fine now. Healthy as a horse. So tell me about some of the crime scenes you don't want your mom to know about.' I bit into my cookie. It was fresh and tasted of cinnamon, nutmeg and honey.

'The worst ones were when I was a new uniform,' he said. 'When I first started, I got all the bad jobs. I'd show up in my new pressed uniform with my shiny shoes, and the old cops loved to send me Dumpster diving. Those were the worst. The owner of a pizza joint had been shot to death in a hold-up and I had to search the rat-infested Dumpster behind the place for the murder weapon.'

'What did you do?' I asked. 'You couldn't shoot the rats.'

'No, but I got lucky. A tough old alley cat showed up at the scene, just like he'd been sent as back-up. In fact, that's what I named him – Back-Up. He was a real battle-scarred veteran with one ear. He heard rustling and leaped over the yellow tape. The crime scene people tried to stop him, but I said to leave him alone. Back-Up cleaned that Dumpster out faster than you could blink. Rats were flying everywhere – and some were almost as big as the cat. When it was over, I rewarded him with a can of Fancy Feast. From the way he acted, you would have thought he was dining on caviar.'

'Not bad,' I said. 'Eco-friendly rat removal.'

'For less than a buck,' he said. 'The murder weapon had been dropped down a sewer two blocks away. I had to climb down and search that, too. We caught the killer, a stupid kid who threw his life away – and the store owner's – for sixty-eight dollars. Old

Back-Up patrolled the neighborhood alleys for years and every week I left a can of Fancy Feast for him.'

He laughed, then drank his coffee. I smiled at him, and drank mine. I liked a man who was kind to animals. I also liked the way his hair curled around his ears. His Old Spice was a manly smell.

'Did I ever tell you about the time I had a death investigation in a hoarder's house?' I said, and we were off, swapping stories.

Periodically, we would get up to order more coffee. Then a couple of plates of avocado toast and another round of cookies. In between, I admired the way Chris smiled, and the crinkles around his eyes. I'm a sucker for eye crinkles.

Chris was telling me about investigating a 'shots fired' in a bad neighborhood. 'It was a horrible place,' he said. 'My partner and I were down in the basement. I thought it had brown walls. Then my partner put his hand on the wall and it moved – the wall was covered with roaches!'

I shivered and eyed the raisin in my last bit of cookie suspiciously, then said, 'I once had an investigation—'

'Excuse me,' said Trey, the owner. He was using an old-fashioned floor sweeper to get the crumbs by our table. That's when I noticed it was dark outside, and the other customers had left.

'Good heavens, Trey, how late is it?' I asked.

'Five to seven,' he said. 'We're closing soon.'

'We've talked the afternoon away,' Chris said, standing up. He left a ten spot on the table, but Trey handed it back. 'Thanks,' he said, 'I appreciate it, but you don't have to tip me. I'm the owner. Just come back soon.'

I grabbed my purse. I was so full of coffee, I sloshed. But I felt good. For a couple of hours I'd forgotten that I was a widow and lost the endless burden of my grief. It was fun to talk to another professional who understood my job.

Chris and I walked slowly to the now empty parking lot. When we reached my car, he asked, 'Would you like to go to dinner?'

'Now?' Suddenly, I panicked. Our cup of coffee was turning into an all-day date. I wasn't ready for that. It was too soon. Where would it lead?

'Yes, dinner,' he said. 'Do you like Mexican? We can go to Gringo Daze.'

My panic increased. If I went to a local hangout like Gringo,

I might as well take out a billboard that said, 'Angela Richman is dating Chris Ferretti.'

'Uh, I have plans,' I said.

'Tonight?' He didn't believe me.

'Yes.'

With that, he kissed my lying lips. It was a good kiss, sweet and firm, slightly coffee-scented. I kissed him back, hard. My fingers ran through his hair. Then I pulled myself away, breathing a little too hard. It was the first time I'd kissed a man – really kissed him – since Donegan had died. I didn't know what to think, but I knew I wanted to run.

'I have to go,' I said, slipping out of his arms and into the safety of my car.

'Angela, you will see me again?' He looked forlorn now.

'Yes,' I said.

I put the car in gear and drove to my dark, empty house. All the way home, I cursed my cowardice.

THIRTEEN

After a restless, sleepless night – and don't ask me what was running through my head, I just want to forget it – I finally gave up the fight for sleep at about seven a.m.

It was a warm spring morning and I went for a walk on the Du Pres estate to clear the cobwebs out of my head. The air smelled like flowers and green things. New plants were coming out so fast, I could almost hear them growing.

I was still on call that day, and I hoped I didn't have a death investigation. At least, not another one like yesterday's.

I kept my office cell phone on all day, taking it with me everywhere. Most death investigators go into an office when they are on call, but not me. I lost my office spot because Evarts Evans, the ME, wanted a state-of-the-art shower. I still had a desk in the office, but it was too small to use. And a computer, but it was too old and unreliable.

But good ol' Evarts had a spa with rain shower sprays, six pairs of body jets custom-designed to target his shoulders, middle, and knees, plus a spray for his head, and steam, lights and music. Yes, music. The ME never forgot the case of the woman who was accidentally electrocuted when her radio fell into her shower. He had a set of JBL wireless waterproof speakers.

A spa like this required extra space. The ME and I had an unspoken agreement – I got my freedom (as long as I stayed in touch with the office), and he got his stone-clad shower.

Don't get me wrong. Evarts wasn't a bad guy, but he was a bit of an operator. He convinced the Chouteau County Commission that this luxury shower was necessary for his job and they bought it – both his argument and the spa. He also had a practice putting green in his office. He was a scratch golfer, unless he was playing an important member of the local gentry, when he knew how to lose gracefully.

In the name of compassion, he justified politically smart decisions. He'd rule that a bigwig's suicide was an 'accidental death.' He gave the tricky cases to his hardworking assistant ME, my friend Dr Katie Kelly Stern.

I couldn't drop by and see Katie this morning. She was doing Dr Bob's autopsy.

Instead, after I ran some errands, I wanted to go to the site of the body dump. I had to find out if there was anything to help our case against Briggs Bellerive. The investigation had been dubbed the Women in the Woods by the press. They still swarmed the area like blowflies on a corpse. Each day, a passel of reporters were sent out to the scene in case the investigators found something – or someone.

Dana Murdoch, the forensic anthropologist from City University, had to run this gauntlet every working day, keeping a tense silence as the reporters lobbed questions at her. I knew she usually forgot her lunch, or got by on snacks, so I stopped by Gringo Daze, my favorite Mexican restaurant, and ordered two lunches to go. The grease-spotted bags smelled heavenly, and it was only out of friendship that I resisted attacking them.

It was eleven-thirty by the time I got to the entrance of the site, way back in the woods. I politely pushed through the throng of reporters, then showed my ID to the uniform on duty. By then, it was another sweltering spring day. Once again, I admired the

newly green trees and flowering redbud and dogwood as I trekked
to the site, but I was sweating by the time I got there.

Dana was excavating under a white tent, to keep the press from
seeing her work. Helicopters flew over daily, hoping to see her
unearth the dead women.

Dana was tall and sturdy with short red hair and shrewd
brown eyes. Not much escaped her notice. Unlike many redheads,
her skin was tanned a golden brown. She came out of the tent
carrying a trowel and a small brush. Her boots, khaki shorts and
T-shirt were all liberally smeared with mud. She wiped her
sweating forehead, left a brown streak on it, then pulled off
her work gloves.

'Angela!' she said, her face lit with a smile. 'This is a surprise.'

'I brought lunch.' I held up the bags.

'Even better. I was about to dine on a pack of peanuts and
bottled water. What else brings you here?'

I told you she was shrewd. 'I did the first body inspection
and I wondered what you've found so far.'

'Pull up a chair,' she said, dragging out two lawn chairs from
alongside the tent. She carried over a foam cooler, put it between
our chairs, pulled out two bottles of cold water, and put the lid
back on. 'That's our table.' She looked into the brown bag of food.
'This smells good. What did you bring?'

'Guacamole, fish tacos and flan,' I said. 'Let me bring you up
to date on what I know.' I didn't worry that Dana would tell
anyone. She was as silent as the graves she worked. She crunched
chips and guacamole while I filled her in on what we had.

I told her about the note the victim had tucked in her shoe, and
Dana whistled. 'Briggs Bellerive? She named him? I don't live in
the Forest and even I know his name. That guy's at every local
charity event between here and St. Louis. He gave major money
to both the senate and governor's races. Definitely rich and famous.'

'Also connected,' I said.

'You're going to have a hard time pinning these murders on
him.'

'We know. We've found some things when we searched his
estate and now we're waiting for word on whether it's enough for
an arrest.'

We ate our slippery fish tacos with our laps full of napkins.

Another reason I was glad we were out in the woods – this lunch was a messy business. Tacos are best tackled in the company of good friends, with no other witnesses.

Over flan, we talked about Dana's findings. 'I started with the oldest body,' she said. 'My guess is it's been in the ground about three years, but don't quote me. There was some plant growth over the grave, and fortunately, the plants were annuals.'

Unfortunately, I wasn't as keen a gardener as my mother.

'That means they grow back every year?' I said.

'Right. A biologist took the plant stems and roots. She said they had at least three rings. That usually means three years.'

'What kind of shape was the decedent in?'

'Not bad. She was almost totally skeletonized, but the victim was buried deep enough that the scavengers didn't get to her and scatter her remains. Some remnants of her hair and clothing survived. We know she was a blonde.

'Judging from the clothing, I'm guessing the woman was either a runaway with little or no money, or a sex worker, probably a streetwalker.'

'A streetwalker? In the Forest?'

'I doubt it,' she said. 'The cops would chase her off. But the Stroll in St. Louis is only forty minutes away. The killer could have picked her up there.'

'Series killers often start with sex workers,' I said. 'They're the most at risk.

'What was she wearing that makes you think she was in the so-called oldest profession?'

'It appears she had on black plastic boots, a short skirt made of some sort of synthetic material, and a fur-like jacket,' Dana said. 'The good thing about those fabrics – polyester, rayon and plastic – is that they last for years. Not as long as silk and wool, but long enough to help us.'

'What was her age?'

'Late teens, early twenties, but don't hold me to it. I'd like to get her on my table in my lab. I want to get a look at her sternum, where the ribs join. That's a good indicator of age. But judging by the teeth and the lack of arthritis, she was definitely young.'

'Oh.' I felt a stab of sadness. 'She'd barely started her life before it was over.'

'And a hard life it was. This wasn't a rich girl, not judging by those clothes.'

'Anything else?'

'I think she was right-handed. That's just a guess right now, but the upper arm bones on the right side are wider.'

'What was her race? Can you tell?'

'Caucasian. No children. She's never been pregnant.'

'I've heard you can tell that in a skeleton. Is it easy?'

'If she'd had a child, there would be a series of pockmarks about the size of shotgun pellets along the inside of the pelvic bone. Those are caused by the tearing of the ligaments during childbirth. It's a violent process. Mind you, we can't tell how many children a woman has had by looking at her bones, but we can tell if she'd been pregnant, and this woman wasn't.'

'Any tags on her clothes or name tags?' I asked.

'None. Those were deliberately cut out. The killer also cut off her fingertips – the distal and intermediate phalanges on both hands are missing. The killer used a saw.'

I shuddered. 'I hope the cuts were post-mortem.'

'The killer thought he was so smart. He did everything to hide this woman's identity. He cut off her fingertips, cut out any clothing labels, threw away any ID. But he missed one thing.'

'What?'

'She had breast implants,' Dana said. 'Most implants have a lot number and a serial number. The manufacturer compiles this information into a data registry that can be accessed in order to track down the patient about a safety concern or product recall. But it's a big help to law enforcement. We'll know her name soon. Funny, isn't it?' Dana said. 'How many men look at a woman's chest and never see her?'

FOURTEEN

Chris called me twice that day, but I didn't pick up his calls. The same for the next day. Each time he asked me out to dinner. I was too confused to answer. I didn't know how I felt about him. His kiss caught me by surprise.

On the third day, when I continued to ignore his calls, he drove to my home. I peeked out my window and saw him parking in the driveway about six o'clock on a warm spring night.

He pounded on my door. At first, I didn't answer. I was in no mood for visitors.

'Angela,' he said. 'I know you're in there. Do I have to break down the door for a police welfare check? No one's seen you in three days!'

'I'll be down in a minute!' He wasn't going away. I might as well get it over with.

I'd been mooching around the house for the last three days in a sweatshirt and jeans. Now I ran a brush through my hair, put on a slash of lipstick and changed into a clean white blouse. I didn't know whether to be pleased or angry that he came to my house. Did I want a so-called 'masterful' man in my life? Or was Chris a controlling bully? Whatever was going on, I was going to find out right now.

I flung open my front door, prepared to give him a piece of my mind.

Chris handed me a big bunch of daffodils, the color of spring sunshine.

'Angela!' he said. 'I'm so glad you're all right. I was worried about you.'

'Nothing to worry about,' I said. 'I just like to be by myself.' I sounded snippy, but I didn't care.

'Since you didn't want to go out to dinner with me, I've brought you dinner.' He held up a foam cooler and burlap tote bag and smiled. 'May I come in? Please? I don't want to be a stalker. If you don't want dinner, I'll go away and never call you again.'

Dinner. Hm. That was tempting. When I went into hibernation, like I did for the last three days, I lived mostly on tea, toast and scrambled eggs. And speaking of tempting, Chris looked damned good in a starched white shirt and jeans. Smelled nice, too. Coffee and Old Spice.

'Well . . .'

'Good,' he said. He was in my living room, examining my bookshelves. 'I like this room,' he said. 'It has a good feel.' He was right. It did. I liked the leather couch and the worn Oriental rug.

'My father built those bookshelves,' I said. 'This used to be my parents' home. I grew up here. The kitchen is this way.'

He carried the cooler into my kitchen and set the cooler on the round oak table. I was still carrying the bouquet of daffodils like a demented bridesmaid. I quickly found a vase, cut the stems, and put the flowers in water. Their springlike scent filled the kitchen.

'The kitchen,' he said. 'That's the heart of the house.'

'That's what my mother always said.' I was glad I'd put three days of coffee mugs and dirty plates in the dishwasher and turned it on. The kitchen was presentable.

'I wasn't sure if you ate red meat,' Chris said. 'I hope you like wild salmon.'

'Love it,' I said.

'How about honey-grilled salmon?' He took the top off the cooler. Inside were four salmon fillets, small covered plastic dishes, and a cast-iron skillet. 'I have all the ingredients and I can make it quickly. The grilled vegetables are ready to go into the oven.'

He took out a large glass dish with broccoli, cauliflower, new potatoes and red peppers in neat rows. They'd been drizzled with oil. 'May I put them in your oven?'

'Yes, of course.' Thank goodness I hadn't stuffed any unwashed pots in there. One advantage of staying home for three days was I'd done the housework and laundry.

He set the oven on broil, then said, 'And last, but not least.' Chris produced a chilled bottle of Clos du Bois 2006 Riesling.

'It's a crisp wine. Not too sweet. Now, if you don't mind, I'm going to take over your kitchen for a bit.'

'Fine with me,' I said. 'I'll set the table.'

I got out my new white place mats and napkins, then used my mother's best flowered china and silver. I polished the water and wine glasses with a towel, and set them out. With the bouquet of daffodils and the thin, shining crystal, it was a good-looking table. I didn't bring out any candles. Those would be too intimate. I was glad Chris didn't bring me roses. Donegan always gave me roses.

I sat on a wooden stool and watched Chris cook. The peppered salmon steaks were on a plate. He'd added butter to the cast iron skillet, and it was nicely browned. He sautéed the chopped garlic, and added honey, soy sauce and lemon juice with small, expert movements.

'That smells delicious,' I said.

'That's what I intended.' He deftly added the salmon, then put the whole skillet in the broiler. 'It will be ready in five minutes. The veggies are about ready, too.'

Meanwhile, he uncorked the wine and poured two generous glasses. 'Sit down and relax,' he said. 'I'll bring your dinner over.'

So I sat and let myself be served. From the tote bag he produced a bag of crusty rolls and two ramekins of fresh butter. He plated the salmon and vegetables and set them down in front of me. I enjoyed the fragrant smell. Chris brought his own plate to the table and sat down.

I lifted my wineglass. 'To the chef!' I said.

'To the hostess,' he said, clinking my glass. 'Thank you for letting me barge in and have dinner with you.'

I decided to ignore that comment. Instead, I took a forkful of salmon. The honey, garlic and soy blended perfectly. 'This is heavenly. Where did you learn to cook?'

'My mother,' he said. 'She was a single mom, and didn't believe in what she called "gender-associated stupidity." So I had to learn how to cook, clean house and do laundry – all those things many men are never taught. My sister, Julie, had to learn how to change a tire and the oil on our car. Once, Julie shrieked when she saw a furry spider in the kitchen and asked me to kill it. Mom put Julie in charge of home wildlife removal – ants, spiders, roaches and mice.'

He paused for a moment to try his own salmon, then said, 'I don't mean that our home was overrun with bugs.'

'Every house has a few critters,' I said. 'Your mother sounds like quite a woman.'

'She was,' he said, and his face was suddenly sad. 'She died of breast cancer a year ago. I still miss her.'

'My mom went that way, too,' I said. Over the warm food, we talked about our families.

'We were both lucky to grow up in good families,' I said. 'I need that reminder for my job. Especially after encountering people like Samantha Scott.'

'What I don't understand,' Chris said, 'is why she didn't just divorce the bastard.'

'Money,' I said. 'It's at the root of so many marriages in the

Forest. Some people will do anything to keep their comfortable lives.'

'Until they can't take it any more,' Chris said. 'That's when I get a call – or you do.'

We were off the topic of our happy families before the stories turned too sappy. I was relieved. Now we swapped stories about dysfunctional families we'd known – and they were many.

'I had to do a welfare check on a family,' Chris said. 'Nice, suburban family. Big new house. Well-cared-for. The father worked for a bank. Mom didn't work outside the home. The school said the little girl hadn't been to classes in four days. I went to the house and found the front door open, and the mother passed out in the front hall. Turns out she was addicted to oxy. The seven-year-old girl – a sweet little thing – had stayed home from school to take care of the baby because "Mommy was sick."

'Daddy was on a business trip in San Francisco. When I called him, he said he knew his wife had a "little problem with pain pills" but told me "she'd get over it." He was outraged when I had his wife admitted to the detox ward and called child protective services for the two kids. He screamed at me that "this doesn't happen to people like us."'

'Except it did,' I said. By this time, I was mopping the last of my sauce on my plate with my roll.

'How about coffee and dessert?' Chris said.

I rose to make coffee. 'I have some vanilla bean ice cream in the freezer.'

'And I have homemade chocolate truffles,' he said. He pulled a blue dish out of the tote bag, and there were a dozen round truffles.

'You made these yourself?'

'They're not that difficult,' he said. He tried to look modest, but it didn't work. I quickly made us coffee.

While it brewed, Chris said, 'These four are coated with pecans, these have chocolate sprinkles. These four have espresso powder and the last group have Dutch process cocoa.'

'What's Dutch process cocoa?'

'It's sometimes called European chocolate. It has a more intense chocolatey flavor than natural cocoa. It's also darker. Oreo cookies are made from Dutch process cocoa.'

The coffee maker was giving its final blurps and burbles. I poured us both coffee and brought dessert plates and forks for the truffles.

With that, my phone rang.

'Sorry, Chris,' I said. 'That's my work phone. I have to take this.'

It was Katie. 'I have the final results for your search of the Bellerive estate,' she said. 'Can you meet me in my office at eight a.m. tomorrow?'

'Of course,' I said. 'Can you tell me anything now?'

'Not a peep,' she said. 'They'd have my head – and my job. The department is terrified of leaks. I'll see you and Jace in the morning.'

She hung up. I saw that Chris had cleared the table. I gave him the news. 'That's good, isn't it?' he asked.

'I don't know,' I said. 'Katie wouldn't give me a hint.'

'Drown your sorrows with a truffle.'

He didn't need to ask twice. I tried one with Dutch process cocoa first.

'So?' he said. 'Your verdict?'

'It's creamy and smooth,' I said. 'And it tastes nothing like an Oreo.'

I took another sip of coffee to clear the palate, then tried the truffles with chocolate sprinkles.

'Equally good,' I said, and reached for a pecan truffle.

'Downright amazing.'

'What's your favorite?' I asked.

'Espresso,' Chris said. So I tried that one, too. We'd – OK, mostly me – had gone through half a dozen truffles in about five minutes.

'Let's take our coffee into the living room,' I said.

Chris looked up at the kitchen clock. 'It's nine o'clock,' he said. 'I better go.'

'No, it's OK. Stay and talk,' I said.

But he was already packing the dishes he'd brought into the cooler. 'At least let me clean those for you,' I said. 'You shouldn't take home dirty dishes.'

'Wouldn't think of it,' he said, adding the dirty skillet to the pile.

'What about your truffles?'

'They're your truffles now,' he said, and before I knew it, he was out the door.

As his car drove off into the spring evening, I thought, Damn. He didn't even kiss me.

I was more confused than ever.

FIFTEEN

At eight the next morning, Jace and I were crammed into Katie's coffin-sized office, with barely enough room to move. Once again, I drew the short straw and got stuck sitting on the wire chair, a contraption Torquemada would have coveted for his torture chamber. Jace perched on the edge of Katie's desk.

I kept my work cell phone out. I was on call today, and hoped all the Forest denizens would stay alive until Katie finished.

I stifled a yawn – I'm not a morning person. Jace looked alert and eager, with an irritatingly sunny smile. He was ready for the results of our search warrant and expecting good news.

Katie was wired. I could feel the energy radiating from her. She wore her usual brown suit and sensible heels and couldn't stop pacing. She'd moved her paperwork piles to the top of the filing cabinet, and had a breakfast spread for us on her desk: bagels, cream cheese, fresh fruit and hot coffee.

Jace eyed the food like a hungry teenager. 'Is this a victory celebration?'

'More like a consolation prize,' Katie said. That wiped the smile off Jace's face. He poured two cups of black coffee, and handed one to me.

'OK, I have the final report,' she said. 'If you want to get it direct from the horse's mouth, you can spend the day chasing down the experts. Or I can tell you everything at once.'

'Go ahead,' Jace said. The smile was back – sort of. He looked like he was facing a firing squad and trying to look brave.

Katie finally sat down behind her desk. She was in full lecture mode.

'Jace, your warrant said you could search Briggs's house and anywhere or anything on the property, including any outbuildings, vehicles, sheds, and storage containers.'

We nodded. I reached for a cinnamon-raisin bagel and spread it with cream cheese. The carbs would cushion the shock of what came next. I could tell Katie was warming up for an ugly surprise.

'As I said before, Terri Gibbons, the victim I examined, was garroted with garden twine. The cause of death was manual strangulation, possibly auto-erotic. The victim was strangled with green garden string made from jute. You recovered a ball of jute string during the search.'

'Right.' Jace's smile looked hopeful.

'The string you found was a nearly new ball. It had no connection to the string used to kill the victim, except that it was the same brand. And that's not much help, either. That string is sold in most garden stores, all Home Depots and on the internet. So anyone can buy it anywhere, any time.'

It was painful to watch Jace's smile crumple and slide off his face. 'I wasn't expecting much from the string anyway,' he said.

I suspected Jace was trying to make himself feel better. 'But what about the death car?' He pasted the smile back on and waited.

'Right,' Katie said. 'The Range Rover that was ruined because the housekeeper left two hundred pounds of barbecue meat to rot inside it.'

'Barbecue, my eye!' Jace said. 'You can't fool a homicide detective's nose. There was a decomposed body in that Range Rover. I could smell it.'

'Maybe,' Katie said. 'But the spoiled barbecue meat contaminated the DNA results. They came back as "animal protein." That's what we are – animals. I suspect Bellerive used the Casey Anthony dodge.'

'The what?' I said.

'Casey Anthony,' Jace said. 'Didn't she kill her little girl a couple of years ago?'

'The police and prosecutors said she did,' Katie said. 'She was indicted for murder and a slew of other serious charges, along with four lesser counts of providing false information.

'Listen hard,' Katie said. 'This may save your ass if you're ever accused of murder. Casey Anthony lived in Orlando, Florida. She was arrested on suspicion of killing her two-year-old girl, Caylee, and the story went worldwide. Caylee was reported missing by her grandmother, who said she hadn't seen Caylee for a month, and her daughter would only make excuses for the toddler's whereabouts. The grandmother told 911 that Casey's car smelled like a dead body had been in it. The cops searched the car and used a cadaver dog, who picked up the scent of decomp in the trunk.

'An expert said an air-test sample from the car *also* showed the presence of human remains in the trunk.

'Casey went on trial for capital murder – the prosecution wanted the death penalty for this child killer. They painted her as a party girl who didn't want a child. The experts piled in and testified that the odor in the trunk was definitely a decomposing body – Caylee's body.

'The jury didn't buy the murder charges. The trial was the goatfuck of the century.'

Jace blinked at Katie's blunt language and said, 'The experts did seem to be stumbling all over one another.'

'I didn't realize she got off,' I said. 'What happened?'

'Turns out there was a bag of decomposing garbage in Casey's car trunk, and that threw off the DNA results,' Katie said. 'So, if you've been hauling bodies in your car, toss a couple of pounds of hamburger in the car trunk. Or, in Bellerive's case, two hundred pounds of decaying barbecue meat. He moggled up the results good and proper. Your so-called death car is useless, Jace.'

Jace seemed resigned. 'What about the clove gum?' he asked.

'Yes, Briggs chews it,' Katie said. 'But so what? It's common. I can buy it by the case on Amazon.'

'So we have nothing?' Jace looked like a five-year-old who'd just heard there was no Santa Claus.

'Have you talked to the careless housekeeper yet?' Katie asked him. 'The one who ruined the Range Rover?'

'No, but I will.' He set his cup down on the desk so hard it sloshed coffee everywhere. Katie handed him a pile of napkins and he mopped up the mess – and helped himself to a plain bagel. I fixed myself another cinnamon-raisin.

By this time, Jace's disappointment at the news had turned to outrage. 'Bellerive is smart, Angela. He's taunting us. We'll get him.' He took a murderous bite out of his bagel.

I heard a soft whimpering. 'Is that you, Jace?' I asked.

'No,' he said, with his mouth full. 'It's coming from under the desk.'

We both looked down and saw a fat yellow puppy waddling out from under Katie's desk. He put his big paws on my shoes.

'He's adorable,' I said, picking up the pup and scratching his fuzzy ears. 'Katie, when did you get a puppy?' I cuddled the furball and he licked my nose with his pink tongue.

'Yesterday. His name is Cutter,' Katie said.

'He's a cute little fellow,' Jace said. 'What flavor?'

'He's a Lab-golden mix,' Katie said. 'Eight weeks old. I tried to leave him at home in his crate, but he cried.'

'And you couldn't leave him at home,' I said.

'He's just been separated from his mother,' Katie said.

I scratched the pup under the chin, and he bit my nose.

'Ow!' I said, more from surprise than pain.

'What did he do?' Katie asked.

'He bit my beezer.'

'Bad dog!' Katie swatted the pup on his black nose and he whined.

'It's OK, Katie, he didn't hurt me.'

'I don't care,' Katie said. 'It's a bad habit. It has to stop.'

'Why do you call him Cutter?' Jace asked.

'It's what I do,' Katie said.

'You're a lucky pup,' I said to Cutter. 'You could have been called Autopsy.' The pup slurped my hand.

'Or Slice and Dice,' Jace said.

Katie gave Jace some serious stink eye. 'Don't you have a killer to catch?'

'Uh, yeah.' Jace took an onion bagel. He gave Cutter one last pat, and headed for the door. I started to hand Katie the pup and leave with Jace when she said, 'Angela? May I talk to you for a minute?'

She checked to make sure that Jace was gone, then asked, 'How was your salmon dinner with Chris?'

I couldn't hide my surprise. 'How did you know I had dinner with him?'

'Hell, the whole Forest knows. The way he carried on at the Forest Meat and Fish Mart, I thought he was picking out a diamond engagement ring. I was in the line behind him. You wouldn't believe the questions: was the salmon fresh? When did you get it? Had it been previously frozen? Farm-raised or wild caught? I had to help him pick out the fillets.

'You didn't answer my question. How was dinner?' she said.

'Fine.' I was wary. Katie was going to grill me.

'Only fine? A hunk like that?'

'He's an excellent cook,' I said.

'A hot guy who can cook, who's straight and single. That's every woman's dream. And all you can say is he's a good cook.'

'He's a very nice man,' I said.

'Nice! Nice is for maiden aunts and second cousins. Did you get anywhere?'

'We ate all the salmon.' I snuggled closer to Cutter and petted his warm fur.

Katie gently took the cuddly puppy out of my hands. Cutter whimpered. So did I.

'That's not what I meant. Did you jump his bones?'

'That's private!' I said.

'You didn't, did you?' Katie said. 'You're still sleeping with a dead man.'

'I'm still in love with my late husband, if that's what you mean.' I sounded chillingly formal. To my great relief, my work cell phone rang. I was never so happy to take a call.

'Jace! You need me already?'

'I'm at the scene, Angela. It's a doozy. Hurley Street.' He gave me the address.

'I'm on my way. I'll be there in five,' I said.

'Gotta go,' I told Katie. 'Death investigation.'

I gathered up my purse, phone and another bagel. 'Thanks,' I said, waving goodbye with the liberated bagel.

'You can run, Angela, but you can't hide. You'll have to face facts someday!' Katie shouted as I ran out of the ME's office.

SIXTEEN

I was called out to the unattended death of an elderly woman – an all too common occurrence in my profession. The Hurley Street address Jace gave me was a neat two-bedroom bungalow, now surrounded by two patrol cars, an unmarked and an ambulance. The neighbors were out on their lawns watching the commotion.

This was a quiet blue-collar neighborhood. Normally quiet, I should say. When I arrived at the house, I saw two women on the green lawn – one in her forties and the other somewhere past fifty – screaming and punching each other.

'Give it to me, bitch!' The blonde – the taller one – had a handful of the chunky brunette's hair. She held it at the roots to make her opponent stay still – an impressive barroom fight technique – and punched her in the face. These weren't girly punches, either. The blonde delivered real bashing blows. Both women were screeching.

Jace was trying – and failing – to break up the fight. 'Ladies!' he shouted over the racket. 'Stop. Right now!' They ignored him.

The blonde landed a right hook in the brunette's stomach. The sturdy brunette rocked back on her heels but she stayed standing and kicked the blonde in the knee. The blonde howled in pain. Now her knee was bleeding.

Three paramedics were standing at the edge of the altercation, watching as if they'd bought tickets to see the fight. The neighbors had picked their favorite and were cheering whenever she landed a blow.

The blonde hauled off and punched her opponent in the nose. Now the brunette had blood on her flowered top. That stopped the fight for a few seconds.

Both women were gasping for breath.

When they stopped swinging, I quickly stepped between the two and elbowed them both in the ribs. In my high school days, those bony elbows cost me many penalties on the basketball court. I was pleased they were as sharp as ever.

'Hey, watch it!' the brunette said to me. She was still gasping for breath.

'That's assault, lady,' wheezed the blonde, but she let go of the brunette's hair. The brunette shook herself.

The blonde said, 'Officer! Did you hear me? This woman assaulted me!' She pointed at me.

'It's Detective,' Jace said and introduced himself. 'Assault? I didn't see anything, ma'am. But the two of you seem to have a problem. Why don't you both cool off? All right, people, nothing to see. Go home!' he yelled to the crowd, which had edged to the driveway. The two uniforms, Mike and Brian, dispersed them.

Meanwhile, Jace went over to confer with the paramedics, who shook their heads and looked sad. Jace took some paperwork from them, and they drove away, emergency lights and siren off. They couldn't revive the victim, which was why I was here.

Now that the two women were no longer tearing at each other, I got a good look at them. They were attractive opposites. The blonde was tall, slender and stylish, though bedraggled from the fight. The collar was ripped on her silk blouse, a button was torn off her jacket, and her knee was bleeding. Her nylons were in tatters.

The brunette was short and chunky with luminous skin, a pink flowered top and black pants. She had three deep scratches across her right cheek, a bloody nose, and a bruise was coming out on her forehead.

'It's her fault,' the blonde said, her voice a controlled shriek. 'She stole our mother's ring.'

'I did not,' the brunette shouted. 'I took *my* ring. Mother promised it to me when she died.'

'Liar!' the blonde said. 'She gave it to me because I'm the oldest! You mutilated Mother's hand to get that ring!'

'Quiet!' Jace shouted. 'Or I'll arrest you both for disturbing the peace!'

I could hear both women breathing hard. The blonde tried to put herself back together. The brunette realized that she had a torn right sleeve on her flowered top and pushed it up to hide the rip.

Jace demanded, 'First, what are your names and how do you know each other?'

'I'm Shirley Davis,' said the brunette, 'and that blonde bitch is my sister, Ellen Tollman. My *older* sister.'

'I may be older, but I look ten years younger,' Ellen said. Actually, she spat the words. She really did. 'I didn't chunk up like you did!'

'You didn't have the stress of caring for Mother,' Shirley said. Her pale skin was red with fury. 'I was with her night and day. That's why she gave me her ring. Because I took care of her. You just dropped in from time to time and played Lady Bountiful.'

'I brought her gifts,' Ellen said. 'Chocolates, flowers and books. But Mother liked me because I was pleasant to be around.'

'She gave me the ring!' Shirley shouted.

'When?' Ellen said, her voice a snarl.

'When you weren't there. As usual. Last Thursday!'

'Then why didn't she take it off and hand it to you?' Ellen screeched.

'Because it reminded her of our father. She wanted to keep it until she died!'

'Liar!' Ellen cried.

'SILENCE!' Jace roared. I'd never seen him so furious.

Both women gulped and instantly went quiet. The brunette whimpered a bit, and dabbed at her bloody nose with a tissue.

Jace marched to a black wrought-iron table and chairs on the lawn, and pointed to Shirley, the brunette. 'You sit here!' he said.

He carried the other chair to the driveway, where the ambulance had been and pointed to the blonde, Ellen. 'You sit there!'

Both women sat, but continued the searing glares at each other.

I'd been dragging my DI kit across the lawn. I set it on its side near the table and used it as a seat. Then I pulled out my iPad to take notes.

Shirley was still dabbing at her bloody nose. It was leaking slightly, but didn't appear broken.

'When did you last see your mother?' Jace asked.

'Last night,' Shirley said. 'I live just down the street. Four doors away. I tucked Mother in most nights. Last night, I stopped by about ten o'clock and she asked for a cup of tea. I brewed her some chamomile. She sometimes has trouble sleeping. She complained it was bitter, so I put honey in it, and talked to Mother while she drank her tea.'

Bitter? That was odd. I wasn't a tea drinker, but chamomile wasn't bitter. It tasted like old sweat socks to me.

Shirley was still talking. 'After Mother finished her tea, I helped her to the bathroom – she's a little unsteady – and back into bed. She wanted to watch the TV in her room, so I made sure she was comfortable, then closed the drapes, checked that the back door and basement door were locked, turned off the living room lights, and went home.

'This morning, I stopped by at six o'clock to make Mother breakfast before I went to work – I do intakes at the hospital – and I found Mother on the floor of her bedroom. She appeared to have had some kind of stroke. I called 911, but the paramedics were unable to revive her.' Shirley suddenly turned angry. 'They looked at her and left her on the bedroom floor! I demand to know why!'

'Oh, you do, do you?' Jace said. 'You tried to cut off your mother's finger, but you're worried she didn't get proper treatment?'

'I have the right to know!' Shirley said.

'Here's what happened,' Jace said. 'Your mother had been dead for hours – maybe as many as seven or eight. The paramedics found signs of livor mortis on her back, buttocks and the backs of her legs. That means the blood had pooled in her body after her heart stopped pumping it, and it stained her skin purple in those areas. There was also significant rigor mortis, which means her body was rigid. She was dead and there was nothing they could do about it. They called her doctor and corralled her drugs, then called me. When did you remove your mother's ring?' Jace asked.

'After I called my sister,' Shirley said, 'I told the paramedics I wanted to be alone with my mother.'

'And they thought you were a grieving daughter,' Jace said. 'Instead you tried to saw off your own mother's finger. Didn't the paramedics tell you not to disturb the body?'

'I didn't! I left her right where she was.'

'Except you cut off her finger with a steak knife,' Jace said.

'She had arthritis,' Shirley said. 'It was hard to get my ring off over her knuckles. And I didn't cut her finger off. But I did help myself to what was rightfully mine.' Her voice defiant, oozing injured innocence like pus from an infected wound.

'Mother wanted me to have that ring. And things disappear at times like these. After Great-Aunt Ethel died of a stroke, we never did find the ruby pendant she always wore. The family thought the morgue attendants stole it, but we couldn't prove it. Besides, Mother was gone. I couldn't hurt her. No one can hurt her. Not any more.'

'You had no business disturbing the scene. Now, I'd like that ring, Ms Davis,' Jace said, his voice dangerously low. 'I'll put it in evidence for safe keeping, but you must hand it over.'

'What if I call my lawyer?' Shirley said, suddenly sounding bold. She had her hands on both hips, challenging Jace.

'Fine with me,' he said. 'You can tell the lawyer that I'm arresting you for abuse of a corpse. You skinned your mother's finger to get that ring.'

I shuddered when Jace said that. It was unprofessional, but I couldn't help it. Shirley was so greedy she'd cut the hand that fed her.

Jace held out his hand, and Shirley reluctantly put the ring in his palm. I'm no jewelry expert, but it was a fair-sized pear-shaped diamond in a rose gold setting, with smaller square-cut diamonds on the band. The sparkle in the morning sun was blinding, and light danced across the lawn.

'Angela,' he said, 'will you photograph this ring and put it in an evidence bag, please?'

I got out my point-and-shoot camera that I use for death investigations (it takes better photos than my cell phone) and photographed the ring from several angles, then noted that it had been taken from the decedent's finger. I was grateful I didn't see any shreds of skin on the ring.

Technically, the ring should have accompanied the body to the medical examiner's office, but I made an exception in this case. Jace wanted that ring for leverage.

'May I go now?' Shirley asked.

'No, you may not,' Jace said. He still sounded angry. 'When the evidence tech gets here, she's going to fingerprint you and take a DNA sample. And I'm sure Ms Richman has questions for you. She's a Chouteau County Death Investigator.'

Shirley looked like she was about to object, but Jace said, 'I wouldn't say anything if I were you. Not unless you want to face those "abuse of a corpse" charges. How would SOS feel if one of their employees was arrested for that – mutilating her own mother?

'Sit here,' Jace said, 'while we go talk to your sister.'

I rolled my DI case over to the drive, and leaned against a patrol car while Jace talked to the other sister.

Ellen's eyes were red from weeping, but she'd smoothed her hair and straightened her wrinkled skirt. She had three broken fingernails and blood trickled down her knee.

'When's the last time you saw your mother?' Jace asked.

'This morning,' Ellen said. 'She was dead on the floor of her bedroom and her ring finger was nearly hacked off. With a steak knife!' She burst into tears.

'That's not what I meant,' Jace said. 'I need to know when you last saw your mother alive.'

'Yesterday,' Ellen said. 'I brought Mother her favorite chocolates – Godiva. Shirley had taken Mother to the doctor, Dr Carmen Bartlett. Dr Bartlett said that Mother was in good health for her age. If she took her medicine she could live for years. She'd also read the neurologist's report and said Mother was slipping mentally, and we should seriously consider putting her in a memory care unit. I told Shirley I would look for a real estate agent to sell the house, so we could afford Mother's care.'

'Did you have power of attorney?' Jace asked.

'No, Shirley did. She handled the day-to-day care.'

'Did your mother have any savings?' Jace asked.

Ellen shook her head. 'Just Social Security and an insurance policy from our father's death. Mother used that money to buy Shirley the house down the street, so Shirley could take care of her. My husband has MS, and I work full-time. I can't visit as often as I would like.'

Suddenly, Ellen's eyes looked like shards of dirty ice. 'Mother bought her that house!' she repeated. 'That's why she wanted me to have the ring. Our father gave that to Mother on their fiftieth wedding anniversary. She never took it off.'

She turned and gave Shirley a look that should have seared her fair skin. 'Until my own sister hacked up Mother's hand to steal her jewelry.'

SEVENTEEN

I looked at Shirley, the caretaker daughter, a pretty brunette who'd taken a steak knife to her dead mother's arthritic finger for that sparkling ring. She looked ordinary in the best sense of the word, but there was something off about her mother's death. I didn't believe Mrs Davis had died suddenly of a stroke, and I'd been at a lot of older people's unattended deaths. I hoped Katie got the autopsy – she was always thorough.

The sun was beating down on the metal lawn table, and my black DI suit was hot. I'd put my long brown hair in a ponytail. Sweat was running down my forehead. Shirley also seemed to be feeling the heat. She brushed her dark hair off her forehead, and revealed the bruise from her sister.

I called up the 'Death Scene Investigation Form' on my iPad. Jace gave me the decedent's name – Ruby Randall Davis – the case number, and the time Mrs Davis was pronounced dead.

'Ready?' said Jace.

Shirley had calmed down enough to give me most of her mother's demographic data for the DI form. With Jace glowering at her, I think she was afraid to say no.

Shirley said her mother was seventy-seven, wore soft contact lenses and used reading glasses. Mrs Davis was small and underweight.

'Mother was five feet tall and weighed eighty-nine pounds,' Shirley said. 'But don't let her small size fool you. Ruby was one tough woman. Ten years ago, Mother had stage three breast cancer, and needed a double mastectomy, radiation and chemo. She bounced back, but she wasn't quite the same after Father died two years ago.

'After his death, she starting failing rapidly. She needed a walker outside the house. At home, Mother got around with a cane. She took medication for arthritis, hypertension and adult-onset asthma.

'All the things that happen when you get old,' Shirley said, and her shrug dismissed her mother's ills. That was another false note.

'Lately, Mother had memory issues. She left a pot of tomato soup on the stove and nearly burned down the house. The fire department had to put it out. That's why I checked on her every morning and night. I wanted to make sure everything was turned off and she didn't hurt herself. Ellen came in the afternoons, when she could. She behaved badly this morning, but I'm sure it was just stress due to our mother's death.'

I wasn't sure at all. I suspected that Ellen and Shirley had a long, unhappy history. And I kept hearing those false notes.

'Ellen's a payroll clerk for a St. Louis car dealership company, and her husband's sick a lot with MS, so she couldn't make it to see Mother as often as I did.

'Mother's neurologist said she was showing signs of dementia. My sister and I were discussing putting her in a memory care unit. We'd have to sell her house to pay for it, and Mother really didn't want to move, but after the burned soup episode, we knew we'd have to make a decision soon. At least she got to pass in her own home.'

She sighed dramatically.

There it was – another one. There were more false notes than a grade school band recital.

'What did your mother have for dinner last night?' I asked.

'Mac and cheese – her favorite – a chocolate pudding cup and orange slices.' Shirley's brown eyes widened and she tried on a smile, like she was telling a happy story.

'Does your mother have a will?' I asked.

The smile vanished. 'No, she didn't like lawyers,' Shirley said. 'She told us what she wanted to happen to her things: Ellen would get Mother's house and I'd get the diamond ring.'

'I was supposed to get that ring!' Ellen said. The tall blonde sister had quietly made her way across the lawn and stood by the wrought-iron table with her arms crossed. I was afraid she'd start the fight all over again, but Jace barked, 'Go back and sit down, Ms Tollman, unless you want to go to jail.'

She went, but she gave her sister a murderous glare.

I'd finished questioning Shirley. Sarah 'Nitpicker' Byrne, the CSI tech, had arrived. Today, her hair was a vibrant magenta. Sarah took Shirley's fingerprints and then Ellen's.

When Nitpicker finished printing the sparring sisters, we both went inside to examine the scene. Jace came with us and left a uniform to watch Ellen and Shirley.

The house was painted pale green with dark green shutters and a dark green door with a polished brass knocker. At the door, we all put on protective booties.

Inside, the house had that strange stillness that settles over a home when the owner is deceased.

We walked straight into a neat living room. The lights were on and the curtains were drawn.

'Who turned on the lights?' I asked Jace. Questions like these could help determine time of death and corroborate Shirley's account.

'The paramedics,' Jace said. 'They also turned on the bedroom and hall lights.'

I put that in my 'scene information' form. I added that the weather was warm – seventy-nine degrees. The temperature inside the house was seventy-eight according to the thermostat, and my thermometer agreed. I photographed both of them.

The living room had a green damask couch and matching easy chair, both with see-through plastic covers. I was glad I didn't have to sit on them on a day like today. Silk flowers brightened the polished coffee table. A plastic runner protected the pale green wall-to-wall carpet. The carefully protected furniture had outlasted its owner.

I photographed the living room. The police would also video it, but my photos would go directly to the medical examiner.

We followed the plastic runner down a narrow hall to the master bedroom, painted pale pink. The bed was on the south wall and it had been slept in – the covers were pulled back on the east side, and the pink flowered spread trailed on the carpet. The two lamps and the overhead light were on and the pink flowered curtains were still drawn.

Ruby Davis was on her back, six feet from the bed, lying face-up on the pink wall-to-wall carpet. Her head was pointing northwest.

'Did the paramedics move her?' I asked Jace.

'Yes. They said they turned her over. That's when they saw the livor mortis.'

I took multiple photos of the hall and bedroom – wide shot,

medium and close ups. These routine actions calmed me. Next, I photographed the deceased.

Ruby was wearing a high-necked blue cotton nightgown. It appeared that she'd had reconstructive surgery after her mastectomy, though I couldn't remove her gown to check. Her short gray hair was in foam curlers. My stomach turned when I saw Ruby's wedding ring finger.

'Holy crap,' Sarah said. 'What happened to that poor woman's finger?'

'Her loving daughter wanted Mama's ring,' Jace said. 'She sliced the old woman's finger into hamburger to get it over her arthritic knuckles.'

'There's the knife,' I said. On the floor next to Ruby's body was an ordinary wooden-handled steak knife, with bits of flesh in the serrated edges.

'Oh, jeez, there's some of the woman's skin still in the knife,' Nitpicker said. 'How low can you go?'

I'd seen worse – much worse – as a death investigator, but deliberately disfiguring this harmless old woman hit a nerve. I felt queasy.

Do your job, I told myself. You're a professional. I bagged the knife. It would go to the ME with the body.

'Was the ring mentioned in the will?' Sarah asked.

'There is no will,' I said. 'I suspect most of Mrs Davis's estate is going to lawyers' fees.'

There was little blood – Ruby had already been dead – but the thin, fragile old flesh had been brutally chopped. The nails on both hands were unbroken, but the knuckles were swollen to the size of acorns, and the small, fragile fingers had been brutally twisted by the disease.

I took close-up photos of the postmortem injury and noted the cause and that Jace had the disputed diamond ring. That answered the question: 'When decedent was discovered, were any items removed by family, EMS, etc., prior to the investigator's arrival? If yes, explain.'

I did, in detail.

Then I described the finger injury in the 'specific marks of violence on body' section. I placed a paper bag over the injured left hand and secured it with evidence tape.

Ruby had no bruises, but varicose veins snaked over her pale legs. Her feet were bare and clean. The body was almost completely stiff from rigor mortis. Full rigor often happened about twelve hours after death, though that wasn't completely reliable.

When I finished examining, measuring and photographing the front of the body, I took a clean white sheet out of a zip-lock bag I carried in my kit, and spread the sheet on the bedroom floor.

Jace and Nitpicker helped me turn the body onto the sheet, so I could examine the back. Thanks to the rigor mortis, the body was difficult to move.

The decedent had soiled her nightgown when her bowels and bladder released. I saw the dark purple-red patches of livor mortis on the backs of her legs and shoulders. I lifted her gown. She also had patches on her buttocks. I photographed and measured the livor.

Finally, I finished my examination of the body.

I continued examining the scene. A pair of white nightstands flanked the bed, and the one on the east side appeared to be the one Ruby used. It held a pair of reading glasses, the TV clicker, a paperback mystery, and a flowered teacup. There was about a spoonful of tea in the bottom of the cup and maybe a quarter-teaspoon slopped in the saucer. I used a clean eyedropper to suck up the liquid and deposited it into a Tupperware container for testing.

Directly across from the bed on the north wall was a white mirrored dresser with a pink leather jewelry box, a vase of pink silk flowers, and a small boxy TV.

Next to the dresser, under the wall light switch by the bedroom door, was a nearly new black purse – Kate Spade brand – and a white wicker wastebasket.

'Is that the decedent's purse?' I asked.

'I don't know,' Nitpicker said. She opened the purse with her gloved hands and checked the matching black wallet. 'The ID is for Ellen Tollman,' she said.

'There's an iPhone in a black case in the wastebasket,' I said.

'Is it the decedent's?' Jace asked.

I photographed the phone inside the basket, then pulled it out. It was on. I swiped the screen, but it needed a password to open.

With that, Mike, the uniform, knocked on the bedroom door. He was a twenty-something cop who looked too young to shave.

'Detective,' Mike said. 'One of the daughters says she dropped her purse near the door in her mother's bedroom. The blonde, Ellen.'

'Bring her in,' Jace said. 'And both of you put on booties. Make sure the other sister, Shirley, stays outside.'

'My partner will watch her,' Mike said.

He was back shortly with Ellen in tow. She'd made some effort to put herself back together. Her blonde hair was smoothed and her jacket was on straight, but the torn collar on her blouse stuck straight out.

'Is that your black purse on the floor by the wastebasket, Ms Tollman?' Jace asked. He pointed to the white wicker wastebasket.

'Yes,' Ellen said, her voice shaky. 'And why is Ms Richman holding my cell phone?'

'I found it in the wastebasket,' I said.

'It must have fallen out of my hand,' she said. 'I was shocked when I saw Mother.'

'If it's yours, open it,' Jace said. He took the phone from me, and held it out to Ellen. She touched it with her right index finger, and it opened. Jace made her go to the settings to further verify the phone. 'OK, it's yours.' He handed it back to her.

Meanwhile, I was photographing and bagging the contents of the wastebasket: two used tissues smeared with pink lipstick, a piece of paper with a telephone number jotted down, a grocery list (eggs, chocolate, bread and coffee), an empty bottle of Visine eye drops, the empty box for Visine Original Redness Formula, and a Walgreens bag with a receipt inside. I kept hoping I'd find something, anything, that could prove Ruby Davis didn't die of natural causes.

'Wait!' Ellen said. 'What's that Visine doing in there? Mother didn't use it.'

'Why not?' I said.

'She wore soft contact lenses,' Ellen said. 'Visine has a preservative that discolored them.'

I opened the Walgreens bag and found a credit card receipt for Visine, two chocolate bars and a can of mixed nuts.

'Does your sister use Visine?' I asked.

'No,' Ellen said. 'She wears soft contacts, too.'

'Jace,' I said, 'may I see you in the kitchen?'

We walked into the small, bright kitchen that had recently been repainted blue. The blue-flowered curtains looked new. 'Do you know that Visine is poisonous if swallowed?' I asked.

'I thought it gave you the runs,' he said.

'No, that's an urban legend, spread by a movie called "Wedding Crashers." Visine contains tetrahydrozoline. Drinking it can cause breathing problems, high blood pressure, headaches, seizures and coma.'

'How did you know that?' he asked.

'One of my first cases was a little girl who drank her mother's Visine. It killed the child. I'll never forget that. Mrs Davis was small and underweight. If one of her daughters gave her Visine . . .'

Jace finished my sentence: 'In that bitter cup of tea. Let's ask Nitpicker to print the receipt, the Visine bottle, the box it came in and the teacup,' he said. 'I can trace that transaction and the store's CCTV should show who made the purchase.'

Nitpicker printed all the items. Both daughters had good reason to want Mrs Davis dead. Their mother was slipping into dementia, but her body was relatively healthy. The sisters were going to have to sell Ellen's inheritance to put their mother in a memory care unit, which would quickly eat up that money.

Then there was Shirley, the pretty brunette, stuck caring for a woman who took up all her time.

Finally, Nitpicker announced, 'The prints on the Visine bottle, the box and the receipt definitely belong to Shirley Davis. The decedent's prints are not on any of those articles. There is one other set of prints on the receipt, but they are not the decedent's. The teacup has the decedent's and Ms Davis's prints on it.'

Here was the proof. The detail that had been nagging at me. Chamomile tea wasn't bitter. It was too bland to be bitter. That's why this scene was off – way off. Ruby Davis didn't die of a stroke. She was murdered. Ellen had supplied the clue to send her finger-sawing sister to prison.

'Well, looks like I get to take Mrs Davis's greedy daughter down to the station for a talk,' Jace said.

His smile left me chilled, even on this warm spring day.

EIGHTEEN

I needed to shake off this bad death investigation. I had to wipe away the appalling sight of Ruby Davis's skinned and butchered finger, as well as my dealings with her greedy daughter, Shirley.

The best way to clear away those festering feelings was to ride my favorite horse on the Du Pres estate. I'd earned the right to ride American Hero after I'd rescued him from a stable fire.

After the fire, the Du Pres stables had been restored to their original magnificence. They were more luxurious than most of the homes in the Forest, including mine. The stables had originally been built for the family's carriage horses in 1905. Those were long gone, but like a lot of super-rich people, old Reggie Du Pres kept OTTBs – Off the Track Thoroughbreds – as pets and riding horses.

Bud, the man in charge of the stables, was lean, leathery, and somewhere in his sixties. His official title was stable hand, but Bud knew how everything worked on the Du Pres estate. He liked to say, 'Owning a thoroughbred is sort of like dating Elizabeth Taylor in her later years: still beautiful, with a great past.'

Bud also liked to say, 'Rich people are like potatoes. The best part is underground. All they care about are their ancestors.' Of course, he saved that radical thought for me, not for old man Du Pres.

I could see the stables from my upstairs bedroom window. After I finished Mrs Davis's death investigation and signed the paperwork for the body removal, I drove home and filed my report. I tossed my DI suit in the laundry. I wanted to wash away any trace of the Davis family. Then I changed into skinny jeans, an old chambray shirt and riding boots, brought out the bags of carrots and pepper-mint candy I kept for the horses, and walked toward the stables.

As I got closer, I could smell the spring grass and flowers, with an overlay of horse manure. I didn't mind – it was a clean, honest smell.

My first stop was at Eecie's stall. I had to honor the queen of the stable. Her official name was East Coast Express. She was a big bay – that's a brown horse – with a tiny white star on her forehead. Eecie had a pet, a pygmy goat named Little Bit, who hung out in her stall.

Eecie snorted when she heard me, and I fed her peppermints, until Little Bit stood on his hind legs and poked his head over the stall door. I pulled out a carrot for the goat, but Eecie nudged him out of the way.

'Eecie,' I scolded. 'Let Little Bit have a carrot.'

Only after Eecie had chomped five carrots was the goat permitted to have one. I patted Eecie's velvety nose and went to the next stall.

American Hero's stall was mahogany with stained glass windows, and a brass nameplate on the stall door. Hero was indeed heroic with his shiny dark hide and white blaze. He nickered when I approached his stall. I leaned over the top of the door and hugged his neck. Hero stuck out his huge tongue and I gravely shook it. A horse's tongue feels thick, warm and wet.

Some people think I'm joking when I tell them I shake a horse's tongue. But it's true. You can do it, with the right horse. With Hero and me, it's our favorite greeting. I used to be afraid to touch the powerful thoroughbred, especially when I saw those big yellow teeth. But thanks to Bud, I learned to trust the horse. Hero's always gentle and careful with me.

I gave Hero carrots and peppermints, and was patting his white blaze when Bud walked in with his soda can spittoon. Smoking is forbidden in the stables, so Bud chews tobacco. I try to ignore this disgusting habit.

'Here to see your pal in the middle of the day?' Bud asked. 'Must have had another bad death investigation.'

Not much got past Bud. I could tell him anything about my investigations because I knew he'd never blab. The only thing Bud ever talked about was horses.

'The worst case of greed I've ever seen, Bud. A woman tried to cut off her dead mother's finger to get her diamond ring.'

Bud shook his head. 'And people wonder why I spend all day with animals. You want me to saddle up Hero?'

'Yes, thank you.'

With that, my work cell rang. I excused myself and went outside to take the call. By the time I answered it, the caller was gone, but he'd left a message. 'Angela, it's me. Chris. Sorry to use your work phone, but I don't have your personal cell number. Would you like to go out to dinner with me? A real dinner, in a restaurant? Please let me know.'

Would I? Did I? I didn't know, but I'd worked out many dilemmas while riding Hero. By the time I returned, he was saddled. Bud gave me a boost onto the big horse and we were off.

The spring sun shone on Hero's rippling muscles and shiny coat. He broke into a canter, and we were running across the pasture, the wind in my face, blowing away my bad mood.

Hero could sense my mood better than many humans. Now, when I had to decide what to do about Chris, I slowed him to a walk, and he ambled along, letting me think.

I wanted to have dinner with Chris – I really did. But I felt like I was cheating on my husband, Donegan. Yes, I know Donegan was dead – and every time I thought those words, I felt like I'd been stabbed in the heart. But Donegan wasn't dead to me. When I had dinner with Chris at my house, I couldn't help comparing him to my late husband – and Donegan won every time.

He was constantly with me. I could see him in our house: sitting in his favorite chair or walking in the garden. He seemed to linger in the kitchen shadows when Chris made our dinner. At night, I could feel him make love to me, the way we did when we were new to each other. And then I would wake up, lonelier than before.

Had I idealized the man I'd married until he was no longer human? In my dreams he never snored loud enough to wake me up. Or destroyed a clean bathroom with one shower. He never ate sandwiches without a plate and trailed crumbs all over the house.

But I loved Donegan – even the imperfect parts. Well, most of them. And ghosts don't leave crumbs in the living room and wet towels on the bathroom floor.

Maybe another dinner with Chris would help me see what he was really like – his good points and bad ones. There was no reason to feel guilty. I had meals with Jace all the time. Except Jace wasn't interested in me as a lover. He was happily married.

It was time to find out Chris's imperfections. I was sure he had them. At forty-one, I wasn't too old for love. Perfect memories were cold comfort on the long nights.

My work cell rang. This time, it was Jace. I reined in Hero and answered it, hoping I didn't have another death investigation today. Hero stood patiently while I took the call, eating the pasture grass.

'Angela, I need your help,' Jace said. 'You remember Rosanna McKim, Briggs's housekeeper. Did you know her?'

'Sort of. I went to school with her older sister, Diana McKim. Rosanna is about eleven years younger than me.' A memory of a teenage Rosanna flashed in my mind: she was a curly-haired blonde with blue eyes and a big smile. One of those people who's so enthusiastic that being around her can be tiring.

'What about their mother?'

'Lisa McKim. I know her to say hi to. I see her at the super-market sometimes. She likes to talk about her girls. Diana is a sales rep for a big whiskey company in New York. And Rosanna works – I mean, worked – for Briggs.'

'Have you talked to her mother recently?' Jace said.

'Come to think of it, no,' I said.

'I have a problem, and I need your help. Lisa McKim reported her daughter missing three weeks ago, shortly after she was fired. Rosanna was upset about being fired, but told her mother she would look for a job after she went on vacation. She wanted time to think about her future. She was sorry to lose the job, but she didn't like Briggs – he was rude and what she called "grabby." Rosanna told her mother she tried to never be alone with Briggs. She was taking her severance pay and going on a Caribbean cruise that sailed out of Port Everglades in Fort Lauderdale. She promised to call her mother when she arrived. She never did.

'Mrs McKim waited two days, and then filed a missing persons report with the Chouteau Forest PD.'

'Who handles our missing persons?' I asked. 'We're too small to have a missing persons bureau.'

'Right. Her call was sent to the crimes against persons detective on duty, Ray Greiman.'

'Uh-oh,' I said.

'Right,' said Jace.

'I tried to track down Rosanna to talk to her about Briggs,' he said, 'but no luck. A check with the airlines showed Rosanna did not fly out of St. Louis on the expected date, and her name was not on the cruise ship's manifest. She'd paid for the plane ticket and the cruise, but never showed. The bank said she'd cashed her severance check and her paycheck. She had about five thousand dollars in her checking account, untouched.

'I called Mrs McKim and asked to talk to her about her daughter and she got angry at me. She said, "If my daughter's such a slut, why do you want to find her now?" Then she started crying.'

'My guess is Greiman said something to her,' I said.

'That's what I think. Look, I know you're not supposed to investigate cases, but could you go with me when I talk to Mrs McKim?'

I paused for a moment, and rubbed Hero's gleaming neck. If Greiman filed a complaint about me interfering in his investigation, I could lose my job. But there were other DI jobs, and I didn't have any children. I was single. I was free. I could take the risk. I had a Hero with me.

'Yes,' I said. 'I'll do it. What time?'

'What about four o'clock this afternoon?'

'Done!' I said. 'I know where she lives. I'll see you there.'

He hung up. And while I was still feeling brave, I called Chris and left a message. 'Thanks for calling. I'd love dinner tomorrow night at Gringo Daze, my favorite Mexican restaurant. And here's my personal cell number.

'Let's go back home, Hero,' I told my horse. 'You've worked your magic again.'

NINETEEN

Lisa McKim, the missing housekeeper's mother, lived in a white 1960s split-level with black shutters. Lisa met Jace and me with a warm smile at her front door. She ushered us through a mirrored hall into a formal living room with a beige damask couch, pastel upholstered chairs, and a silver tea service on a serving cart. The furniture was polished to a high gloss, and the couch looked brand new. I suspected the room was rarely used.

Lisa was in her early fifties, but looked at least ten years younger. She was a trim woman with dark, curly hair. I could see where

Rosanna got her energy and enthusiasm. Lisa wore dark skinny jeans and a pink blouse.

Jace and I sat on the pale, pristine couch. 'Would you like coffee?' Lisa asked. 'It's ready. All I have to do is pour.'

'That sounds good,' Jace said. Lisa rolled the cart over to us and fixed three black coffees with a sugar cookie on each saucer. She took the pink chair next to the couch and we got down to business.

'I want to apologize for what I said yesterday, Detective,' Lisa said, looking at her well-manicured hands. 'I was rude to you, and you didn't deserve it. But that other detective – that Ray Greiman – insulted Rosanna! He acted like my daughter was . . . is . . . has . . .' Lisa stopped, unable to find the right words. She kept wringing her hands and finally burst out with, '. . . has loose morals!'

'What did he say, Mrs McKim? What did you tell him? We need to hear the whole story.'

'When I called the police station to report Rosanna missing—'

Jace interrupted. 'Excuse me, I'd like to hear your story from the beginning, please. First, did your daughter let two hundred pounds of raw meat rot in Briggs's new Range Rover?'

'Absolutely not!' Lisa was indignant. 'My daughter is extremely organized and very competent. Yes, Briggs said he was going to have a party on a Saturday, right before she disappeared. He told her to order the meat the Thursday before the party, and she went to the store in person to place the order.'

'Which store?' Jace asked.

'The Forest Specialty Meat and Fish Mart,' Lisa said. 'Nothing but the best for Mr Bellerive. He doesn't eat supermarket meat. Briggs told my daughter he was going downtown – downtown Chouteau Forest, that is – for lunch, and he'd pick up the order Friday afternoon, the day before the barbecue. Saturday was Rosanna's day off – he'd hired staff for the event – and she spent the day with me.'

'Wait,' Jace said. 'Did he *tell* your daughter he was picking up the meat, or did he give her a written order?'

'He texted her. She sent me a copy of it after he fired her. She was terribly upset by his accusations. His *false* accusations. Here.'

Lisa brought out her cell phone, and called up an email from

Rosanna. It said, *Mom, here's a screenshot of the text from that lying creep:*

R, no need for you to go downtown. I'll pick up the meat after I have lunch in the Forest. The liquor, wine and beer will be delivered today about 4 p.m. As soon as they arrive and you've checked them in, you can go. Start your weekend early. BB

I took a sip of coffee. It was rich and strong. Just what I needed.

'Now you've seen his text,' Lisa said. 'The drinks were delivered at four-fifteen, according to my daughter. She inventoried them and put everything away, then checked the other party supplies. Once she finished, she texted Briggs at five-o-two. I have that one, too. See?'

She opened another email with a screenshot.

Mr B, the wine and beer arrived a little after 4. The wine and liquor are stored in the pantry and the beer and soda are in the Sub-Zero. I've checked the other party supplies and called the caterer and confirmed our order. Their number is on the notepad by the fridge. The caterer will start setting up at 3 p.m. tomorrow. Everything is ready for your party. I'm leaving now, but you have my number. If you have any problems, please call me. R

'Did Mr Bellerive call your daughter that weekend?' Jace asked.

'No, and Rosanna spent the weekend with me. She had her cell phone on the whole time. We had a girls' weekend. We went out for a nice dinner at Solange on Friday night. They have the best prime rib. Saturday, we had a spa day and Saturday night we had wine and pizza, and watched chick movies. We giggled like girls. Sunday morning we went to church – St Philomena's – and then out to brunch at the Forest Inn. We had such a good time. Now that my daughter's older, she's more like a friend.' Lisa sounded wistful and her eyes were red. I thought she was holding back tears.

'What is your daughter's relationship with her employer?' Jace asked.

'It's not good. In fact, my daughter was quietly looking for another job, one outside the Forest.'

'What was the problem?' Jace asked.

'He was sexually harassing her,' Lisa said. 'She was documenting as much as she could – she kept a diary. As soon as she had a new job, she was going to consult a lawyer.'

'Where is this diary?'

'On her laptop,' Lisa said. 'She backed up her files daily and sent me copies for insurance.'

'May we read them?' I asked.

'Yes, of course. Anything that will help. I figured you'd want it, so I made you a copy on this thumb drive.' She held up a purple thumb drive. 'Would you like it, or Ms Richman?'

'I'll take it,' I said. 'I'll have time to look at it when I'm on call next.'

As soon as I volunteered, I felt a knot in my stomach. Now I was actively investigating the case, as Jace's pseudo-partner. If Greiman found out, he'd have me fired.

I put the thumb drive in my purse.

'Would you like more coffee, Ms Richman?'

I did, but I didn't want Lisa distracted by hostess duties. 'Thank you, no,' I said.

'We can read it in the diary, but what issues did she have with Mr Bellerive and when did they start?' Jace asked. He quietly crunched on a cookie while Lisa spoke.

'Rosanna lived at Briggs's house. She had her own apartment off the kitchen – a sitting room-office, bedroom and galley kitchen. It was nicely furnished. Free room and board was a good deal, and her salary was generous.'

'Did you search her apartment, Jace?' I asked.

'Yes. We didn't find anything. But we didn't know it was Rosanna's apartment, either.'

'I still have the key,' Lisa said, 'if you'd like to search it again.'

'I'll have to ask Briggs's permission,' Jace said, 'and I don't think he'll give it.'

Lisa picked up the thread of her narrative. 'To answer your questions, the problem started six months ago, about a month after Rosanna was working there. Briggs became handsy – if he gave Rosanna instructions, he'd put his hand on her arm, or her shoulder. She'd politely brush it off, and his hand would "accidentally" touch her bosom. He'd guide her through a door with his hand around her waist, and it would slip to her behind. She asked him several times to stop. She had her cell phone on, so some of those exchanges were recorded. She sent them to me, of course. They're on that thumb drive, Ms Richman.

'Four weeks into her employment, Briggs asked her out. Rosanna said no. She knew he dated a New York model, Desiree Gale. They weren't officially engaged, but she was his main girlfriend, lover, whatever they call adults who see each other all the time. My daughter knew he treated Desiree like a princess. She'd served them late-night suppers of champagne and cold lobster.'

'Did Ms Gale ever stay the night?' Jace asked.

'Yes, occasionally. Briggs also liked to go out late at night and pick up young women. Nobody from the Forest – he'd go to St. Louis or one of the suburbs to find them. My daughter thought some of these women might have been prostitutes or hitchhikers. They would spend the night, too, and sometimes she would hear screams coming from Briggs's bedroom – and not screams of delight, if you know what I mean. Rosanna worried about those girls and thought her boss might have been hurting them – on purpose. She always checked to make sure the girls left. Briggs usually sent them away by Uber, and Rosanna could hear the drivers pull up near her rooms. She was always relieved when they left.'

'How old were these women?' Jace asked.

'They were young – very young, in their early twenties or maybe even underage. My daughter wasn't sure. Rosanna told me late one night, she heard someone rummaging in the kitchen like a hungry bear. Rosanna put on her dressing gown and found one of Briggs's pick-ups. She asked the girl what she was doing. The girl, whose name was Destiny, said she was hungry. Rosanna fixed her a ham sandwich and gave her an apple, a bag of chips, and a soda.

'Destiny stuffed the chips, apple and unopened can of soda in her backpack, and ate the sandwich like she was starving. My daughter fixed her another sandwich and opened a Coke. She sat down at the table while Destiny wolfed down that food. Destiny was a rather pretty blonde, with very white skin. She wore a grubby white tank top, cutoffs, and flip-flops, and her feet were dirty. Destiny had a thick navy-blue wool scarf wrapped around her neck.

'My daughter thought that was odd. Why was this young woman

wearing a heavy navy scarf with such summery clothes on a warm
night? She asked Destiny if everything was OK, and the girl said
yes. "Are you cold?" my daughter asked. "Is that why you're
wearing that scarf?"

'My daughter said Destiny looked fearful and said, "No, I don't
want my boyfriend to see what he did to my neck." Rosanna
figured the girl had a hickey or love bite or something.'

Or something, I thought. Like bruises from near
strangulation.

'The girl was still hungry, so Rosanna fixed her a third sandwich
and gave her a bag of cookies. That's when her Uber driver pulled
up outside the kitchen door. Destiny tucked the sandwich and
cookies in her backpack and ran out to the car.

'Oh, here's something else!' Lisa said. 'Whenever Briggs
had any women stay overnight, he cleaned his own room – dusted
and vacuumed it and changed his own sheets. He even washed
them. Rosanna said he wouldn't even let her empty his wastebasket.
He took out his own trash. She thought that was very strange.'

'Did she ever see that trash?' Jace asked.

'No.'

'How often did Briggs bring women to his home?' Jace asked.

'Nearly every weekend,' Lisa said. 'And sometimes during the
week. Desiree, the big-time model, stayed over twice. My daughter
said the other women who stayed were young and shabby, pathetic
little creatures.'

'Did Briggs ever date any of these young women twice?' Jace
asked.

'Never, not in the seven months my daughter worked there. They
were strictly one-night stands. After a month of these shenanigans,
Briggs asked my daughter out. She told him no. She thought it was
a bad idea to date her employer, and she didn't like the way he
treated the young women he picked up. She wasn't going to be
another notch on his bedpost. Besides, she is dating a nice young
man named Kevin.' Lisa lowered her eyes, then said, 'I'm hoping
Kevin gives her a ring on her birthday in May.'

Jace leaned forward and said, 'When did your daughter start
looking for other work, Mrs McKim?'

'Right after Briggs asked her out. He'd become more insistent,
and she was afraid to be alone with him in dark rooms or hallways.

She spent many of her days off here with me or Kevin. She was becoming discouraged about the job search. During our girls' weekend, I told her she could live with me until she found a job. She could have her old room back.

'But my girl had her pride. She said she'd stick it out another month, and then quit. But she didn't get the chance. That despicable man blamed her for the spoiled meat, and fired her when she came back Sunday night. I couldn't believe it!'

Lisa McKim was almost shouting now. She took a deep breath, then a sip of coffee, and said, 'Of course I believe he'd do something like that. Briggs is a crook!'

And a killer, I thought.

'Even though he blamed her for the spoiled meat, he still gave her a good severance package – twenty thousand dollars – and a good reference.'

'So he was paying her to go away,' I said.

'Yes, and despite the money, Rosanna was furious. She's always loved the ocean, and she told me she wanted to go on a cruise to get her head straight. I offered to go with her, and so did Kevin, but she said she wanted to be alone for a week.

'She emailed me her itinerary. I've made you both copies.' Lisa handed us both a stack of paper.

'As you can see, Rosanna was supposed to take a Southwest Airlines nonstop flight to Fort Lauderdale for her cruise, which left the next day from Port Everglades. Rosanna promised she'd call me when she got to her cruise hotel – she was staying overnight at a DoubleTree hotel. They had a free shuttle to the cruise ship.

'The day Rosanna left, I waited until midnight to hear from her. Nothing. That wasn't like her. I checked if Rosanna's flight had been delayed. It had landed on time in Fort Lauderdale. I called the hotel and she hadn't checked in yet.

'Now I was really worried. I called her boyfriend, Kevin, and several of her friends. No one had heard from her that day, after she'd told them she was taking a cruise.

'I checked her bank accounts – she'd given me access – and she'd cashed the twenty-thousand-dollar severance check with her phone app. It was in her savings account. But her checking account was untouched. I called Briggs and asked if he'd seen my daughter.

He said, "No. She cleared out as soon as she was fired." I could almost hear the "good riddance" after that, but he didn't come out and say it.'

'How was your daughter planning to go to the St. Louis airport?' Jace asked.

'By Uber. Briggs claimed an Uber driver picked her up, but I can't find out which one – I don't have the warrants or whatever you need to check that.

'All I know is my daughter was fired – unjustly. She supposedly packed her things, bought a plane ticket and a Caribbean cruise, and vanished on Briggs's doorstep.'

TWENTY

After Lisa McKim's impassioned speech in defense of her daughter, we fell silent. Bright, bubbly Rosanna had vanished, and Briggs Bellerive was behind her disappearance. I knew it, and so did Jace and her mother. And there was nothing we could do about it.

I stared at my empty flowered cup and ate the rest of my cookie. Finally, Jace broke the loud silence with, 'What did you tell Detective Greiman when you spoke to him?'

Lisa's face reddened with anger and her hand trembled so much her thin china coffee cup rattled against the flowered saucer. Finally, she composed herself enough to say, 'Before I can talk about that man, I'll need more coffee.'

'May I help?' I asked, and started to stand up.

She waved me back into my seat. 'No, sit back down and make yourself comfortable. I have another pot ready in a Thermos in the kitchen. I'll bring it right down.'

Lisa carried the silver coffee pot upstairs. We could hear her rattling around in the kitchen. She was back a few minutes later with a fresh pot of coffee and a full plate of sugar cookies.

She poured coffee for all three of us, then took a deep breath and said, 'This is very hard to talk about. I don't know where to begin.'

'How about if I ask you questions, and you answer them?' Jace said. His smile was reassuring and his voice was soothing. 'When did you decide to call the police?'

'The morning after Rosanna didn't show up in Fort Lauderdale. I stayed awake all night, walking the floors and waiting for her call. In the morning, I talked with her friends. I called Diana, her older sister, and Rosanna's boyfriend, Kevin. No one had heard from Rosanna after she told them she was taking a cruise.

'By now, I was heartsick. I called 911 and the operator said I should make a report with the detective on duty and sent me to Ray Greiman. He came here in his fancy suit and shiny shoes, a real slick.' I heard the contempt in her voice. In fact, her sentiments about Greiman echoed mine. It was difficult for me to remain silent.

'He asked me about Rosanna, her hobbies, her friends, and her boyfriends. Especially her boyfriends. He was particularly interested in the number of men she'd dated. I gave him a recent photo of Rosanna, her cell phone provider and bank account information. He said he'd get back to me in a day or two. While I waited for that detective to call me back, I couldn't eat or sleep.'

Looking at Lisa, I could see she wasn't exaggerating her distress. Under her skillfully applied make-up, her face was haggard.

'I was frantic,' she said. 'I didn't hear from Greiman for three days. I couldn't wait any more. I called him and he said he'd talked with Rosanna's employer.' Lisa stopped for a moment.

'What did Briggs tell the detective?' Jace asked.

The color rose quickly on Lisa's pale face, until she was nearly stroke red. 'Briggs lied! That son of a – a B – said my daughter had men at her apartment several times a week. He said one of her most frequent callers was a large black man, built like a football player, and the other male visitor – another muscular man – wore a turban.'

'A turban?' I said. 'Like someone from India?'

Nothing like playing to the Forest prejudices, I thought. Pretty, white Rosanna was consorting with foreign men. Big ones.

'Yes. Briggs said they were drinking and had loud parties until all hours of the night. He had to ask Rosanna to turn down the music in her apartment several times. He told Greiman that if he hadn't fired Rosanna for incompetence, he would have fired her for her outrageous behavior.'

'And Greiman believed that?' Jace asked.

I squeezed my hands to keep my mouth shut.

'Oh, yes! When I protested that my daughter would never behave that way, the detective said, "Well, you are her mother. You'd be the last to know." I felt like he'd reached through the phone and patted me on my head.'

I knew that feeling, too. I struggled to keep quiet.

'I was furious, and Greiman told me to calm down, that getting hysterical never settled anything. I said I wasn't hysterical – that was a very prejudiced word to use when describing a justly angry woman. He told me not to hide behind "a bunch of women's lib stuff." Except he didn't use "stuff." He used the other S-word.

'When I told him about my daughter's diary and Briggs's unwanted touching, he said, "Look, ma'am, Mr Bellerive is a rich and attractive man. Any woman would want to date him. Better yet, get pregnant by him."

'"Pregnant!" I shouted.

'"Yes, pregnant!" That disgrace for a detective said, "If your daughter had Briggs's bun in her oven, she'd be set for life. One little DNA test and she'd never have to work again. Briggs told me that she begged him to jump her bones, but he refused. When he turned her down, she started that diary out of spite."'

Lisa was so upset she was gasping for breath. I reached over and patted her hand, and poured her more coffee. She thanked me and took a long drink.

I could feel my fury growing, and I had to keep my feelings under control. It was hard to believe people still talked that way in this day and age – until you heard it. And I heard it a lot from Greiman. He was a good old boy. He always sided with the most powerful person in any debate. It was the secret of his success in the Forest. There was no question who held the power in this contest. Lisa and her mom lived in what some locals called Toonerville, the working part of town.

Lisa had recovered enough to continue her story. 'That ignorant detective believed every lie Briggs told him. The two of them smeared my daughter's reputation. Greiman told me, "A man in Briggs's position can't be too careful. He's super-rich, handsome and connected. Women throw themselves at him all the time. He has to do everything he can to protect his reputation."'

Lisa was talking faster now that her anger had surfaced. "'And what about my daughter's reputation?" I said to him. OK, I shouted it. I admit I'd lost my temper again. Greiman said, "Well, Briggs said your girl was kind of a free spirit. Very attractive. Any man would want her – but a bit of a . . . well, she got around, ma'am. And she wasn't prejudiced, either. She liked white men, black men, Muslims." Then he added, "Briggs said he isn't gay or anything. He likes a pretty woman as much as any other man. But he was afraid her playground was an international destination, if you know what I mean, and not a safe place for a man like him."'

'I had a hard time controlling myself,' Lisa said, 'but I realized I had to, for Rosanna's sake. I asked him if he knew where Rosanna was. He said, "Oh, yes. I'm quite sure Rosanna has run off with one of those men – her night-time party pals – or maybe both of them. She sure did like her dark chocolate."'

'What!' I said.

'He did!' Lisa said. She was defiant now. 'He really said that. I told him, "Then why hasn't she used her bank accounts or credit cards since she went missing?"

'You know what he said? He said, "She doesn't have to. All a good-looking young woman like Rosanna has to do is put out a little, and any man would pay for her company. And the darker they are, the more they like blondes."'

I gasped in shock. 'No! Not even Greiman would say that!' Jace looked at me, and I instantly regretted my unprofessional outburst.

'Oh, yes, he did,' Lisa said. She was trembling with rage.

Jace took control of the conversation and tried to calm Rosanna's mother. 'Mrs McKim, I'm sorry that Detective Greiman upset you. But your daughter's case has intersected with one of my cases now and—'

Lisa interrupted him. Her voice was so faint I had to lean forward to hear her. 'No,' she whispered. 'Please, no. You're the detective working the Women in the Woods case, aren't you? Tell me you haven't found my baby.'

'No, Mrs McKim, so far as I know, your daughter is not one of the young women found in the woods.'

I heard those weasel words, 'so far as I know,' and hoped Lisa McKim didn't. We still didn't know who the other two women were, but their remains were too old to be Rosanna McKim.

'Yes,' Jace said, 'I am working the case of the three women found in the woods.'

Lisa let out a mournful wail.

Jace interrupted it with, 'Only one has been identified, and I'm almost certain the other two women are not your daughter, though their remains have not yet been identified. But Briggs remains a person of interest.'

'I knew it! I knew it!' Lisa said. She looked almost jubilant.

'Mrs McKim!' Jace raised his voice. 'Listen and listen closely. There is not one shred of evidence to connect Briggs Bellerive with the disappearance of any woman. Do you understand?'

She nodded yes.

'Briggs is a powerful man and if you say anything now, he'll walk away free. Do you understand?'

Lisa gulped twice, then said, 'I do, Detective. And I appreciate you and Ms Richman listening to me and taking myself and my daughter seriously. Now let me tell you something: I believe my daughter is alive and that beast is hiding her. You have to find her.

'And if you can't and it's too late, I want you to bring my baby home so she can sleep in the Forest cemetery next to her grand-parents. Please don't let Rosanna become nameless bones in the woods, a horror show for some hiker to trip over.'

With those brave words, Lisa McKim dissolved into tears.

TWENTY-ONE

I woke up the next morning to a gentle spring rain. It was the kind of rainy morning that makes you want to roll over and go back to sleep. That's exactly what I did, since I had the day off. I finally woke up again at ten a.m., brewed some coffee and took it upstairs to bed, where I luxuriated in the sound of the rain drumming softly on the roof.

I washed my hair for my date with Chris that night and did my nails. The house was due for a cleaning, but what I really wanted to do was check out Mrs McKim's intriguing thumb drive. It was still in my purse. I could practically feel it pulsing in there, sending out signals to me.

I loaded the dishwasher and turned it on, then decided more cleaning would ruin my manicure. Besides, that tantalizing diary was calling my name. I put on another pot of coffee, and stuck the thumb drive into my iPad.

Armed with a mug of hot coffee, I sat at my kitchen table and scrolled through Rosanna McKim's diary to the first entry, about six months ago. It was a long email.

Monday, October 7, 2019
Dear Mom,

You've always had my back, but now I need you to be my back-up. Like I told you last weekend, Briggs is really handsy. It's like working for an octopus. And today he asked me out.

'Wanna go on a bar crawl?' he said. 'I know some great dives.' He acted like he expected me to be overjoyed. That was his idea of a first date. A bar crawl! And dive bars at that! What a lowlife.

I told him no thanks. I wasn't interested. I said it was a bad idea for an employee to date her employer. If he thinks I'm a housekeeper with benefits, he's got another think coming. Anyway, he barely said anything to me the rest of the day. We avoided each other and that was fine with me. I went to bed about 10 p.m. and made sure I locked my door.

I know what you're going to say, Mom – I should come home this instant. I can have my old room while I look for another job.

But jobs that pay like this one are hard to come by, especially when all I have is a degree in English Lit. If I quit, I'll be hustling fries at Mickey D's or pounding a cash register and making minimum wage – if I'm lucky. Plus this job includes room and board. So for now, I'll avoid Fumble Fingers and keep on working. Don't worry. I can handle him.

But in case there's a problem, I'm starting this diary to keep track of him on a daily basis. I'm backing it up in the cloud – and sending a copy to you – each week.

Monday

You already know about this day. B asked me out. I refused. No further contact.

Tuesday

B got up early and was out of the house all day. I went to bed early. NFC (no further contact).

Wednesday

Ditto

Thursday

B was very friendly this morning. Too friendly. He patted my shoulder and told me what a good job I was doing, and his hand slid down to my right boob. I removed it and told him to keep his hands off me. He apologized.

B left the grounds after supper – about 6 p.m. – in his Beemer and came back about 8:30 with a girl. I could see the two of them out my kitchen window. I hid behind the curtain the way our nosy neighbor, Mrs Crane, used to watch our street. The girl was very thin and pale and looked underage. She wore a skimpy, shiny red dress and red heels. Her blonde hair hung down past her waist and needed a wash. She was tipsy and stumbled when she walked. Was she a sex worker? Was I being too harsh? Maybe she was just a poor girl who hung around dive bars.

B took her upstairs and about thirty minutes later I heard her moaning, followed by muffled screams. They sounded like screams of pain. They were so loud, I heard them all the way back in my apartment. I was sure he was hurting that girl. I tried to go to bed but couldn't sleep. I was too worried. The screams and moans lasted until after 1 a.m.

I stayed awake until I heard a car in the drive at 1:21. The girl climbed into the back of an Uber, a black SUV. She seemed OK. Does Briggs like kinky sex? Was the girl's screaming part of the thrill for him? None of my business, as long as the woman was safe. Once she was gone, I fell asleep.

Friday

B called me into his office and said he had a date with Desiree Gale Saturday night and he was bringing her home for a cold supper. He wanted lobster, a fresh fruit salad, and good chocolate, and I was to make sure the champagne was iced. Once I finished those duties, B said I could have Saturday night and Sunday off. I called Kevin. He was thrilled. Me too. I said I'd pack a bag and spend the weekend at his apartment.

I spent the rest of the morning running around the Forest like crazy, buying lobster, greens, and fresh fruit from specialty shops. I stored the food in the fridge, then drove forty miles to Maplewood, all the way to the edge of St. Louis, to get the dark chocolate B likes from a shop called Kakao, which makes its own chocolate. I'll have to get you some, Mom. It's superb.

By 4:15 p.m. I was in the kitchen pantry, bent over, stocking the lower shelves, when I felt something brushing my bottom. I swatted it and discovered I'd slapped Briggs's hand. He'd slipped into the pantry when my back was turned. I stood up and said, 'Do NOT touch me ever again!' The miserable weasel backed away, saying, 'Sorry! Sorry! It was an accident! I was trying to get a bottle of Burgundy.' I didn't like that sly grin on his face, but the Burgundy he wanted really was on the lower shelf. Thank gawd I have the weekend off and can spend quality time with Kevin.

According to Rosanna's diary, the next six weeks were variations on that first week. Briggs got up early one or two days a week and didn't come home until late, usually at the beginning of the week. He often went prowling for women on either Wednesday or Thursday nights. The ones he brought back were nearly inter-changeable – thin, pale, very young, with shabby clothes. All had long hair. Four were blondes, two were brunettes, one had lime green hair and another girl's was baby pink.

During their visits, Rosanna wrote that she could hear the women's screams in her quarters at the back of the house. Rosanna thought they might be in real pain. She was unnerved and always waited anxiously until an Uber came and took the women home, usually around one or two in the morning. Rosanna convinced herself that these women were in Briggs's home consensually, and hoped that those screams were partly fake.

None of Briggs's pick-ups stayed overnight, and all of the women – with the exception of Destiny, the hungry girl with the wool scarf around her neck who raided the kitchen for food – did not appear hurt. Briggs never had Rosanna prepare any food or refreshments for these visitors, and she was never allowed to clean Briggs's bedroom after the encounters.

Rosanna was always given the weekends off and she usually spent them with either Kevin or her mother. But as the weeks continued, the strange goings-on at Briggs's home began to weigh on her.

On Wednesday, January 15, she wrote:

It's one of B's pick-up nights. He left the house after dinner, and I'm dreading his return. He's going to bring home another pathetic, scrawny creature and abuse her, and there's nothing I can do about it. I can't call the police, no matter how loud she screams. This is the Forest, and they'll do whatever B wants and believe any fairytale he tells them. Looks like I'll be up most of the night, waiting for that poor girl to leave.

By March, she was writing, *B brought another bone-thin bone-white girl home tonight. This one has pink hair. It's 10:25 p.m. and she's screaming her lungs out. I cannot take this much longer. I HAVE GOT TO FIND ANOTHER JOB!*

Rosanna spent the rest of the evening online, applying for work. None of those applications panned out.

In the entries for the week before Rosanna disappeared, Briggs's behavior grew more aggressive. He brought home two bedraggled women, *both dirty blondes, and I'm talking about the condition of their hair, not the color.* Their screams kept her awake until three o'clock. *The Uber driver arrived at 3:20 a.m. and took them both away. They were able to walk out of the house to the SUV. Thank gawd!*

On Friday, Rosanna's last day before the barbecue, Briggs found the housekeeper alone in the linen closet at about ten a.m. She wrote:

I thought I'd locked the door from the inside, but B must have a key. I was putting away a stack of fresh bedding when he wrapped his arms around me and kissed me – hard. His breath smelled like whiskey. I pushed him away, and shouted, 'Don't you EVER do that again!'

He said, 'Hey! I find you irresistible. Is that so bad? I couldn't help myself. That's a compliment.' He had to be drunk. I was afraid to be alone with him in the linen closet. I made sure I'd backed out of there first. Then I said, 'Inappropriate and unwanted touching is not a compliment. I'm putting you on notice. Touch me again and I'll quit.'

I ran to my quarters and made a cup of tea. My hands were shaking so badly I could hardly drink it. B sent a text saying he would pick up the meat for the barbecue after his lunch. I logged in all the supplies at 4:15 p.m. and texted Briggs at 5:02 p.m. that everything was ready for the barbecue. Then I packed and was out of there.

The last entry in the diary was after Rosanna was fired for leaving the meat in the Range Rover. She was furious, and sent the texts that corroborated her story to her mother, then cashed her final paycheck and severance using her phone app, found a Caribbean cruise and hotel, bought a last-minute plane ticket to Fort Lauderdale, and texted her family and friends she was leaving. She wrote:

It took me about half an hour to pack my things. I only had a few photos and some clothes here, and they fit into a suitcase and a gym bag. Briggs is knocking on my door. I assume he wants to say goodbye. I'm storing this and sending it to you, Mom. I'll stay in touch.

And that's where Rosanna's diary ends and the mystery begins.

TWENTY-TWO

Rosanna's audio files were next, the ones she'd recorded on her cell phone. Now I would hear Briggs's harassment in detail. I wasn't looking forward to it. Reading the housekeeper's diary already made me angry.

My little iPad was grinding its gears, struggling with the huge file, when my cell phone rang. It was Jace, asking what I'd found on the thumb drive.

'I just finished reading Rosanna's diary,' I told him, and gave him a summary. Jace took notes and asked me to repeat several points. 'It's time I had a serious talk with Mr Bellerive,' he said.

'Be careful, Jace,' I said. 'He'll be filing a complaint about you before your car makes it through his gates.'

'I'm not going to be a Forest lapdog,' he said.

'I admire your courage,' I said.

'And? What's the rest of that sentence?'

'I hope you have a job when this is all over.'

'I will,' he said. 'And Briggs will be in jail.'

I hoped he was right. I wanted him to be right. But he was a seasoned cop and I'd lived in the Forest all my life. I knew money often trumped truth.

A quick glance at the clock told me it was almost six o'clock. Time to get dressed – really get dressed – for my date with Chris. I spent time with my make-up. Not too much, just enough to give my face definition and color. I brushed my shoulder-length dark hair until it shone. Tonight, I was wearing it down, not pulled back in a practical ponytail.

Then I opened my closet for my dinner dress. For too long, I'd regarded clothes as utilitarian slipcovers. But tonight I wasn't going to wear black – not my plain black DI pantsuits, or even my favorite black cocktail dress. It was time to add some color to my life.

I brought out my hot pink dress with the butterfly sleeves. The sleeves were banded in black and I liked how they moved when I walked. Paired with black heels and my favorite silver bracelet and earrings, it was a classic look.

When the doorbell rang at precisely seven o'clock, I was ready.

When I opened the door, Chris said, 'You look amazing.'

'So do you,' I said. He wore a blue button-down shirt that looked like it had been made for him. No tie this time. His collar was open and I caught a glimpse of just the right amount of chest hair. I don't like men who are manscaped or ones who are hairy beasts. Chris was just right. He smelled good, too: Old Spice and coffee. His hair looked newly cut.

I could see he'd shined up his Mustang for the occasion. I was touched.

My walkway was lined with spring flowers. The last of the red tulips and yellow daffodils were still blooming, and the redbud tree was a purple cloud.

'Nice garden,' he said. 'Your work?'

'No, can't take any credit for it. My mom planted them. She was quite the gardener.'

'So was my mom,' he said. 'And my grandmother. My grand-father was a plumber and a carpenter. He'd retired by the time I came along. I remember him sitting on his front porch, smoking cigars. He had a pewter smoke set. I still have it, even though I don't smoke.'

On the way to the restaurant Chris and I talked about our parents, and grandmothers – all the good memories we had. Then we shifted the conversation to our grandfathers and I think we were down to quirky first cousins by the time we got to Gringo Daze, the Forest's most popular Mexican restaurant.

Inside the big beige stucco building, soft Spanish guitar music played. The bar was crowded with locals, as usual. Eduardo, the owner, was on duty. He was a handsome, dark-haired man, lean as a bullfighter. He met us with a smile and two menus. My high heels tip-tapped across the Spanish tiles.

Eduardo gave us a large table near the fountain. I was relieved to see that the table in the secluded alcove by the fountain was occupied by another couple. A young pair in their twenties. They were holding hands and staring into each other's eyes as if there was no one else in the restaurant. I wasn't ready for that kind of privacy.

The server brought us chips and salsa and asked if we'd like guacamole. Chris looked at me and I said yes. We ordered drinks – a Dos Equis beer for Chris and a glass of chardonnay for me. Both came quickly, and the beer was in a frosted glass. By the time the server returned with the big, brown bowl of mashed avocados, we were ready to order. I wanted my usual – chicken fajitas. Chris ordered chile rellenos.

The guacamole vanished before our entrées arrived. They were steaming hot, and my fajitas were sizzling in a little frying pan. I built my fajitas on the warm, soft tortilla, loading it with a carefully calibrated amount of salsa, guacamole, chicken, red and green peppers. I left out the onions.

Chris took a bite of the chile rellenos and said, 'This is perfect. Just the right amount of oregano. Have you ever made these?'

'I'm not much of a cook,' I said. 'My default meal is scrambled eggs or roast chicken from the supermarket.'

'Cooking bores you that much?' he asked.

'No, I like food – good food. But I'm not a good cook. I'm too easily distracted. I'll whip up something and put it in the oven and then I'll get wrapped up in a story on the internet and the next thing I know, I have a pan of burned food. I can turn a sauce into charcoal. I once burned boil-in-the-bag lima beans.'

'Now you're bragging,' Chris said, and laughed.

'Hey, it took me weeks to get burned plastic out of that pot,' I said. 'But I can't resist penguin videos.'

He took another drink of his beer, then said, 'I know what you mean about distraction. For me, cooking is a different kind of distraction. I can forget about a bad scene at work by chopping vegetables and experimenting with different flavors. I enjoy the challenge of a new recipe. Back to my question: have you ever made chile rellenos?'

He looked at my blank face and answered his own question. 'Obviously not.

'They start with poblanos.' He pointed to his half-eaten pepper with his fork.

'You char these big suckers until they're black. After that, you stuff them while they're hot into a zip-lock plastic bag so they steam. That makes them tender and easier to peel.'

'How do you peel a poblano?' I asked.

'You have to remove most of the char on the outside. When you char them, your whole place smells like roasted poblanos, and that's a smell they ought to bottle and sell as perfume.' Now he was concentrating on finishing his poblano before it went cold.

'Sounds wonderful,' I said.

'It is. I'd like to cook for you, Angela. What kind of food do you like?'

'Anything, really.'

The server quietly removed our empty plates. I took another sip of wine. It was cold and dry, just the way I liked it.

'Give me a hint,' Chris said. 'Do you like Thai, Chinese, Mexican, French, or good old Southern cooking?'

'I like them all – but not too spicy or covered in sauces.'

'How adventurous are you?' he asked.

'About what?' I said, and then wished I hadn't.

He laughed, and took another sip of beer. 'You blush beautifully.'

I struggled to get the conversation back on track. 'I don't eat crickets, ants or grasshoppers.'

'And I don't cook anything that can be killed with a can of Raid,' he said.

'I'm not a big fan of weird cuts like tongue, hearts, gizzards and sweetbreads,' I said. 'Or liver. I really hate liver.'

'Even pate foie gras?'

'I don't believe in torturing geese.'

'Fair enough.' He held up his frosty beer glass and said, 'I solemnly swear that no geese will be force-fed for my dinners. All long-necked honkers will remain unharmed. But I can't speak for the safety of any cows, fish and chickens.'

I laughed. He looked so comical holding up his beer glass, I couldn't help it.

The server brought two orders of flan. 'With the compliments of the owner,' he said.

We spotted Eduardo at the host stand and raised our glasses in thanks. He smiled and waved.

Chris ordered coffee for both of us. It went well with the creamy custard in caramel sauce. Over dessert, Chris told me funny stories from his time as a patrolman in St. Louis.

'So I arrested this guy in an iffy neighborhood. Caught him red-handed, taking a fistful of cash out of a broken cash register in front of gas station.

'He told me he was taking a walk – alone at three a.m., mind you, in an area where I wouldn't go without my weapon – and he saw "someone" had broken the big plate glass window on the gas station.

'"Must have used a rock," he said. "In fact, I think they used that rock right there." He pointed to the rock next to the broken cash register.'

'Helpful,' I said, 'but how did he get the cash register open if it was offline?'

'You can open them with a credit card,' Chris said. 'There's even a YouTube video to show you how. It takes a little practice, but I suspected this guy had had plenty of it.

'Our man said he walked inside the gas station to make sure everything was OK. And he had no idea how the one hundred bucks cash – the exact amount the owner kept in the cash register – got into his pocket, and the little bits of glass on his clothes must have come from the window.

'I asked where he lived and he gave me his address. It was a rooming house two streets over. I asked his name, and he told me it was James Bond.'

'As in Double-O-Seven? Was he wearing a tux?'

'Nope, gray sweatpants and a T-shirt that read, *Buy Me Another Beer. You're still ugly.*'

'Charming.'

'I asked Mr Bond his real name, and he said Tom Smith.'

'You've got to be kidding.' My laugh turned into a snort.

'I'm not making this up. I asked Mr Smith if he had a middle name and he said, "Laird." And then he spelled it – L-A-I-R-D. He said his grandmother was Scots–Irish.'

'She must be so proud,' I said.

'Anyway, I took him in for a talk at the station, and checked his name in the computer for wants and warrants. He had warrants under both names – Tom Laird Smith and James Bond – for first and second-degree burglary. He was wanted even under his alias!'

We both laughed, and that's when I heard the sound of chairs scraping across the tile. The servers were mopping the floor.

'Looks like we've closed down another place,' Chris said.

'This is becoming a habit,' I said.

'A good one, I hope,' he said, and took my hand.

TWENTY-THREE

My dinner with Chris had passed so quickly I wasn't even aware it was over until the servers started closing the restaurant. When the server brought our check, I insisted on paying. We argued at first – in a friendly fashion. Finally, he said, 'OK, you can pay – on one condition. I insist on cooking dinner for you at my place.'

'Deal,' I said. My voice shook a little, though I wasn't sure why.

He smiled and said, 'I'm sorry you'll have to wait two weeks, though. Mike is going on vacation and we're short-handed until he gets back.'

I felt an odd pang at that news.

We walked hand-in-hand through the empty restaurant and deserted bar to his car. The only sounds were the splashing fountain and my heels clicking on the tiles. Don't ask me what we talked about walking through the restaurant or on the ride home. I just know we were at my house way too fast.

The full moon turned my old stone house and spring garden into a silver fantasy. Chris walked me to my door, and we stood on my front porch. Suddenly, we were both silent. Awkwardly silent. Then he lifted my chin and kissed me. Slowly at first, a little tentatively. His lips were soft and dry and he tasted of coffee and flan. His kiss became hard, and I wrapped my arms around him. Then we were leaning against my house, the cold stone pressing against my back. I'm not sure how long the kiss lasted, but finally I came up for air. I was panting slightly and suddenly afraid.

'Thank you,' I said. 'For a lovely evening.' I pulled myself out of his warm embrace, ran inside and shut the door.

'Angela, wait!' he cried. 'Please! Let's talk. We can sit out here on the porch if you want. Please!'

I couldn't resist that final plea. I carefully opened the door and stepped outside.

'Are you OK?' he asked. 'You look so wary, like you expect to be hurt. Did I do something wrong? Did you have a bad time? Am I a bad kisser?'

I sat down on the porch swing and patted the seat next to me. He sat, but not too close.

'No, you're good,' I said, then took a deep breath and started. 'I enjoyed our evening. It was a wonderful break from my work, which has been very intense lately.'

'I understand.'

'You do, far more than most people,' I told him. 'You have a good sense of humor, and I like that. You're a terrific storyteller – very entertaining.'

I looked at him. The moonlight had bleached away the small signs of aging around his eyes, and he looked young. And oh, so attractive.

'As you know, my husband Donegan died two years ago. So I'm a . . . widow.' I hated that word. It sounded like death itself. As soon as I mentioned it, I felt draped in suffocating layers of black, like a Victorian woman in mourning.

'I know,' he said. 'You must have loved him very much.'

'I did. His death was unexpected – Donegan had a heart attack while teaching and by the time I got to the hospital, he was . . . he was . . . gone.'

'That must have been tragic,' he said. 'You didn't even get to tell him goodbye.'

'I didn't. I barely remember the funeral, I was in such a daze.'

I had one memory, which I couldn't bring myself to say out loud. It was after the prayers were said over the open grave. The coffin had been lowered but not yet covered up. Someone handed me a red rose to toss on top of Donegan's coffin. Throughout our courtship and marriage, Donegan had given me red roses. I watched the rose fall. I heard it land on the coffin lid and I felt my heart break.

'Angela?' Chris asked. 'Where did you go?'

I shrugged and shook my head. I could feel the tears welling up, and I didn't want to cry.

'You were there, weren't you? Back at the funeral?'

I nodded, grateful I didn't have to answer.

'Angela, I lost my wife, too. Not the way you lost your husband, so maybe I have no right to compare my pain to yours, but she's gone, too. Forever. I'd loved Carrie since high school and I thought we had a good marriage. Sure, I knew I wasn't at home as often as I should have been, but her father was a cop, so I thought she understood what the job required and knew how to take being alone.

'Turns out she didn't. She told me over and over that she needed me to be home more often, but I didn't listen. Or maybe I should say, I listened, but I didn't hear what she was saying. Then Carrie was in a car accident and the dispatcher couldn't reach me. I didn't find out what happened until I got home at ten that night, and a neighbor ran over to tell me. Carrie had broken her leg and was in the hospital.

'I drove to the hospital with lights and siren and when I got there, she was in surgery. The doctor had to insert a pin in the bone. It was a difficult surgery, and when she came out of it, she never forgave me for not being there with her. Apologizing didn't work. Carrie said she'd had enough. When she left the hospital, she went home to her mother's house and filed for divorce. I didn't want the divorce, but Carrie insisted. When the divorce was official, she moved to Hawaii, and I haven't seen her since. After her mother died, she had no reason to come back here.' Even by the dim porch light, I could see the sadness shading his eyes.

'I'm sorry, Chris. You must have really loved her. What does she do for a living?'

'She's a decorator. You won't believe how she fixed up our house – it was just a plain old two-bedroom ranch. The inside was a showcase, but the kind of showcase you can live in. Carrie had a real flair for color. She'd show me how she was going to put two colors together and I'd think – well, that will never work. But it did. She had endless patience with clients. Some of those women would agonize over two shades of eggshell paint as if they were two doors with a live tiger hiding behind the wrong choice.

'Carrie liked rooms with lots of light, plants, and bright colors. She waited every year for summer. I guess it's no surprise she ended up in Hawaii.'

As Chris talked about his ex-wife's talents, he grew more enthusiastic, and I felt uneasy. Was I jealous of a woman forty-one hundred miles away? Ridiculous. Finally, he stopped.

'After the divorce, I could retire – I'd put in my twenty years – so I did. I'm not interested in riding a desk. I had the retirement party, opened my presents, then went home and crawled into the bottle for about six months, thinking about my ex and what I did wrong. I got tired of the pity party, and decided I needed to go back to work. A friend told me the Forest PD was looking for patrol officers.

'What I like about this job is it's never boring. And I was bored – bored to death.'

'So bored you went back to a dangerous job? You could get shot on a routine stop.'

'See, that's why I like to talk to someone who understands the job. I can't tell you how often someone tells me that I was lucky to retire "so young." They don't understand the job stress, or what it's like to work in ice storms, or work twenty-four hours without sleep and then come back in after two hours of sleep.

'I missed the risk and the adrenaline boost. I never know what's going to happen next, and I like that. I see people at their best and worst. Like when I went with you to inform Mrs Scott, that surgeon's wife, her husband was dead.'

'That was definitely a low point,' I said.

He reached for my hand. 'That wasn't entirely a low point. I got to have coffee with you. And tonight we had dinner. I loved talking with you, Angela. You're beautiful, bright, and funny – and a good listener.'

He kissed my hand gently, and said, 'I know you love your husband, and you always will. But I hope you will have room in your heart for me, too.'

I was touched by his sweet, old-fashioned gesture. 'I enjoyed your company, too. Please be patient with me. It's not easy to start dating again.'

'I'll wait,' he said. 'You're worth it. And you're still on for dinner – even if it's in two weeks?'

'Yes,' I said, and pulled him close for a long, sweet kiss.

TWENTY-FOUR

I woke up early the next morning, and felt like I was floating. I hadn't been this light-hearted in years. My date with Chris had been a good one. I remembered his coffee-scented kisses, soft but hard, urgent and insistent. I didn't feel like those kisses had betrayed Donegan. He was still with me, still in my heart, but he was a benign presence now, not a disapproving one.

After coffee and toast, I took a half-hour walk around the Du Pres estate on a perfect spring morning. The sun seemed to shine brighter, and I saw new life and color everywhere. By the time I got back to my white stone house with the gingerbread porch, it was only eight o'clock.

I changed out of my jeans into my black death investigator pantsuit and flat lace-up shoes, then pulled my long hair into a serviceable ponytail. Yep, that's what women who worked in some branch of law enforcement wore, not the sexy high heels and short skirts you see on TV. When we could be spending our day crawling on the floor of some filthy flophouse, a short skirt won't work. If we have to run, heels will hobble us. And long, flowing tresses get in our face.

I was on call for work today and hoped I didn't get any horrible death scenes. In fact, I prayed the whole population of Chouteau Forest would be extra careful and healthy and stay alive.

My work cell phone rang. Please don't be a gruesome investigation, I thought. I checked the number and got the answer to my prayers – or so I thought.

It was my boss, the chief medical examiner, Evarts Evans. What was he doing in the office so early? He was usually on the golf course at this hour, buttering up some bigwig.

When I answered the phone, the professionally affable ME sounded abrupt and angry. 'Mrs Richman!' he said. It was a demand.

Uh, oh. Normally, he called me Angela.

'Yes, sir?' My voice was trembling.

'I need to see you in my office immediately, if not sooner.'

'Of course. I'm on call today, sir.'

'You will be if you still have your job when I finish talking to you!'

Now he was shouting. Evarts never shouted.

'I'm on my way, sir.'

'I expect you in this office in ten minutes, do you understand?'

I did. I also understood there would be no time to stop by Katie's office to find out what was going on. I felt like I'd been kicked in the gut with a combat boot.

I made it to the medical examiner's office in the back of Sisters of Sorrow Hospital in nine minutes, all the while thinking about my recent cases. Who'd complained about me? It had to be someone powerful. Was it Mrs Scott, wife of the plastic surgeon who'd been caught dead with his squeeze? Did Jace and I demonstrate insufficient deference when we broke the news? I didn't think she could be a problem.

I noticed some flowers blooming by the road, and suddenly my hands felt itchy. Where did that come from?

Oh, right. Briggs Bellerive. When Jace and I went to his mansion for the search warrant, Briggs gave me a big bouquet of flowers that had seriously creeped me out. But that visit was in the line of duty, wasn't it?

Not with Briggs's talent for twisting the truth. Did that slippery snake complain? If so, Jace and I had made a powerful enemy indeed.

I didn't have any more time to worry. I'd arrived at the hospital. The lot was unexpectedly crowded, and the only parking spot was between two funeral home pick-up vans. The shiny black unmarked vans with the dignified silver scrolls on the side seemed like an omen. My career was between dead and deader, and I didn't know why. I'd find out in a minute.

I quickly punched the code into the door to the ME's office and ran down the hall.

Evarts was alone in his massive office. His door was closed, another bad sign. I knocked tentatively and was admitted with a low growl. The ME's office was furnished like an expensive men's club, with a forest green carpet, leather wing chairs, and Edwardian fox-hunting prints by the English artist George Wright.

Once, when I complained to Katie about the prints, she said, 'Well, what was he supposed to hang on the walls? Autopsy photos?'

The door to his luxurious bathroom (the one that had claimed my office space) was shut. Then I saw the worst sign of all: his practice putter was propped against the wall in his office putting green. He was too upset to golf.

I took a deep breath and entered. Evarts was behind his massive desk, a copy of the president's Resolute desk in the Oval Office. It was dustless and empty, except for one slim file folder. As I hiked across that vast green carpet, I saw my name on that folder.

Evarts's milk-mild face was red with suppressed anger. He glared at me with a laser gaze, as if he could bore holes in me. I know all the 'how to succeed' books say to wait until the boss speaks first, but I couldn't. I was too scared.

'You called, sir?' My voice was a terrified squeak.

He didn't ask me to sit down in one of the leather chairs across from his desk, so I hung onto the back of one to steady myself.

'Mrs Richman,' he said, in a voice that was like an arctic wind. 'I've received a formal complaint you are interfering in a police investigation. Two formal complaints, in fact.'

This time I kept silent. I didn't know what to say.

He opened my file folder and frowned at it. 'Detective Raymond Greiman says you are acting as an unauthorized partner to Detective Jace Budewitz, interfering with Detective Greiman's investigation into the disappearance of Rosanna McKim, Mr Briggs Bellerive's housekeeper.'

Evarts's words were cold, slow and deliberate. I could almost see Greiman in the room, wearing his TV-ready blue shirt and Hugo Boss suit, smirking at me. My anger burst through my caution.

'What investigation? He's not doing anything!'

As soon as those words shot out of my mouth, I regretted them.

'Detective Greiman says there's no need for further investigation of this case. It would be a waste of department resources. This young woman is what we used to call "loose."' Evarts was the poster boy for mansplaining. I wanted to slap his smug face.

Evarts must have seen my face because he held up his hand and said, 'I know I may sound politically incorrect, but the missing young lady has had multiple sexual partners and she could have run off with any one of them.'

'Says who? Who's saying Rosanna's had sex with a lot of men?'

'Detective Greiman, of course.'

Greiman, the man who hopped into bed with any badge bunny who gave him a second look, had the nerve to brand a woman as 'loose.' At least I didn't say that.

'Does Detective Greiman have personal knowledge of Rosanna's sexual behavior?'

'Of course not!' The old boy puffed up like the toad he was. 'That's outrageous. Detective Greiman is a decorated officer.'

'Then where did he get the information about Rosanna's sex life?'

'From her employer, Mr Briggs Bellerive.' He said the name reverently. 'She was his live-in housekeeper for seven months.'

'And what if I told you Rosanna said Briggs had been sexually harassing her and she was looking for another job? A safer job, away from an employer she described as an octopus. That means he had his hands all over her.' I wasn't above some 'womansplaining.'

Evarts started sputtering like an old car, but I kept talking. 'Rosanna also said that Briggs went out one or two nights a week and brought home young women. Some of them were underage pick-ups, and most were grubby and bedraggled. He took them up to his bedroom and Rosanna could hear them screaming throughout the house – with pain, not pleasure.'

'That's slander, Mrs Richman,' Evarts said. His piggy little eyes gleamed with malevolence. 'Detective Greiman warned me that you might say something like that. He told me Miss McKim had propositioned Mr Bellerive, and when he turned her down – after all, he's dating an international beauty, Desiree Gale – Rosanna began spreading lies about him. That's what that kind of woman does.'

'What kind of woman?'

'An unmarried young woman who is looking to catch herself a rich husband.'

'You do know that Rosanna has a steady boyfriend?' I asked.

'She wouldn't be the first woman to dump a steady boyfriend for a better match. Any girl would jump at the chance to marry Mr Bellerive – especially a Toonerville girl. Miss McKim is twenty-nine. Back in my day, we called an unmarried woman that age an old maid. They get frustrated when they're that old.'

He must have seen the fury on my face, because he put his hands up and said, 'I'm a little older than you, Mrs Richman, and I've seen a lot more human behavior. Especially in the war between the sexes.'

'Rosanna McKim didn't spread gossip about Briggs Bellerive,' I said. 'She hung on as long as she could because the job paid well. But she was looking for another one. She was afraid to be alone with Briggs. He attacked her in the linen closet.'

'And where did you get that information, Mrs Richman?'

'From Rosanna's mother.'

'Well, of course her mother would say that.' Evarts seemed to pity my stupidity. That look was quickly replaced with a crafty expression. 'Why were you talking to Miss McKim's mother?'

'She's a family friend. I went to school with Rosanna's older sister, Diana. While I was at the house, Mrs McKim gave me Rosanna's diary. She kept a day-by-day account of life at Briggs's house and sent her mother the diary as a back-up. Mrs McKim copied it onto a thumb drive.'

'Why would Mrs McKim give her daughter's diary to you instead of Detective Greiman, who was in charge of finding her daughter?'

'Because Greiman has no interest in solving the case,' I said. 'He talked to Mrs McKim and then talked to Briggs. He swallowed every lie Briggs fed him, hook, line and sinker!'

'Mrs Richman! You forget yourself. I am your supervisor.' He pounded his desk, and looked me square in the eye. 'Don't you forget that Briggs Bellerive is one of our most respected citizens. And he has filed a complaint against you. He says you were rude and intrusive and had no business barging into his home.' Evarts was pointing his pudgy finger at me. 'May I ask why you went with Detective Budewitz when he served the search warrant on the Bellerive property?' he asked.

'Because the detective asked me to.'

'Oh? Why was that? Was he lonely? Did he need protection? Or was he in need of your matchless detective skills?'

'No, he asked me because he thought I knew Briggs. I explained that I didn't really know him, I'd only been to a charity event at his house once, but Detective Budewitz really wanted me to go with him.'

'Are you having an affair with Detective Budewitz?'

At first I couldn't answer because of the shock. As I recovered, I bit my tongue and counted to three before I said to the swine, 'An affair! Jace is a devoted family man.'

'Married men have been known to cross the line.'

'Detective Budewitz doesn't. And your question is slander, sir, so please be careful.'

'Come now, Mrs Richman. You seem to have a preference for police officers. You were seen canoodling with Officer Christopher Ferretti at Gringo Daze.'

'Canoodling? What is this? High school?'

'I used that term to avoid a more unpleasant word, Mrs Richman. That's how I really heard this news.'

The F-word, I thought. I bet he got that tidbit from Greiman, too.

'Yes, I went to dinner with Chris Ferretti,' I said. 'And yes, we are dating. And yes, there's a big difference between Chris and Detective Budewitz. Chris is single. I don't date married men. Ever!'

'Mrs Richman, I'm going to ask you three questions and I know the answers. If you lie to me, you will be fired. Do you understand?'

I nodded. I couldn't figure out if he was bluffing about knowing the answers or not.

'Answer me! I want a verbal answer!' Evarts pounded his desk again. Harder. If his replica desk wasn't built like a fortress, it would have collapsed. His face was so red I hoped he'd soon show up on Katie's autopsy table.

'Question one,' he said. 'When you decided to visit your good friend Mrs McKim' – I could hear mocking quote marks around the words 'good friend' – 'was Detective Budewitz with you?'

'Yes.'

'Two. Did you read the copy of the diary on the thumb drive and report to Detective Budewitz?'

'Yes.'

'Three. Did you also make a report to Detective Greiman?'

'No.'

Now he took a piece of heavy stationery out of my file folder and said, 'Just as I thought, Mrs Richman. That's why I've prepared this official letter of warning for your permanent file. I'm providing you with a copy. Please remember that two more written warnings and I can fire you for disobeying orders. You will not get unemployment benefits. You have no business playing detective.'

I was so angry I couldn't move. I was stuck to the floor.

'You can leave my office, Mrs Richman. Because you answered truthfully, you still have your job. For now. Good day.'

TWENTY-FIVE

My heart was pounding and I was dizzy with rage after my encounter with Evarts. I fled down the hall to Katie's office, flung open her door without knocking and walked straight into Jace. The detective looked surprised.

Katie pushed forward to examine me. 'Angela! What's wrong?' Her plain, serious face mirrored her concern.

I tried to talk, but I was so angry I was gasping for breath. Evarts had left me speechless.

'Slow down.' Katie guided me around her desk and made me sit in her chair. There was barely room for the three of us in the claustrophobic space, so Jace perched on the flimsy wire chair near the door. It creaked ominously.

Katie had a full mug of hot coffee on the desk blotter. She grabbed a spoon, some fake creamer and sugar packets out of a drawer, and whipped up a brew that was more caffeine milkshake than coffee.

'OK, take deep breaths – several deep breaths, dammit! Breathe, Angela!' Katie's voice was rough but somehow soothing. I followed her orders and felt a little calmer.

Katie handed me the coffee mug and said, 'Drink this. All of it.'

I took a sip and made a face.

'Yeah, I know. It tastes like sugared cat piss, but it's what you need right now. Hold your nose and drink it. You have to tell us what happened. Both of us. This is war.'

While I swallowed the vile concoction, Jace filled me in on what had happened to him.

'Greiman filed a complaint against me,' he said. 'A formal complaint. So did Briggs's lawyer, and that one is even more serious. Briggs's attorney says I've been harassing his client and the search warrant was unnecessary interference.'

As I tried to gulp the disgusting beverage, I thought that Katie had nailed it: it did taste like sugared cat piss, with top notes of tar and chalky powdered milk.

Jace looked like he was having a hard time, too. His usual boyish countenance seemed older. Thin lines cut the corners of his eyes and dark circles hung under them. He'd nicked himself shaving and had a tiny bit of toilet paper stuck to his neck near his ear.

He talked quickly, and I heard anger and disappointment in his voice. 'Greiman says I'm meddling in his missing persons case, the disappearance of Rosanna McKim. He claims Briggs's housekeeper ran off with one of her many boyfriends, and further investigation is a waste of department resources. I said there was no proof Rosanna had a lot of lovers. I told Greiman that her mother said she had a steady boyfriend.

'Greiman sneered at that and said, "Exactly what you'd expect her mother to say. Who's going to admit their darling daughter is the town pump?"

'Greiman said Briggs told him Rosanna was a slut who came onto him. When he turned her down – and why would he screw a Toonerville tramp when he was dating an international model? – she made up stories about him harassing her. Greiman said that was the oldest female trick in the book, and any man would understand it.

'He got really ballistic when I mentioned Rosanna's diary,' Jace said. 'Greiman said she started writing a bunch of lies to cover her own skanky ways. That's when Greiman said I was too tight with you, Angela, and I was trying to turn you into my partner. And since the search warrant didn't give us anything useful, I've been told not to go near Briggs Bellerive and his house. His lawyer has threatened to sue us sideways and bankrupt the department.

'In this room, we all know that Briggs is guilty. He killed those three women and terrorized and abused we don't know how many more. We have to find a way to get around Greiman and arrest that killer.'

At last, I'd finished Katie's foul potion. Awful as it was, the caffeine and sugar were kicking in, and I felt a little better. At least I was able to talk.

'I just left the office of that miserable worm, that hypocritical bastard, Evarts Evans. He accused me of having an affair with you, Jace!'

The blood drained from Jace's face. 'But, Angela, that's not true! I'd never even think you're a woman. I mean, you are, and I like you, but just as someone I work with. Not like you're not attractive or anything. I mean, you are, but I don't—'

His sentences were so hopelessly tangled, I stepped in and rescued him. 'I know, Jace. Evarts is too dumb to understand that men and women colleagues can form working friendships. Greiman planted that idea in Evarts's head, and his manure-filled brain was a fertile spot.'

Katie snorted. 'Why don't you just say our boss has shit for brains? What did Evarts do that has you so upset you were speechless?'

'He gave me a written warning,' I said. 'I'm being warned for "playing detective" and assisting Jace. He put it in my permanent file.'

'Evarts did that? Really?' Katie looked shocked. 'I didn't think he had enough balls to try something that drastic.'

'His pair is owned by the Forest fat cats, and someone must be squeezing them hard,' I said.

'You're making an appointment with Monty,' Katie said. 'He'll have that letter taken out of your file.'

Katie believed her lawyer lover was invincible.

'I know Monty can do that,' I said. 'But I'm worried about backlash. I'm afraid if I win that battle, Evarts will remove the letter from my file, but he'll get revenge in little sneaky ways.'

'Monty's good at fixing that problem, too,' Katie said. 'And you have to fight that reprimand.'

'When this is over,' I said. 'Meanwhile, we have to bring down Briggs.'

I knew my brave words sounded ridiculous, like some kid making a promise in a tree house fort. But I meant them.

'And while we're talking revenge, how do we get Greiman?' I asked.

'We don't,' Jace said. 'He's not worth it. Besides, he's like a cockroach that can survive a nuclear blast. He'll crawl out of the ruins bigger and stronger than ever.'

I laughed. 'Jace, I'm awed by how well you are learning the ways of the Forest.'

'I'm learning the way I always do – the hard way,' he said.

'All right, enough with the dramatics from you two,' Katie said. 'Let's get down to business. You're going to be watched – in fact, you already are. Angela, I knew about your dinner date with the new hire, Chris Ferretti, by eight this morning. You ate chicken fajitas, by the way, and he ordered chile rellenos. I also knew you two were going at it hot and heavy on your front porch until nearly two in the morning.'

I felt my face burn scarlet and cursed my ability to blush at age forty-one.

'I didn't – we didn't—'

Katie cut me off with a laugh. 'Angela, the Forest is a small town, and despite its money, in many ways it's a hick town. That's what they do in small towns – watch one another. People-watching is the local sport, right after backstabbing. Everyone knows when the neighbors sneeze. They particularly like to track single women. So for now, assume someone is always watching when you leave home.

'Also, assume that someone is keeping track of your work phone calls, and possibly listening in. From now on, when you and Jace have to call each other, use your personal cell phones, not your work numbers. Exchange numbers right now.'

We did, while Katie watched. Then she gave her next instruction. 'Jace, when you get home today, tell your wife why Angela's number is on your personal phone. Definitely tell her about the accusations.'

Jace hesitated and looked alarmed. 'I'm supposed to tell my wife that people are saying I'm having an affair with Angela?'

'Yes,' Katie said. 'Get it out in the open before that rumor causes problems. Rumors die when they're exposed to the light. If you don't do it now, someone will be happy to "enlighten" your wife about the so-called facts.

'Finally, if you and Angela need to meet, call me on your private cell and I'll set up a meeting here, in my office. It's the one place that's safe for you two without raising eyebrows.'

Suddenly she tensed and said, 'Shh! What's that?'

'I don't hear anything,' Jace said.

'I do,' Katie said. 'Someone's coming down the hall.'

She peeked around the edge of the door, then hissed, 'Damn.

It's Evarts. If he sees us together, he'll know we've been conspiring. Hide! Jace, stay behind that door and make yourself as small as possible.'

Good luck, I thought. Jace was six-foot-two and about one-ninety.

Katie shooed the big detective behind the door, then said, 'Angela, get under my desk. Now!'

I felt like I was in a French farce. I crawled into the kneehole of Katie's desk, hunched over on all-fours. She sat down in her chair and her foot landed on my left hand. I fought hard to keep from screaming in pain.

There was a brief knock on the door, and it opened slightly.

Katie stood up, and I moved my hand just in time. I guessed she went over to the door to keep Evarts from coming into her office and getting too comfortable.

'Dr Stern,' Evarts said, 'do you have any information about when we'll get the identification on the two decedents in the woods? The forensic anthropologist, Ms Murdoch, hasn't given me an ETA yet.'

'I talked with Dana yesterday,' Katie said. 'She said it would be another ten to fourteen days before the victims would be ready for us. We caught a break on one, though. The woman had breast implants, so we'll be able to trace her.'

'Humph!' Evarts sniffed. 'I wonder why Ms Murdoch didn't call me with that information. I *am* in charge here.'

And out on the golf course in the morning, and at lunch for three hours in the afternoon, I thought.

Evarts sounded petty and petulant, but Katie rushed in to soothe his feelings. 'Oh, Dana knows that. She called me because she didn't want to bother you. She knows your time is important.'

I fought to keep from laughing. Katie, you're shameless, I thought. But her topnotch job of boss-buttering seemed to work. I could almost hear Evarts's ego inflating as she spoke.

'Well, yes, of course. I have been busy. That's very thoughtful of her, very thoughtful. You'll continue to keep me informed, won't you?'

'Oh, yes, sir,' Katie said.

Then it happened. My work cell phone, which was in my jacket pocket, chimed.

'Is that your phone?' Evarts asked.

'My phone?' At first, Katie didn't seem to recognize the ring tone, but she recovered quickly. 'Oh, yes, yes, my phone. Let me get my purse.' She kept her purse in the file cabinet drawer. I heard a drawer slide open and the zipper on her purse. Katie was frantically rummaging in her purse.

Meanwhile, I fumbled around in the dark kneehole, trying to turn off my phone. I caught a glimpse of the number. Damn. It was Ray Greiman, probably calling me for a death investigation, and I was turning off my phone. There would be hell to pay later. I was expected to answer quickly. Finally, I got the ringing to stop. I breathed a quiet sigh of relief. I'm sure Katie did, too. I heard the file drawer slam shut.

'I also wanted to warn you that we must be careful whom we accuse,' Evarts said. 'The search warrant served on one of our finest citizens, Briggs Bellerive, did not yield a shred of evidence. His lawyer has warned us that any further contact with him would constitute harassment.'

'I understand,' Katie said.

'I had a talk with Mrs Richman today. We received a complaint that she'd been interfering in a police investigation.'

'Angela?' Katie did a good job of sounding surprised. 'She's the best DI we have. I'm always happy when I get her on a case. She takes the kind of meticulous notes that stand up in court. Anyone that thorough is bound to offend people sometimes. But she's good – she's very good.'

'Yes, well.' Evarts cleared his throat. 'If she does as she's told, there won't be any further repercussions.'

'I hope so,' Katie said. 'I'd hate to lose a good staff member.'

'Well, I'll let you go, Dr Stern. Please keep me informed on that anthropologist's findings.'

'Yes, sir,' Katie said. 'I certainly will. Have a good day.'

She shut her office door, then whispered, 'OK. Stay quiet and in place. Sometimes he comes back because he forgot to tell me something.'

My hands and knee were aching, but I stayed quiet. So quiet, I could hear whimpering.

'Katie? Is that your puppy, Cutter?'

'Yes,' Katie said. 'He's in a basket on the other side of the file cabinet. I moved the cabinet to make room for my pup. That's why the room is even smaller. I was terrified he'd make a sound when Evarts was in here.'

She peeked down the hall again. 'It's empty. You and Jace can come out now.'

I crawled out from under the desk and dusted off the knees of my pantsuit. Jace and I had some pup therapy, both of us scratching and cuddling the little gold fluff ball. He was growing fast.

Cutter licked Jace's face. Then, snap! The pup bit Jace right on the end of his beezer.

'Ouch!' Jace said, and dabbed at his nose with his handkerchief. Cutter had drawn blood.

'Bad dog! No! No!' Katie said, and carried the disgraced pup to his basket.

'I'm sorry, Jace,' Katie said.

Jace grinned. 'That's OK. This love bite will be easy to explain to my wife.'

TWENTY-SIX

'Where the hell have you been?' Greiman roared at me when I phoned him from my car. 'I called you eight minutes ago. I've been sitting with my thumb up my ass, waiting for your call.' He was rude, impatient and sneery, but that was the answer I'd expected.

'I couldn't call back. I was in a meeting.'

'Oh? A meeting? You do know your job is to stay in contact at all times? Does Evarts know about this?' Greiman demanded.

'Evarts was there.' Well, he was. That was technically true. Greiman didn't need to know I was hiding under a desk. Besides, the creep shut up when I said the magic word – Evarts.

'We've got a traffic fatality on Gravois,' he said. 'One dead teenager, the other seriously fucked.' Nice language, I thought. Really professional. But I wasn't going to take the bait.

'What's the address?' I asked.

He gave it to me and said, 'Traffic is backed up for half a mile.'

'I'll be there as quick as I can,' I said.

Fifteen minutes later, thanks to some semi-legal maneuvers like driving on the shoulder to a chorus of furious honks and flipped middle fingers, I made it to the scene. I parked in a muddy spot by the side of the road and hauled out my death investigator's suitcase.

This section of Gravois cut through majestic limestone bluffs, with green woods on either side of the narrow, winding two-lane road. Under less dire circumstances, it was a scenic drive.

I threaded my way through the patrol cars and other official vehicles, including an ambulance with flashing lights, and a red fire truck with shining chrome. Firefighters in turnout gear and helmets were swarming over the car, a black sporty coupe with blood on the windshield.

The accident scene was hidden from prying eyes by portable screens. I stepped around the screens to find Greiman. He was dressed in charcoal gray Hugo Boss pants and a light gray sweater. I took childish glee in seeing his pricy Fendi footwear caked with an inch of sticky clay soil.

'What happened?' I asked Greiman.

'The car was speeding, missed a curve and hit that rock face.' He pointed to a towering limestone cliff with a long white horizontal gash in the stone.

'The car flipped over twice, slid across the road and ended up hitting that tree on the passenger side.'

The car broadsided the tree, a thick black walnut a good sixty-feet tall, and caved in the passenger side of the car almost to the center console. The windshield on that side was cracked and spattered with blood. I caught a glimpse of a mangled body in the passenger seat, and heard someone moaning in the front seat. The fire department would have to take the car apart to free the passengers.

'The firefighters are using the Jaws of Life to extract the two passengers, both males, aged seventeen,' Greiman said. 'The kid in the passenger seat is dead.'

'Do you know who he is?' I'd have to do the death investigation on his body.

'Jared Dunning. He is – or rather, was – a linebacker for the Forest High football team. He was being scouted by four college teams. I know his stats, too. Kid was custom-built for that position: he was six feet two inches tall and weighed two-hundred-thirty pounds.'

'Poor kid,' I said. 'All that promise cut short.'

'The driver – Chad Du Pres – is also on the team. Another big guy. Six one and two-forty. He's alive but badly injured, possibly paralyzed from the waist down.'

'Is he the Forest High star running back? Henry Du Pres's grandson?

'That's the one. This accident is going to destroy the team's prospects.'

And a lot more than that, I thought.

'His grandfather showed a lot of foresight,' I said, 'and it's going to save Chad. The Jaws of Life will get the old man's grandson out of that wreck alive.'

'The kid would be better off dead, if you ask me,' Greiman said. 'He won't be able to play football ever again.'

'What happened to him is tragic,' I said, 'but he's young, healthy and rich, and science has made great advances with spinal cord injuries.'

'I can tell you this – I'd rather be dead.'

I'd rather he was dead, too. I fought hard not to answer him back. The damaged car looked like a bag of blood had exploded inside.

Chad was the child of either very good luck, or very bad, I wasn't sure which. Henry Du Pres was one of old Reggie's cousins. The Du Pres had their fingers in every pie – and cash drawer – in the Forest. Henry's oldest daughter, Caroline, was in a big wreck on the Dan Ryan Expressway in Chicago some years back, and the Jaws of Life saved her.

I give Henry credit. He made it his personal mission to get the Jaws at the Chouteau County fire department, and donated seventy-thousand dollars of his own money for tools and training. Most small fire departments couldn't afford these expensive lifesaving tools.

Now the equipment he'd bought was going to save his grandson, Chad. A firefighter covered Chad with a protective sheet to keep the fine powdered glass out of his eyes, and turned on a Sawzall, a kind of machine-powered saw. The firefighter deftly cut out and removed the cracked windshield in two neat pieces.

While he worked, I opened my iPad and began the preliminary information for a Vehicular Related Death.

I noted the accident took place on an open two-lane road in a wooded area, and the car was southbound. The speed limit was twenty-five miles per hour, because of the sharp curve. The accident took place in daylight, at 10:34 a.m. The temperature was seventy-two degrees. The weather was clear and sunny. The roadway was asphalt and had a ninety-degree curve. A yellow sign with a blinking light warned, SLOW! DANGEROUS CURVE.

There was no debris in the roadway, no deadly 'rising sun over a hill' factor – no reason at all for this fatal one-car accident except stupidity.

A woman firefighter with a face shield had started up the noisy hydraulic Jaws of Life cutter tool, a two-pronged machine that resembled a giant can opener, and began working on the driver's door. The cutter's mouth opened and closed. It could snap a doorpost like a twig and cut through the door like it was aluminum foil.

While she worked, I wrote down the vehicle's details. The crushed car was a sweet ride, 2020 Nissan Z 3702. Later, I would discover it only had 19,012 miles on it. Black, with a black interior, it had been a real beauty, and I wondered if it was a birthday present for the promising running-back. I noted the Missouri license plate number.

The mechanical chomping stopped for a moment, and I saw a strapping young paramedic talking to the driver, Chad, who was moaning under the protection.

'Chad,' the paramedic said. 'Stay with me, buddy. This will be over soon. We have to keep you covered just a little longer.'

'Jared . . .' the injured driver said. 'Why . . . won't he . . . answer me? Is he . . . mad at me?'

'No, Chad, he's not,' the paramedic said. I was close enough to see the sadness on his face, but he kept it out of his voice. He looked like a bodybuilder, somewhere in his early twenties. His hair was brown and buzzed.

I wondered if Chad couldn't see the mangled body of his friend and teammate next to him, or if he was too shocked to comprehend what had happened.

'How come I . . . can't move . . . my legs?' Chad asked.

'We'll have a doctor look at you and find out.' The paramedic didn't lie, but he didn't tell the injured young man what he suspected was the full truth, either.

'Chad, I have to ask you some questions,' the paramedic said, 'and I want you to answer honestly. The doctor may have to do surgery and it's important that you tell me what really happened. Do you understand?'

'OK.' Chad's voice sounded slurred.

'Chad! Stay with me. Did you and Jared have anything to drink this morning? Maybe a couple of beers? Some of your dad's bourbon? A little Captain Morgan, maybe?'

'No . . . We're . . . in training.' Chad's answer wrung my heart.

'I'm not judging, Chad. Just asking. You understand that?'

'Yes.'

'Did you use any controlled substances – pot, coke, crack, happy dust . . .?'

He rattled off some names I'd never heard before and ended with 'Did you take anything, Chad? Any pills or powders? Please, it's important.'

'No . . .' Chad's voice was growing weaker.

The paramedic turned to the female firefighter with the Jaws of Life and said, 'How much longer?'

'Less than five,' she said.

The paramedic was back talking to the injured driver. 'OK, Chad, are you there? Are you with me, buddy?'

'Uhh,' said Chad.

'Can you tell me what may have caused this accident? Did a rabbit run out in front of your car? Or a deer? What ran out in front of your car?'

'No . . . no deer. It was Mom.'

I figured the poor kid was hallucinating.

The paramedic said, 'Your mom ran out in front of the car?' I heard the disbelief in his voice. He signaled to the firefighter to hurry.

Chad sounded impatient. 'No . . . Mom not here . . . Mom caused this.'

'How?'

'Mom . . .' With that, the hydraulic Jaws of Life started again, prying the car apart like a tin can, and I couldn't hear any more.

TWENTY-SEVEN

T he firefighter had predicted the time of the grand opening correctly. Five minutes later, the once-snazzy sports car was reduced to rubble. Despite the paramedic's entreaties, Chad had stopped talking and slipped into unconsciousness.

Under the blood, the injured athlete was a handsome young man, clean-shaven with even, well-defined features and the choirboy-pink complexion that fair-skinned young men have in their teens and early twenties. Marring this manly beauty was a deep, bloody gash running down his face from his eyelid to his jawline. I suspected he'd need plastic surgery.

Chad's blond hair was cut in a trendy flattop. He wore khaki Bermuda shorts and a green Chouteau Forest High School T-shirt. His flip-flops were in the footwell. He may have kicked them off to drive or lost them trying to control the car when it went into its fatal skid.

Chad was a big young man. Greiman's estimate of six feet one and two-hundred-forty pounds seemed about right. He had a football player's broad shoulders and muscular arms. He was definitely a catch – a good-looking football star with the right bloodline and big bank account. I wondered if that would change now.

The four paramedics quickly and expertly lifted Chad out of the car seat and onto the gurney. The bone was jutting out of his right leg. The paramedic put a tourniquet on the unconscious man's leg, and the four rushed him to the waiting ambulance. The doors slammed with an ominous sound, announcing that Chad's life as a football hero was over. He went off in a blaze of lights and blare of sirens.

Now I had to focus on the death investigation of Chad's friend and teammate, Jared Dunning.

The police tech had videoed Jared's body in the wrecked car at every stage: from the time they arrived at the scene, through the dismantling of the car by the Jaws of Life, to now, when he sat slumped in the stark shell of the sports car.

I opened my DI case, gloved up with multiple pairs, and took my own photos for the medical examiner – wide, medium and close-up shots from both sides of the car – driver and passenger – as well as front and back views.

As I worked, I hoped time would erase the grim sight of Jared's death from my memory. This morning, Jared Dunning had looked much like his friend, Chad. He'd been another privileged, careless youth with golden hair, a handsome fortune and a bright future. Now he was two-hundred-thirty pounds of butchered meat.

I checked the car and noted that the airbags had been disabled on both the passenger seat and the driver's seat sides. If this went to court, the Dunning family lawyers were going to love that information.

Jared had been wearing his seatbelt, but it wasn't enough protection. Jared's face was covered with blood. His elegant patrician nose and strong jaw had been smashed against the passenger window, and some of the skin had peeled off his face. His neck was at an awkward angle, which might have been a sign it was broken. For his sake, I hoped his death was quick.

On a nearby patch of grass, I spread out a clean, sterilized sheet for the body inspection, sometimes known as the body actualization. Then I opened the Scene Investigation form on my iPad.

Four firefighters lifted Jared out of the car seat and gently laid him face-up on the white sheet. I started answering the long list of questions on the form. I'd fill in the demographic data later, probably when I saw his family.

When was the time of death? the form asked.

The paramedics had pronounced Jared dead at 10:47 a.m.

What was the location of the body?

The decedent was in the vehicle's passenger seat.

What direction was the vehicle?

The car had been heading south on Gravois Road.

What was the directional body position?

The decedent was sitting straight up and wearing a seatbelt. He was also facing south.

Again, I listed the weather conditions. The day was becoming sunnier and more beautiful by the hour, a heartbreaking fact I didn't have to mention.

I used Greiman's estimate of Jared's height and weight, then described the decedent's clothing. Like his friend Chad, he wore khaki shorts and a Forest high school T-shirt. Jared's shoes, brown Topsiders, were in the footwell. I was always amazed how many car accident victims wound up shoeless. Pedestrians, too. They were often knocked out of their shoes.

Jared wore no socks – typical for kids his age – and no jewelry. It was unsettling to see this uniform of preppy privilege soaked in blood.

Was the body fresh? the questionnaire asked.

Yes, I wrote.

Beginning to decompose?

No.

Any insects present?

No. That was good news for me. Otherwise, I'd have to gather samples of fly larvae, beetles and other critters, then label and package them. Insect scavengers helped the medical examiner determine time of death. When these creatures arrived and began laying their eggs were vital clues.

Environmental temperature?

My thermometer said seventy-four degrees.

That was the easy part of my examination. Now for the body actualization. I had to document the wounds, starting at the top of Jared's head, and I had to be absolutely accurate. Two wealthy families were involved, and a promising young man had met an abrupt, violent death. Lawyers would be circling like buzzards to grab this accident. The blood complicated my job.

I recorded that the decedent had a deep 'cut-like defect on his right temple.' Actually, it was a deep gash, but I couldn't say that. If this case went to court, as I suspected it would, and that gash turned out not to be a cut, the attorneys would tear apart my testimony.

On Jared's once handsome face, a seven-inch by three-inch flap of skin was torn away, exposing the muscles on the right side of his head. The right eye socket was smashed and so was the right eye. The eye had burst or been torn open, and it leaked vitreous fluid.

I felt suddenly dizzy and leaned against a nearby tree, breathing in the soft green spring air. I needed a break from recording these stomach-turning injuries. I gave myself the usual lecture: get past the 'oh my God' reflex and help this poor man. He died young. He needs your help and respect. Woman up and finish this.

I shook my head, squared my shoulders, and went back to work.

Jared's right side had taken the brunt of the injuries. His right forearm had a compound fracture of the radius, the long bone in his arm. A two-inch jagged piece of bone had pierced the skin. There was a fourteen-inch by three-inch bloodstain on his right arm.

Both hands were a shattered, bloody mess. I had to document the injuries. I saw multiple broken and twisted bones – four meta-carpals (the bones that extended from his wrists), six proximal phalanges (the first joint above the knuckles), eight middle phalanges (the second joint) and two distal phalanges (the finger-tips). Both wrists also appeared broken. I wondered if Jared had held up his hands to protect his face. Both sides of his hands had significant (six by four inches) patches of drying blood, almost as if he was wearing red gloves.

I lifted his blood-soaked shirt and noted a three-inch by five-inch yellow-green healing contusion – in other words, a bruise – on his abdomen. Was this an old football injury?

Jared had an eight-inch cut-like defect on his thigh. If he'd lived, my guess was that deep cut would have needed stitches. There were six cut-like defects on his right knee and four on his left. His right leg had thirty-four cuts, ranging from one-eighth of an inch to six inches, plus four abrasions.

His rather hairy right foot had a patch of blood measuring three-by-two inches. The foot might have been broken. The ME would X-ray the body and see how many fractures there really were.

The firefighters were packing up the Jaws of Life gear. The tools that could take apart a car fit inside a surprisingly small case. I asked the firefighters for help turning over Jared's heavy body, and the woman volunteered.

She was wearing a bulky tan turnout jacket and pants with reflective yellow stripes. From what I could tell, she was blonde, compact and tough.

'I'm Heather Fowler,' she said, introducing herself. 'I'm a new hire.'

With her help, we quickly turned over the body. This side would be easy. A six-inch cut-like defect on the back of the decedent's bare neck and a blood spot that measured twenty-seven by thirty-one inches.

I thanked the firefighter and complimented her on how skillfully she'd turned the muscular body.

'You're strong,' I said.

'I have to be to get hired on in this department,' she said. 'Some days I'm hauling ninety-five pounds of gear. I used to be a paramedic.'

'Can you answer two questions about Chad, the driver?'

Heather glanced at her colleagues and said, 'I've got a minute or so before we take off.'

'Chad said he couldn't move his legs. Is he going to be totally paralyzed?' I asked.

I thought she might have shrugged inside the heavy turnout coat. 'I don't know. I'm no doctor. It could be he was just in shock and there's nothing seriously wrong.

'I do know if he did have an injury it wasn't high up on the spine, around C5 or above, or he wouldn't have been able to breathe or talk to that paramedic. So I doubt he'll be a quadriplegic. That's some good news.

'Since Chad was able to talk, I think the injury might have been in his mid-back. He'll probably be able to move his arms and hands. If he turns out to be a paraplegic – his legs may not work. But there's hope. He can use a wheelchair and even drive a car that has hand controls.'

After this accident, I wondered if Chad would ever want to drive again.

Heather was still talking. 'I've seen other people with his type of injury learn to walk with braces. So if he really is injured, his future's not totally bleak. But he is looking at years of hard work.' She checked her watch and then glanced over at the truck. 'What's your second question? We're about to head out.'

'You were there when the paramedic asked Chad what caused the accident. Chad said, "Mom caused this." Then you fired up the Jaws of Life and I couldn't hear his answer. Did you hear it?'

'Oh, yes,' she said. 'His mother had texted him: "Make sure you come home for dinner tonight. It's important!" She texted that message three times and he didn't answer. When she sent the fourth demand, it had 666 at the end.'

'The mark of the Beast?' I said. 'Why's a nice Forest Mom using satanic symbolism?'

'In this case, 666 had nothing to do with the devil. On an alpha-numeric keypad 666 spells 'MOM.' Sometimes, it's code for "Answer this instant or you're grounded till you graduate from college."'

'So he was reading that furious message from his mother—' I said.

'And went straight to the Devil,' Heather said.

TWENTY-EIGHT

After that horrific death investigation, I had to inform Jared Dunning's family that their golden boy was dead. Detective Greiman begged off, as usual. He always found an excuse to avoid an unpleasant job. Right now, I wanted to be around him as little as possible.

I was glad that Bill Sherman, one of the uniforms, went with me for the notification. He was a lean, seasoned cop in his late thirties, just starting to go gray at the temples. A little age looked good on him.

The Dunning home was ten minutes away and Bill followed me there. The Dunnings made their money in shoes in the nineteenth century, and through wise investments, it continued to grow. Their mansion seemed to symbolize the family. Most of the Forest grandees lived in extravagant mansions – fanciful French chateaus and Romanesque castles. The Dunnings lived in a redbrick Georgian mansion, notable for its austere beauty.

Bill and I parked in the graveled circle out front.

A housekeeper, a stout older woman in a white uniform, answered the door, and I asked to speak to Mrs Dunning.

'Do you have an appointment?'

'No,' I told the housekeeper, 'we do not, but it's important.' Bill and I introduced ourselves and showed our credentials. The woman's face turned pale. She led us into a small side parlor and hurried up the staircase.

The room was an afterthought, meant for tradespeople and unwanted visitors. It had four green upholstered chairs and a carved oak table with spring flowers in a vase. On the walls were more than a dozen photos of Jared, from newborn to toddler to football hero. If there were other children, I saw no evidence of them.

Bill looked at the photos of the triumphant boy. 'I hate this part of the job,' he said, keeping his voice low.

'Me, too,' I said. 'This news will ruin this poor woman's life.'

We heard hurried footsteps and both of us shut up. A tall, dignified, fifty-something woman rushed into the room. She wore flats and a blue striped shirtwaist. White as paper and trembling, she said, 'I'm Natalie Dunning. Who is it? My husband? My son? My daughter? My grandson?'

I knew better than to beat around the bush. I delivered the blow quickly. 'It's your son,' I said. 'Jared. He was in a traffic accident. He died.'

'Noooooooo!' She started to totter. Bill and I grabbed her and helped her sit down. Mrs Dunning rocked back and forth and howled like her heart had been torn apart. I ran out of the room, and found the housekeeper pacing the kitchen, wringing her hands.

'Mrs Dunning needs help,' I said. 'What's your name?'

'Flynn,' she said. 'Susan Flynn.'

'I had to give Mrs Dunning bad news. Her son was killed in a car accident.'

'Jared?' Mrs Flynn's eyes filled with tears. 'That lovely boy is gone?'

'I'm afraid so.'

She wiped away her tears with her apron and said, 'What should I do?'

'She needs hot tea or coffee,' I said.

'For that news, Ms Richman, she needs brandy.'

Susan Flynn quickly searched a cabinet, pulled out a bottle and a glass and followed me to the parlor. There she poured a stiff shot and said, 'Mrs Dunning! Natalie! Here, you must drink this. You've had a shock.'

'My boy's dead!' she cried. 'I want to die, too.'

'Where is Mr Dunning?' I asked.

'In Frankfort,' the housekeeper said, raising her voice to be heard over Natalie's cries of distress. 'He's expected home tonight and there's no way to reach him right now.'

'She needs her family,' I said. 'Can her daughter come now?'

'Alison should be home. I'll call her right now.' Susan Flynn rushed out of the room.

Natalie Dunning had swallowed the hefty shot of brandy. She was slightly calmer and a bit woozy, but she'd recovered enough to ask questions. Each one seemed torn from her heart.

'What happened?' she asked, still trembling.

'Your son was in a car accident with his friend, Chad Du Pres.'

'Wh-where did it happen?' she stammered.

'On Gravois.'

'Who was driving?'

'Chad.'

'Did Chad survive?' She was rocking back and forth again.

'Yes, but he's badly injured.'

'Good! I wish he was dead. I hope he dies, too!' Natalie's eyes narrowed with fury. 'I never did like that boy. Smug and entitled, like all the Du Pres. He drove too fast. Raced that car all over the Forest, terrorizing the neighbors! I didn't want my Jared with him, but they were on the same team. And his father said it was good to know the Du Pres family. Said it would help his future. Ha! What future? The Du Pres family stole it! They killed my boy!'

She was crying now and furious. Rage contorted her features. She stood up, took both hands and tore open her blue-striped shirtwaist dress down to her waist. Buttons popped and flew across the room, revealing a modest full slip, trimmed in lace.

For a moment, I was frozen with shock. Then I said, 'Mrs Dunning, stop, please!'

She shrieked louder, and started tearing at her carefully coiffed gray hair. Stiff with spray, it stood up in hanks. 'I don't want to stop! My boy is dead! He's dead.'

She howled and began beating her head on the wall. Bill grabbed her, trying to keep her away from the wall so she'd stop hurting herself. She bit his hand.

'Ow!' he cried.

Natalie broke out of his arms, ran to the wall of pictures, picked out a big, silver-framed photo of her son in his football uniform, and smashed it against the wall. The glass shattered. She found a pointed shard about eight inches long. Before Bill or I could stop her, Natalie plunged the glass dagger into her left wrist. That skin is surprisingly tough, but she succeeded in slicing her wrist. Blood spurted down her arm.

'He's dead, he's dead, and I want to die, too!' she shouted.

Bill wrestled the glass shard away from her and yelled, 'Angela! Call 911. Get an ambulance.'

I quickly punched in the call and the operator promised to send an ambulance right away.

I called for the housekeeper and Susan Flynn came running back in. 'Natalie's bleeding! What did you do?' she cried.

'Mrs Dunning tried to kill herself,' I said. 'I've called 911 for an ambulance. Is her doctor Carmen Bartlett?'

'Yes.'

Doc Bartlett took care of most of the Forest, and I had her on speed dial. Her efficient receptionist got her on the phone right away. I told the doctor the story and said an ambulance was on the way and would take Mrs Dunning to SOS.

'That poor woman,' Carmen Bartlett said. 'Jared was her whole life. I'm finishing up here at the office. I'll meet her at the emergency room.'

'Thanks,' I said. Carmen was a rare doctor – the kind who cared about her patients.

'Is Mr Dunning home?' she asked. 'He travels a lot for business.'

'He'll get in from Frankfort sometime tonight,' I said. 'But her daughter is on her way over here.'

'Send her to the ER. She can help me work out a treatment plan for her mother.'

I could hear sirens. Flashing lights strobed the room. The ambulance was here. By this time, Natalie was in one of the chairs, weeping. Grief seemed to roll through her body in waves. I met the paramedics outside. There were two – large, muscular men with buzzed hair and oddly boyish faces – and told them what happened. I also asked them to check Officer Sherman's hand. They wheeled in a stretcher.

Inside, the two men filled the small parlor. One checked Bill's hand, then cleaned, disinfected and bandaged it. 'Have you had a tetanus shot recently?' he asked.

'I got a booster shot a year ago,' Bill said.

'Human bites are nasty. I'll give you a script for an antibiotic, just to be safe. Keep this wound clean, and if it shows any sign of infection, don't fool around. Go to the ER. I've cleaned and bandaged the glass cut, too. It's not deep enough for stitches. It should be OK, but if it's not, you know the drill.'

The other paramedic was ready to roll Mrs Dunning out on the stretcher. She was crying hard and didn't seem aware of what was going on.

I shut the front door and turned to Bill. 'Whew. Are you OK?'

He looked at his bandaged hand. 'I'm fine, but I never thought I'd get chomped by a rich lady. This job is full of surprises.'

Susan Flynn brought in a wastebasket, dustpan and broom, and began sweeping up the larger pieces of broken glass on the floor. Her eyes were red from weeping.

'Poor Mrs Dunning,' she said. 'She loved that boy so much. She devoted her life to him. He was a good boy, too. She didn't want him running around with that Chad Du Pres – that boy has too much money and not enough guidance from his parents, and it shows. He was driving too fast in that new car of his. The police stopped him, but they never gave that boy a ticket. He was a Du Pres!

'Every time Mrs Dunning tried to lay down the law and make her son stay away from Chad, her husband would say that the Du Pres were an important family and they could help Jared.'

She was sweeping up the glass with quick, angry strokes of the broom. I picked up the photo of Jared, who was holding a huge gold trophy aloft, and carefully pulled the remaining pieces of glass out of the frame and dropped them in the wastebasket.

'Where should I put this?' I asked.

'In the hall closet,' she said. 'I'll take it to the framers later.'

The front doorbell rang and a young woman burst in. She looked like a slightly older version of her brother, with long blonde hair. 'Where's Mother, Mrs Flynn?' she said. 'What's wrong? You said you'd tell me when I got here.'

She glared at me and Bill. 'And why are the police and this woman in here?'

I introduced myself and Bill and said, 'I have bad news. Please sit down.'

Alison sat and said, 'OK. Enough! Tell me.'

'Your brother is dead. He was killed in a car accident.'

'Jared? Oh, no! Oh, no, no, no! That can't be!' She was crying now. Through her tears she said, 'Was my little brother running around with that Chad Du Pres?'

'Chad was driving the car,' I said. 'He's in the hospital with serious injuries.'

'Where's Mummy?'

'She was very upset and she's been taken to SOS. Dr Bartlett is with her.'

Alison stood up. 'I'll go there right now. This is all Daddy's fault. I tried to tell him that Jared shouldn't be in a car with that Chad. That boy was racing all over the Forest, terrorizing everyone. But Daddy wouldn't listen!'

She ran out the door.

But the blame from that terrible accident lingered.

Chad blamed his mother for texting him and insisting on an answer.

Alison blamed her father. And Mrs Dunning blamed her husband.

Both families would be maimed forever.

TWENTY-NINE

I'd been hoping to sleep late the next morning, after that hideous death investigation. Instead, I was awakened at seven o'clock by a call from Katie.

'Angela, I need you at my office at seven-thirty,' she said. 'It's important.'

'Now?' I said, still sleep-stupid.

'Yes, now. Shower, throw on some clothes, and get over here. I'll have breakfast and some decent coffee.'

I yawned, still too dazed to focus.

'Angela!' Katie shouted. 'I need you at this meeting. Are you coming?'

'I'll be there,' I said.

I longed to go back to bed and snuggle under the covers, but I couldn't. Katie was telling me in code that we needed to meet with Jace.

I stood up – a real achievement in my bone-tired state – stretched and headed for the shower.

Yesterday had taken a lot out of me.

After that nightmarish death investigation, Officer Bill Sherman and I had that emotionally wrenching Dunning family notification. It was nearly four p.m. by the time I got home from that. I threw on my riding clothes – an elegant name for a pair of ancient jeans and a disreputable shirt. I loaded up with carrots and peppermints and headed to the Du Pres barn for horse therapy. American Hero listened patiently to my troubles, and sagely agreed with me. I rode the horse for two hours until my muscles ached, but this time from exercise, not tension.

At home last night, I threw my DI suit along with a load of darks into the washer. Dinner was my usual default meal, scrambled eggs and toast. After dinner, I took a long, hot shower, put the freshly washed clothes in the dryer, and fell into bed. My mattress felt like cobblestones, and I tossed and turned until four in the morning, when I fell into an exhausted sleep.

Now Katie's call dragged me out of bed. After a cold shower shocked me awake, I switched to warm, soothing water. Then I pulled my damp hair into a ponytail, put on another black DI suit and sensible shoes.

Outside, spring had turned the trees the tender yellow green I only saw early in the year. The tulips along my walk were a fiery blaze – red, yellow, orange. Behind them were the purple blooms of my mother's wild phlox. She went into the woods with a shovel and dug them up herself years ago. They prospered in captivity.

My sun-warmed skin felt good. The sky was china blue. In short, it was another perfect spring day, and I was headed to the morgue.

I made it to Katie's office at 7:28 a.m. She'd turned her desk into a buffet, with a big tray of fresh fruit, a basket of muffins and bagels, whipped cream cheese, and two giant boxes of fresh hot coffee. Next to the coffee were two mugs. One read *I See*

Dead People and the other had a Sherlock Holmes skeleton with an earflap traveling cap and calabash pipe.

'Tasteful,' I said, choosing the Dead People mug and pouring myself a cup.

'Gifts from a staffer who's leaving,' she said. 'Feel free to break your cup or steal it.'

Katie looked exhausted this morning – pale, and her brown hair was spiky and unruly. I wondered if she'd had a bad night, too.

I filled a paper plate with berries and melon chunks and topped it with a blueberry muffin.

'I see you caught the fatal accident with the football stars,' Katie said.

I didn't want to talk about that case any more, but I wanted a lecture on my love life even less.

So I said, 'Yeah, it was a bad one. We needed the Jaws of Life to free both of them. The Du Pres kid may wind up a paraplegic and the Dunning kid is dead. I had to inform the family, and Bill Sherman went with me. Dunning's mother bit Bill and collapsed from shock and was taken to SOS.'

'I heard it was a real shit-show,' Katie said. 'It got worse later last night. Old man Dunning called Evarts at home and demanded all the paperwork from the autopsy ASAP. He says he's going to sue Henry Du Pres and "get his last nickel."'

'Wait,' I said. 'Stephen Dunning gets home from a long trip to Europe and all he can think about is suing the De Pres family? With his only son dead and his wife in the hospital from a nervous collapse? Now that's cold.'

'He's so cold, his words freeze in the air,' Katie said.

I laughed, except it wasn't funny. Stephen Dunning had already sacrificed his son for his social ambitions, insisting Jared ride with a kid who drove like a maniac. Now he was trying to profit from his son's death.

'So you did the kid's autopsy?' I took a big bite of muffin. Yum. It had lots of blueberries. Just the way I liked it. The black coffee was hot and strong and the crass mug didn't affect its flavor.

'I started the post at four o'clock this morning,' she said.

Ah, no wonder she looked tired.

'Why so early?'

'Evarts's orders. After Evarts got Dunning's phone call, he knew he'd be tied up for weeks on that case, including depositions and court prep and testifying. It would make a serious dent in his golfing and lunching, so he passed the buck – and the body – to me. He had the nerve to tell me to be ultra-careful.'

'Did you find anything unusual?'

'Besides the fact that a healthy, talented athlete was smashed to shit?'

Katie sounded angry. I knew the wasted life upset her, but she didn't usually let that get to her.

'Was Jared drinking or using drugs?' I asked.

'I don't think so,' Katie said. 'But the tox tests won't be back for a few days. Usually, I can smell if they've been drinking when I open them up. I think the kid was clean and sober. He took his training seriously.'

Katie's news only made the football star's death sadder. She'd finished a bran muffin and was busy spreading cream cheese on a raisin bagel.

'Any idea why Jace wants us here so early?'

'No. He called me at home last night and said he had an idea how to break the Bellerive case wide open, but he'd need both of us for what he called "night work." And before you ask, I haven't the foggiest idea what he means by that. He said he'd get here about eight o'clock and he thought there should be a half hour between the two of you arriving or leaving this building. He'll have to leave first.'

'He's really taking this cloak-and-dagger stuff seriously,' I said.

'He has a wife, a child and a mortgage, Angela. He has a lot more to lose if he gets fired. You can pick up and go anywhere, any time, but he has obligations.

'And while we're talking about you having nothing to tie you down . . .'

Here it comes, I thought. The love life lecture.

With that, there was a knock on Katie's door, and Jace walked in. He looked tired and worried. The Bellerive case was taking its toll on him.

'How nice to see you, Jace,' I gushed, as if we'd been parted for years.

'Good to see you, too, Angela.' Jace greeted Katie, poured hot coffee into the Sherlock skeleton mug, piled cream cheese on an onion bagel and sat on the edge of the desk.

'I really want to nail that sneaky bastard Briggs,' Jace said between bites. 'One key is those young women he picked up in bars and sent home by Uber. I can't check his Uber records without drawing attention to myself. But we can look for the women.'

'We? As in me?' Katie said.

'Yep,' he said with a big smile. 'I need you two to go to dive bars. That's where Briggs hung out. I have his photos.' He showed us a sampling of Briggs's photos from magazine and newspaper sites. 'You can show these around.'

'Whoa,' Katie said. 'There are a lot of dive bars in the far-flung burbs. How are we going to find the right ones?'

'I worked out a system last night,' Jace said, and produced a stack of papers from a folder. 'Rosanna the missing housekeeper said in her diary that Briggs was usually gone about two and a half hours when he was hunting those young women. She thought some of them were sex workers and hung out in dive bars. Judging by his time frame, I figure these bars were within an hour or so of St. Louis. I looked for dives that had histories of arrests for prostitution, soliciting and similar crimes. Now, that doesn't get them all – some of these small-town sheriffs can be paid to look the other way – but I narrowed it down to twenty-four dive bars that we can visit.'

'Twenty-four!' Katie said.

Jace held up two sheets of paper. 'I've divided the list in two. If you and Angela take twelve and I take twelve, we should get through them pretty quick. I've isolated six bars as the top choices and divvied them up. They're the top three on your list.'

'Have you ever been to these bars?' Katie said.

'Some. I consulted colleagues on others. There are no fake dives on that last.'

'What's a fake dive?' I asked.

'A dive bar that doesn't have any duct tape on the seats is a fake,' he said. 'So is a bar that serves twelve-dollar "hand-crafted" cocktails or a bunch of craft beer. Any bar that has "Dive" as part of its name is not a real dive. There's more, but this list of dive bars has been carefully curated.'

'I do believe that's the first time I've heard "dive bar" and "curated" in the same sentence,' Katie said.

'So what are we looking for?' I asked.

'One of the women he picked up. Find out if Briggs hurt her, what he did, what happened that night. Did she feel threatened? I've been shut down. I need a reason to investigate him again. What do you say? Will you do it?'

Katie looked at me. 'Angela, wanna go on a dive bar crawl?'

'How could I turn down that invitation?' I said.

THIRTY

'Angela and I will start the dive bar crawl tonight,' Katie announced.

'Good,' Jace said. 'I will, too.' He glanced at his watch. 'Time for me to leave. Report if you find anything.' He grabbed a muffin and waved goodbye. I refilled my coffee cup and sat on Katie's desk.

'Have you ever been to a dive bar?' she asked.

'Sure. I did the death investigation of that bartender's shotgun murder at the Dew Drop Inn. The rundown bar way out by the highway. It was a mess.'

'Shotgun blasts usually are,' Katie said.

'I mean the bar. It was dirty – all the bar stools had duct-taped seats and stuffing was coming out of the booths. Over the bar was a framed photo of a fat guy on a toilet that read, *The Only One Here Who Knows What He's Doing.*'

Katie laughed. 'Yep, that's an authentic dive bar,' she said. 'I meant have you ever been to one for a drink?'

'I don't think so.'

'OK, I'll give you a short course in how to go on a dive bar crawl. I grew up in the country, so I'm in my element at these bars. First, eat dinner before we go. You'll lay down a base for the night's drinking. Plus, you don't ever want to eat anything at a dive bar. Mostly they sell beef jerky, pickled eggs from a jar – definitely stay away from those little bacteria bombs – and the occasional microwaved Hot Pocket or ham-and-cheese.'

'None of those tempt me,' I said.

'The only safe things are packets of peanuts (those are usually stale) and bags of chips or pretzels.'

'I can do without them all.'

'Don't sit at the bar unless I tell you. Take a table. If the dive doesn't have table service, you'll have to order your drink at the bar. For gawd's sake, don't order club soda or wine. The wine usually has a screw cap and tastes like paint thinner. Order a beer.'

'I don't like beer,' I said.

'I don't care. You don't have to drink it. Just set it in front of you. If you're looking for a craft beer, say with wheat berries and lemon zest, forget it. In a dive bar around here, you get two choices: Bud and Bud Light. Don't get a draft, either. Take a bottle and tell the bartender you don't want a glass – glasses in dive bars are dirtier than the toilets.'

'Thanks for that stomach-turning detail,' I said, and took a big gulp of coffee to wash that thought away.

'What are you going to wear tonight?'

Katie saw my blank look and said, 'Ditch the nun suit. You're not wearing that black pantsuit. Got any old jeans?'

'Sure. My riding clothes – jeans and a chambray shirt – but they're one step above Goodwill rejects.'

'Perfect,' Katie said. 'Do you have any cowboy boots?'

'Just my riding boots.'

'Too upscale.' She checked out my sensible lace-up flats and nixed them. 'You are not wearing those. Any cheap-looking high heels?'

'I've got some red open-toed spikes.'

'Perfect,' Katie said. 'Wear a red belt and dangly earrings and you'll be good to go.

'I'm driving my pick-up. We'll fit in better. We'll start at the top of the list. I'll pick you up at seven o'clock for Claude's Hideaway in Crawford. In the meantime, get some sleep. It's going to be a long night.'

I took some time to pat her golden-haired pup, Cutter. The furball looked angelic. I scratched one velvety ear and he rolled over and made a contented little sound. I left Cutter sleeping in his basket, and headed home to take my own nap.

I awoke at six, fixed a quick dinner and extra-strong coffee to wake me up, and dressed according to plan. I felt silly teetering along in high heels and old jeans, my long gold earrings tinkling, my waist cinched by a red belt. But anything to help get Bellerive locked up.

At seven o'clock, Katie was in my driveway. I climbed into her red pick-up and we drove to Crawford, a small town about forty minutes west that was slowly becoming a St. Louis suburb. Right now, it had the small-town essentials – a Walmart, a gun shop, a diner and two churches. The fruit and vegetable stand was closed, but the new library was open and offering *Free Computer Classes*. New houses advertised as *Four Bedrooms – Only $250,000!* were springing up along the highway exit like weeds.

On the way there, Katie and I were silent, both lost in our thoughts and a little tired. I was grateful for the quiet.

Claude's Hideaway was on a back road, hidden away like an embarrassing relative. A sign with a blinking yellow arrow said, *Turn Here to Party Hearty! Good Times at Claude's Just A Country Mile Away!*

Katie bumped down the rutted road, gravel pinging off the sides of her pick-up. It was indeed a country mile away, which meant it was more like two miles, before we saw Claude's, surrounded by dark woods.

The gravel parking lot was packed with pick-ups, and we could hear loud country music. 'That's Hank Williams Junior singing "All My Rowdy Friends Are Coming Over Tonight,"' Katie said. I liked the music.

Claude's Hideaway was a long, low-slung cinder block building that had once been painted white. A sign proclaimed *Jell-O Wrestling Every Weekend.*

'What's Jell-O wrestling?' I asked, as we crunched across the lot. I had visions of someone eating a giant bowl of Jell-O with a fork.

'Women in bikinis wrestle each another in a pit of Jell-O,' Katie explained. 'Yes, I'm talking about the gelatin dessert. The wrestling match takes place in some sort of blowup kiddie pool for the entertainment of a bunch of drunken dickheads. If you're a supreme ass wipe, you can pay ten bucks extra to spray the wrestlers with a can of whipped cream.'

'Sounds horrible.'

'It is,' Katie said. 'Some hair-bags get off on making women feel bad.'

'What kind of woman would put up with that?'

'A desperate one,' Katie said. 'Don't you go thinking the wrestlers are skanks.'

I didn't think that, but there was no point stopping Katie when she got on her sociology soapbox. 'Let me tell you about Donna, a girl I went to school with,' Katie said. 'She was desperate enough to Jell-O wrestle. She'd lost her job at the packing plant and had to wrestle in blueberry Jell-O. Hated herself for it, but she was a single mom with a little girl to support. She told me, "Nobody ever died of shame." She finally got a waitress job and was able to make enough to feed her kid and keep her clothes on.'

We were at the door. 'Let's hope we're at the right place and can find one of Briggs's pick-ups,' Katie said. 'I'll go first.'

Katie walked into the dimly lit bar and I followed. The place smelled of mold, Pine-Sol disinfectant and cigarette smoke. I saw maybe thirty men – the heavy drinkers pounding it down at the bar and the rest at about ten tables with mismatched chairs. The men were mostly shaggy-haired, many wearing straw cowboy hats with curved brims and cowboy boots. The fat bartender wiped the bar top with a dirty rag. The few women customers were chubby, cute and flirtatious, dressed in sparkly tops and tight jeans, with heavy make-up. They were sitting at the tables with the men.

We walked past the Official Jell-O Wrestling Ring, a roped-off alcove. *Next match Saturday night at 9*, the sign said. *Sexy Sally v. Foxy Fran!* Next to it were two photos of underfed blondes with big breasts, little bikinis, and Farrah Fawcett hair. *Tickets: $10 Admission, $10 for a 12-second whip cream squirt.*

I started reading the Official Rules: *No kicking, punching, biting, hair pulling, gouging, head butting, choking, etc. All participants must remain on their knees.* And finally, to my horror, the last rule said, *If your opponent yells 'stop,' passes out, or is injured in any way then the round ends immediately.*

Katie tugged at my arm. 'Hey, Angela, where did you go? Sit down!'

We took a table near the restrooms, which were labeled 'Pointers' and 'Setters.'

'Yep,' she said, and I heard the satisfaction in her voice. 'Definitely a dive. That sign over the bar confirms it.' Over the bar was a plastic sign that said, *Our credit manager is Helen Waite. If you want credit, go to Helen Waite!*

A thin, hawk-faced, long-haired blonde wearing short-shorts, a T-shirt and tennis shoes showed up at our table. Her name tag read *Jolene*.

'Can I get you ladies a drink?' she asked.

'Beer,' I said. 'Bud, in a bottle. No glass.'

'Same for me,' Katie said.

'Anything else?' Jolene asked.

'No, thanks.'

Reba McEntire was singing 'The Night the Lights Went Out in Georgia' when Jolene returned with our drinks. Katie put a twenty down on the table for our drinks.

'Can I ask you a question, Jolene?' Katie asked.

'Sure, hon. I may not answer, but go ahead and ask.'

Katie brought out a headshot of Briggs Bellerive. It had been cropped so he wasn't wearing a tux. 'Have you ever seen this man in here?'

Jolene laughed. 'Look around you, hon. You see any men like that in here?'

'Not right now,' Katie said. She put another ten on the table.

'I'll gladly take your money till the cows come home,' Jolene said, picking up the bills and giving us a friendly smile. 'But I've never seen that man in here. Thank you for asking, though.'

'Jolene!' the bartender said, and she went back to haul beer to another table.

Katie finished her beer. I took a couple of sips of mine. It was thin and bitter, and confirmed why I didn't like beer. Kenny Rogers was singing 'The Gambler' as we left. Like the wise old Gambler, we knew when to fold.

It took forty minutes to get to the next dive, the Crowbar in Crow Creek. This little town could have been Crawford's clone. The Crowbar was located a little closer to town, but it was in a similar cinder block building. The neon sign read THE CRO BAR.

'Aha!' Katie said. 'Burnt-out neon. Another sign of a dive.'

The lot was just as crowded with pick-ups. The bar's interior was about the same: long, narrow, smoky, with lots of working men in straw cowboy hats and boots. The bartender waved to us and Katie and I took the only empty table in a corner. Our server was named Scarlett and she was just as friendly as Jolene. This time I asked the questions and shelled out the money. Scarlett brought us our bottles of Bud, and when she was ten dollars richer, said she'd never seen Briggs. 'He don't look like our kinda customer, hon,' she said.

The restrooms were next to us. These doors had the generic stick people signs for men and women, except both icons were crossing their legs.

'I feel like that sign,' I told Katie. 'I've gotta go.'

'You're in for a treat,' Katie said.

The women's restroom had two stalls, one with a homemade *Out of Order* sign taped to the door. A slender brunette in cowboy hat, jeans, and a flowered shirt tied under her rib cage was pacing restlessly. 'Wish that lady in there would hurry up. Mother Nature didn't do us any favors in the plumbing department, did she? There's never a line in the men's room. When my boyfriend has to go and it's crowded, he just uses the tree by the Dumpster. I'd get poison ivy if I did that.'

A large woman with short curly hair came out of the stall and looked apologetic. 'It's not my fault there's only one stall,' she said.

The cowgirl ignored her. 'I'll be quick, hon,' she promised. 'It's just number one.'

The large woman washed her hands and left.

Admonitory signs were all over. *If you sprinkle when you tinkle, please be neat and wipe the seat.*

And, *Ladies, please stay seated for the entire performance.*

Last but not least was a big homemade sign proclaiming:

Do Not Flush
Tampons
Maxipads
Paper towels
Used diapers
Kittens and puppies
Hopes and dreams.

The sign was prophetic. So far tonight, our hopes and dreams had been flushed.

THIRTY-ONE

'So what's going on with you and Chris?' Katie asked.

I'd been dreading this question all day. Now I was trapped in Katie's pick-up for another half hour before we got to our last stop of the night, a dive bar in a country town called Harland.

'Chris and I had fun at dinner at Gringo Daze,' I said.

'That's progress,' Katie said. 'This is the first time you've mentioned "fun" and a man's name in the same sentence. What about after dinner?'

'We went to my house and sat on the porch for a bit.'

'And?' Katie said.

'And that was fun, too.'

'So have you slept with him yet?'

'Katie!'

'Don't give me that outraged virgin routine, Angela. I've known you too long. You never talked about it, but I knew you and your husband made the bedsprings rock. You had a glow when he was alive. I saw you turn into a dried-up old maid after he died. You've mourned Donegan long enough.'

Angry heat flooded my veins. 'Who are you to tell me when my mourning is done?' I raged.

'Me!' Katie shouted. She pressed her foot down on the gas and the old truck flew past empty fields, lonely farmhouses and the distant lights of truck stops.

'I earned that right! I'm your best friend! I deal all day with death and so do you. You of all people know how quickly a life can end. Yesterday you saw a young man cut down in his prime and another one crippled for life. Now you have a handsome hunk who adores you. You have a chance to enjoy life with him. Instead you waste your precious time moping around the morgue.'

'I like my job!' I said.

'Yes, I know. You are thoughtful, thrifty, honest, trustworthy – all the Boy Scout virtues. But you're still in love with a dead man.'

'Yes, I am.' I felt the tears stinging my eyes, but tried to hold them back. I needed to make my friend understand what was wrong. Katie had to hear me out.

'When I went out with Chris I enjoyed my time with him, but he didn't make my heart sing.'

I was angry and embarrassed. What the hell? I thought. Where did that come from? Did I really say 'he didn't make my heart sing'? Why was I sounding like a cut-rate romance novel?

'How could he?' Katie said. 'It's too shriveled to let anyone else in.'

I took a deep breath and felt a little calmer. I spoke slowly, but my unsteady voice betrayed me. 'All I'm saying is Chris is no match for Donegan.'

'Of course he isn't,' Katie said. 'Donegan's dead, and grows more perfect with every passing year. Live men burp and fart and scratch their ass. Even the best of them. They leave their socks on the bedroom floor and shaving stubble in the sink. They can be as annoying as hell. But they still make life worth living. I knew Donegan and I know he wouldn't want you living like this.'

I felt my temper explode. 'Where do you get off speaking for Donegan?' I said. 'Now that he's gone, everyone offers me advice and says "Donegan would have wanted it that way." How do they know? How do you know? Maybe he's happy that I'm down here withering on the vine until I can join him?'

'Because Donegan wasn't selfish, Angela, that's how I know. Like the poem says, "The grave's a fine and private place, but none, I think, do there embrace."'

'Andrew Marvell,' I said, feeling somewhat calmer. '"To His Coy Mistress." It was one of Donegan's favorites.'

We'd pulled off the highway. Katie passed an all-night diner and truck stop, and we were driving through Harland, a town of four streets, one stoplight, a post office and two churches. Katie turned left past the Methodist church.

'Oh, was it now?' Katie said. 'That was Donegan's favorite poem? So you know about the part that says:

"But at my back I always hear

Time's wingèd chariot hurrying near."'

I finished the rest of the verse for Katie:

'"And yonder all before us lie

Deserts of vast eternity.'"

'I rest my case,' Katie said. 'In case you need that poem interpreted, nothing happens after you die.'

We pulled into the rutted parking lot of our last stop, Earl's Alibi Room. It was almost midnight and I felt like I was going to turn into a pumpkin soon.

'This crowd may be a little more upscale,' I said. 'I see some Jeeps and an occasional new Toyota, Cadillac and Beemer in the parking lot.'

'Keep your fingers crossed,' Katie said. 'Let's hope you're right and Bellerive went hunting here.'

Earl's was rocking, even at that late hour on a weeknight. It was an old white clapboard two-story roadhouse, probably built sometime in the 1920s. A neon Bud beer sign buzzed in the window like an angry mosquito. A flashing sign promised *Wet T-Shirt Contest Every Wednesday! Free Beer and $25 for the Winner!*

Waylon and Willie were singing, 'Mammas, Don't Let Your Babies Grow Up to Be Cowboys.'

I followed Katie into the big, smoky cave with the blaring jukebox. A sign by the door proclaimed: *Avoid hangovers! Keep drinking!*

Most of the customers seemed to be following that advice. A sign over the long bar read:

Earl's Alibi Charges. If any angry wives or girlfriends phone, our answering charges are:

He just left – $5

He's on his way – $10

He's not here – $20

WHO did you say? – $25

In with the usual mix of shaggy-haired, cowboy-hatted dive bar denizens was a slicker kind of customer: men with sixty-dollar haircuts, designer jeans and Ralph Lauren chambray shirts with little polo ponies.

'This could be the right place,' I whispered to Katie. 'That dude in the two-hundred-dollar chambray shirt looks like he wouldn't know a backhoe from a backgammon board.'

'Check out the servers,' Katie said. I heard a note of hope in her voice. 'They look like Briggs's type.'

A pale, skinny server who looked like she wasn't old enough

to drink was expertly carrying a foaming pitcher of beer through the crowd without spilling a drop. Katie waited until the server had delivered the pitcher to a table and politely asked, 'Miss?'

'Yes? May I help you?' The girl had natural blonde hair down to her waist and small delicate features, like a china doll. Her name tag said *Crystal*.

'We're looking for a table,' Katie said.

'I'll find one for you,' she said. 'Follow me.'

We followed her swaying hair and round rump through the crowd to a table for two behind a pillar. 'Sorry it's so cramped,' Crystal said. 'It's the best I can do tonight. What can I get you ladies?'

'Two Buds, no glasses,' I said.

'Be right back,' she said, and five minutes later, she delivered our drinks. I handed her thirty dollars. 'Keep the change, Crystal.'

'But the beer is only three dollars each.'

'I know. You can keep it. I wonder if you could help us.' I showed her Briggs Bellerive's headshot. 'Do you know this man?'

Crystal shook her head. 'Sorry, wish I could help, but I don't have a good head for faces. It's a real drawback in this job. He just looks like another old rich dude.'

To someone as young as Crystal, thirty-one-year-old Briggs would be old.

'The person you want to talk to is LeeAnn, sitting at the table by the restrooms,' Crystal said. 'She's on her break now, but she won't mind talking to you. She never forgets a face. And, uh, she could use the money. Tell her Crystal sent you.'

She smiled at us and went back to work.

Through the shifting crowd, we caught a glimpse of LeeAnn. She could have been Crystal's older sister. Her features weren't quite as delicate, but her skin was pale and her long hair was a delicious shade of raspberry. Was she 'the girl with the pink hair' that Rosanna the housekeeper had written about? Only one way to find out.

Katie and I picked up our beer bottles and wove our way through the crowd to LeeAnn's table. She was drinking a Coke out of the bottle. Her clothes were inexpensive and a bit worn, but well put together. LeeAnn wore a black satiny long-sleeved top, tight red velvet pants and scuffed red heels. She had a red satin scarf wound around her neck.

'Crystal sent us,' I said. 'We need your help.' I put forty dollars down on the table.

'I don't do three-ways,' LeeAnn said.

'Not interested,' Katie said. 'We just have a couple of questions.'

'You two aren't cops, are you?' LeeAnn's pretty face was suddenly suspicious, hard and much older.

'Nope.' Katie produced Briggs's headshot along with another ten-dollar bill. 'Do you recognize this man?'

LeeAnn's face answered before she did – she flushed deep red and her brown eyes sparked with anger. 'Why do you want to know?'

'Because I'm married to the bastard,' Katie said. 'I'm trying to divorce him and I wanna take him for every nickel. I'm the one with the money in this miserable marriage, and he's got a prenup. When I cut him loose, I have to give him a hundred thousand dollars. But if he's been seeing other women, I don't have to pay him one red cent!'

'Hah!' LeeAnn said. '*Seeing* other women? He's more a hands-on type of dude. Look what he did to my neck!'

She whipped off the red satin scarf and revealed a shocking necklace of bruises on her fragile white skin.

THIRTY-TWO

LeeAnn's slender neck was circled with ugly yellow-green bruises. Deeper, purple ones disfigured the sides of her neck, below her ears. A thin, scabbing cut sliced a straight line across the skin, right at the level of her Adam's apple. She had long, scabbed scratches on her neck.

'Oh, my lord,' I said. 'You poor thing.'

'Ugly, aren't they?' she asked. 'And they're better now. I can show you the photo I took two days after he beat me up. It's even worse.

'These bruises have really cut into my business. I've got other bruises you can't see. First thing the johns do is whip the scarf off to see the merchandise. They have to be awfully drunk or really twisted to want a girl who looks the way I do now, and I'm too afraid to go with those dudes.'

'How did you get those bruises?' I asked.

'Randy gave them to me. The man in the picture.'

'He said his name was Randy?' I couldn't help laughing.

'It's not funny,' LeeAnn said. She was crying now.

'You're right,' I said. 'I'm sorry.' I put down another ten as an apology, and LeeAnn grabbed it and stuffed it in her big black purse, the kind many working girls carry.

Katie handed the girl a tissue and said, 'His real name is Briggs Bellerive. Will you tell us what happened?'

LeeAnn wiped her eyes and said, 'Randy, or Briggs – and what kind of name is Briggs?'

'A rich guy name,' Katie said.

'Well, whatever his name is, he came here one night on a Wet T-Shirt Wednesday. That's one of our busiest nights and I do a lot of BJs in the parking lot. Not out in the open. Only drunk skanks do that. I go to their cars, so it's private-like.'

'We get the picture,' Katie said, her voice kind and soothing.

'Randy offered me two hundred bucks to go to his house. He seemed nice, and he was clean – his nails were manicured and there was no dirt under them. He smelled like expensive aftershave. I never smelled anything like it. When we got to his place, I looked in his bathroom cabinet and it was something called Creed. The box had the price tag on it – four-hundred-fifty dollars! That's almost my rent for a month.

'When Randy said he'd give me two hundred, I told him I'd think about it. Then he offered me three hundred dollars. Now I couldn't afford to turn him down. I told him I'd need a ride home and he said he'd pay for the Uber ride, too.

'He drove me to his place in a real nice Beemer. He didn't talk much, but that was OK. I was enjoying the quiet and the leather seats. It was the nicest car I'd ever been in. We went to the Forest, where all the rich people live. When we got to his house it was a good thing I was sitting down. It was humongous – a real mansion, bigger than the county courthouse. Kind of looked like it, too.'

I flashed back to my memory of Briggs's house – its staggering size, the huge white pillars and the endless walk up those stone stairs.

'We parked in the front and he told me to keep quiet: his housekeeper was a real bitch. I imagined she was some nosy old biddy, like my landlady Mrs Duckett. Anyway, when we got inside I took off my heels. His house looked like a fancy hotel with real oil paintings on the walls.

'We went up this big marble staircase to his bedroom, which was bigger than this place.' LeeAnn waved her thin arm to take in the vast, smoky expanse of Earl's Alibi. 'It had these huge Oriental carpets and furniture like you see in a museum – the stuff with gold all over it named for one of those French kings, Louie something.'

LeeAnn must have seen me smile. I didn't mean to be condescending, but she got defensive when she couldn't remember which French king. 'I've been to a museum, too. I went to the art museum in St. Louis on a field trip once when I was in school, and they had a whole room full of the same stuff.'

'We believe you,' Katie said.

'I told him I had to tinkle and he let me use his bathroom. I swear, it was big enough for a family of four. I snooped in his medicine cabinet, but he didn't have any interesting drugs, just some allergy medicine. No Viagra, either. If they use that, I have to spend a lot of time jump-starting them. My hand gets sore.'

I bit down on my lip so she wouldn't see me laughing.

'He had a whole room, just for his clothes,' LeeAnn said. 'I had a hard time taking it all in. I was looking at all the gold and fancy stuff and he said, "Hey, I ain't paying you to wander around here with your mouth open. Get your ass over here." It sounded like he wanted to get down to business right away.

'So I got businesslike, too. "Where's my money?" I said, and he put three Benjamins on this fancy gold and wood cabinet he called a commode, but it didn't look like no toilet to me. I shoved the money in my bag and he said, "Take off your clothes."'

'Did he offer you a drink or any drugs?' Katie asked.

'Not even a sip of water. At first, he did, you know, regular stuff.' She looked at Katie and said, 'If you're married to him, you know he's nothing special in the equipment department. A couple of pumps and it was over.'

'You've just described my honeymoon,' Katie said.

I tried to turn my laugh into a cough.

Katie glared at me and said, 'But he hasn't bothered me in a while.'

'You're lucky,' LeeAnn said. 'I thought I could go when he finished, and I started to get up, but he grabbed me by the arm and said, "Oh, no, bitch, you're going to earn your three bills." He got on top of me. He's a big guy. I could hardly breathe and I sure couldn't move.

'He reached into some kinda nightstand and took out this green string, like the kind you tie tomatoes with, and he put it around my neck. I screamed, "No!" I told him to stop, but he wouldn't. He kept pulling it tighter and tighter and I thought I was gonna die. I scratched at my neck to get some air and he let up a little bit. I was gasping for breath and telling him to stop. Problem was, strangling me gave him a boner like you wouldn't believe. I didn't think he'd ever get off me.

'The night lasted forever. Sometimes he used the string and sometimes he'd use his hands to strangle me. I passed out twice, but he slapped my face to bring me back. I was sure I was gonna die. There was blood all over the sheets – my blood. I screamed for help, but nobody heard me. Then I figured out he got off on me screaming, so I tried to stop, but sometimes I couldn't. He hurt me bad. I was getting tired and worn out. I wondered how long I could hang on.

'He reached out to strangle me again and this time I bit his hand. Hard. Right on the fat part of his thumb. I was like a pit bull. He started punching me – my tits are black and blue – and yelling, "Let go! Let go!"

'When I let go, he pushed me off the bed and I hit the floor. He kicked me a couple of times in the ribs, and told me to get dressed. His hand was bleeding and he wrapped it in a pillowcase and went into the bathroom. I got dressed as quick as I could – I was shaking so bad I could hardly get into my clothes. I kept a sweater in my bag and I used it to hide the bruises on my arms.

'He didn't come out right away, so I got out my cell phone and took pictures – of the room, the bed, and me. I made sure I got the blood and the bruises on me.'

Katie leaned forward. 'You still have those photos?' she asked.

'Oh, yes. They're on my cell phone.'

'LeeAnn, we need to talk further. Have you eaten yet today?'

'No,' she admitted. 'The money all went on rent and bills.'

'Would you like to go to the all-night diner by the highway for dinner? Our treat?'

'Oh, yes,' she said. 'I'm so hungry.'

THIRTY-THREE

At one-thirty in the morning, the diner was nearly empty, except for a couple of truckers chowing down in a distant booth. The florescent lights had that odd greenish glow they get very late at night. The old diner had big red leatherette booths, a revolving pie stand with six different pies, and the daily specials on a chalkboard. The air smelled of hot coffee and fried grease.

Sandie, a cheerful older server in a pink dress and frilly apron, showed us to a generous corner booth.

'I love your pink hair, hon,' Sandie said to LeeAnn. 'It would be a good match for my uniform.' Sandie's hair was a tightly sprayed gray helmet, and I thought her style would look like cotton candy in pink.

When we sat down, Katie reminded us, 'This is on me, so everybody eat up.'

LeeAnn ordered the chicken-fried steak special with two veg. Katie had apple pie, and since the new day had started, I ordered a breakfast of pancakes and eggs. Sandie brought us a big insulated pot of strong coffee and three thick china mugs. I can always count on truck stops for good coffee.

Once Sandie had delivered our food, LeeAnn started eating like she hadn't had a good meal in a week. I demolished the pancakes and eggs in short order, and Katie methodically worked on her pie, starting at the tip.

When LeeAnn finally came up for air, Katie asked if she wanted dessert and LeeAnn said, 'Oh, yes, could I? One of them pies, please.'

Sandie delivered a slice of lemon meringue pie, and cleared away some of our empty plates. LeeAnn finished her pie quickly, then delicately wiped her mouth with her napkin and said, 'Thanks. I was real hungry.'

'Will you show us the photos now?' Katie asked.

'Let me tell you about these photos,' Lee Ann said, as she opened her cell phone. 'If you're a working girl like me, one who sometimes makes house calls, you've got to take care. Take precautions. I mean, besides the usual.

'Another girl told me to always take a selfie first thing and send it to myself when I'm with a client – to prove I'm at his house and OK. So I usually go into the bathroom and check out the prescriptions and pick some with the john's name on it. This Randy dude had two prescriptions: one was bright red pills and the other was some kinda nose spray.'

We saw a photo of LeeAnn smiling and holding the two prescriptions. She wore heavy make-up on her smooth, pale skin, though I didn't think she needed it, and a silky pink tank top the same color as her hair.

Katie enlarged the photo for a closer look at the prescriptions. 'The red pills are desloratadine and the nasal spray is azelastine, a prescription nasal antihistamine spray,' she said. 'You can see his name here: Briggs Bellerive.'

'I thought that was some kinda nickname,' LeeAnn said.

LeeAnn showed us the photos she took right after the beating, and they were worse than her description. Her neck was painful to look at. It was streaked with fresh blood and the new bruises ranged from a pale pink to bright red. In two days, they'd changed colors ranging from a fearsome magenta to violet to lilac. The string had left a raw, bloody gash.

She'd taken a selfie that showed the beating she'd survived – bruised breasts with big red marks, an ugly shoe-shaped new bruise on her right hip and another on her ribs. She was naked, except for black panties, but there was nothing erotic about this photo. It was a portrait of pain.

'I'm surprised you didn't have any broken bones,' Katie said.

'Me, too, but I sure hurt a lot.'

LeeAnn had also photographed the bed, with its elaborately carved and gilded headboard. The gold sheets were rumpled and streaked with blood. She also photographed a length of green string, stained with blood, coiled in a wastebasket by the bed.

'No wonder Briggs never let his housekeeper clean his room after one of his evenings on the prowl,' I said. 'He couldn't let her see the blood.'

LeeAnn also showed us the photos she took of Briggs's bedroom.

Katie thumbed through them. 'You're right, LeeAnn,' she said. 'This room does look like a museum exhibit. It's all for show. There's not a single personal item in here – not a book or a photograph of his girlfriend or his mother.'

'Oh, that photo is in his walk-in closet,' LeeAnn said, and showed us that area. 'He's got a whole room just for his suits and shoes. Have you ever seen so many clothes for a man? It looks like a department store. There, on that chest, is a photograph of him in a tux with a real pretty blonde lady in a long black dress.' I suspected she was the international model, Desiree Gale.

'I took this photo,' she said.

LeeAnn's face was tear-stained and her pink hair looked like straw. LeeAnn held the photo of Briggs and his lady-friend close to her bloody face and neck, and snapped the picture.

'That's definitely proof,' I said.

'What happened after you got dressed?' Katie asked.

'I took a bunch of photos and then he came out of the bathroom wearing a robe. He had a bandage on his hand and a mean look on his face. "I've called the Uber for you," he said. "Take the stairs, turn left and keep going until you reach the kitchen. Tony will pick you up back there. He drives a white Cadillac Escalade."

'I nodded and tried to get past him. Randy grabbed my arm, squeezed it until I cried out from the pain and said, "And if you have any sense, you won't tell anybody anything." Then he laughed and said, "Not that they'd believe a worthless hayseed hooker like you."

'I made it downstairs. There were enough lights on, so I took more pictures.' LeeAnn stopped to show us slightly out of focus photos of the massive foyer, dining room, hallway, and finally the kitchen, all on her phone.

'They're kinda blurry because I was crying and my hands were shaking,' she said. 'I stopped crying before Tony the Uber driver showed up. He picked me up in a brand-new Escalade. Here's that photo.'

'You can see part of the license plate,' I said.

'That's good,' Katie said. 'What happened next?'

'I didn't talk much on the way home. I slept most of the next day. I've never ridden in so many fancy cars in one day, but I didn't care. And I'm really sorry I went with that man for the money. I've lost a lot of work, thanks to him.'

'Did you go to the hospital for your injuries?' Katie asked.

LeeAnn laughed. 'This is the sticks. The closest hospital is fifty miles away and I ain't got any insurance.'

'Did you file a complaint with the police?' Katie asked.

LeeAnn stared at her, dumbfounded. 'Didn't I tell you what he said? He threatened me. He said I was a hayseed hooker. He's obviously rich and important. If I went to the police, they'd want a freebie – at the very least a BJ.'

'Not all of them,' Katie said.

'Maybe not in your world, but you've got money and you've been to college and you can get lawyers. Somebody like me can't go up against a big shot in the Forest. You know what the last big city cop called me? A sidewalk stewardess! That's a slightly nicer way of saying I'm a worthless hooker.'

'Look, LeeAnn, you've obviously met some bad apples—'

LeeAnn gave a snort that sounded like Hero. 'Yeah, tell me about it. A whole barrel of them. Look, Katie, I'm a graduate of the school of hard knocks. Phi Beta Kappa, baby.'

'I know a good lawyer,' Katie said. 'One who's not afraid to go up against people like Briggs. And he lives in the Forest.'

Uh, oh. Did Katie know what she was getting Monty into?

Katie raced on ahead. 'You can still file a complaint. Even if you're a sex worker—'

'I'm a hooker,' LeeAnn said. 'Doesn't make what I do any different because you dress it up in pretty words.'

'I don't care what you call yourself,' Katie said. 'You should file a complaint against this Briggs. Even if you agreed to rough sex – and you say you didn't – you still have the right to say "Enough! No More!" and he has to stop.

'And you have the photos to document what happened. You could go to the cops and show them your photos and swear out a complaint. You're a victim of assault and you've got information. Then they could arrest him.'

'So? He'll get his lawyers to get him out of trouble and he'll come looking for me,' LeeAnn said. 'And if he kills me, nobody cares about a dead hooker. I know. One of my friends disappeared two years ago after she got into a car with a john. I reported her missing and nobody did anything.'

'What was her name?' Katie asked.

'Paisley,' she said. 'Paisley Parker. She was eighteen.'

'I'm sorry,' Katie said.

'Yeah. That's life. You're a nice lady, Katie, but what I'm trying to tell you is you're high up and I'm down low and there's no way you can raise someone like me to your level.'

'OK, I get what you're saying,' Katie said. 'But I want to make you a deal. Will you sell me your photos?'

'You can have them for free,' LeeAnn said. 'You've been so nice to me.'

Katie put a hundred dollars in tens on the table. 'You've got to do a couple of things before you can have that money,' she said. 'First, I want you to send me those photos. All of them.'

Katie gave LeeAnn the number to text. She waited a few minutes until the photos came in on her phone. 'OK, got them. Now what's your name? Your real name, not your trick name.'

'LeeAnn's my name,' the young woman said. 'Last name is Higgs. LeeAnn Sadie Higgs.'

'Thank you,' Katie said. 'Last thing. Text me your address. Your real address. I'll know if you make one up.'

Katie waited for the ping on her cell phone, checked the text message, then handed LeeAnn the hundred dollars. 'Thanks,' she said. 'This will help big-time.'

Sandie came back with a warm smile to clear away the remaining dishes. 'Anything else I can get you ladies?' she asked.

'Yes,' Katie said. 'My friend would like to order lunch to go. What kind of sandwich do you want, LeeAnn?'

'I'd like ham and cheese on white bread,' she said. 'And chips and a pickle.'

'Throw in a piece of that lemon meringue pie while you're at it,' Katie said. 'Then bring me the check, please.'

'I do appreciate your help,' LeeAnn said, 'and the extra food.'

'You deserve it,' Katie said. 'Hang onto your phone, will you? I may need it for my court case.'

'Anything you want,' LeeAnn said.

Sandie was back with the to-go order and the check.

'Thank you, ladies,' LeeAnn said. 'Now I need to go home and get some sleep.'

From our window, we watched LeeAnn make her way across the brightly lit parking lot to her old beater of a car. Her long pink hair blew in the wind like the banner of a defeated army.

'She doesn't know it yet,' Katie said, 'but she's going to help us nail that SOB.'

THIRTY-FOUR

I gathered up my purse and stood up, abandoning that comfy diner booth. Before I could leave, Katie said, 'Sit back down, Angela. I'm going to call Jace.'

'Now? It's three in the morning.'

'Right. And we're both hopped up on high-octane black coffee. With all that caffeine, we won't be able to sleep for hours. I bet you Jace is still working. We might as well meet here. It's a safe place. I guarantee nobody from the Forest will be in a truck stop diner in Harland, Missouri at three a.m.'

Katie dialed the detective's cell phone and put her phone on speaker so I could listen.

Jace answered on the second ring. 'Katie?' he said. 'What's happening?' I could hear Waylon Jennings singing 'Honkytonk Angels' in the background.

'We caught a break,' she said. 'With photos.'

'Hot damn!' he said, raising his voice. 'I've been getting nowhere fast.'

'Where are you?' Katie asked.

'An after-hours joint in Jefferson County. I'm the only sober one in here.'

'We're sitting in the diner at the turn-off to Harland. Come join us for a meeting.'

'Does the diner have country music?' he asked.

'No, just Muzak. I'm listening to a blanderized "Strawberry Fields Forever."'

'Just so the songs don't mention Mama, the Bible and cheating hearts,' he said.

'No chance. And I promise the pie and pancakes are good and the coffee is outstanding.'

'I'll be there in thirty minutes,' he said. 'I'm starved. Have the coffee ready.'

Katie waved over our server Sandie, and told her we'd be expecting someone else. She wiped down the table in our booth, reset it with clean napkins and utensils, and brought us fresh water glasses and coffee cups.

'You ladies enjoy your coffee,' she said. 'I'm waitressing until six a.m.'

Jace made it to the diner in twenty minutes, and he looked like the walking dead: dark circles under his eyes, beard stubble and an oily sheen to his pale skin. Sandie bustled over with a new insulated pot of hot coffee and took Jace's order for the Long Haul Special: three eggs, three pancakes, hash browns, a T-bone steak and toast, all for $6.99.

'You're a brave man to order steak in here,' I said.

'I'm so hungry I could eat an old boot,' he said, and poured himself more coffee.

Jace's food arrived shortly. The fried T-bone covered the whole platter, and the eggs and hash browns were piled on top. The stack of pancakes got a separate plate. Katie and I moved our water glasses to make room for all his food.

Jace dug in, first breaking the yolks on his sunny-side-up eggs so they coated the hash browns, then eating his way through the greasy, glorious mess, until he got to the steak. He wrestled with it on the plate like he was trying to cuff an unruly suspect, but finally managed to subdue it and eat it.

'How was your steak?' I asked.

'It was a good boot,' he said, and grinned at me. 'It fought back, but it had real flavor.' He took a long drink of coffee, then started covering his pancakes with syrup. I gathered they were dessert.

Katie and I waited until he'd finished the pancakes and downed at least two more cups of coffee. His color was better and he seemed a bit less tired. He crunched toast drenched in butter while Katie told him who we'd found at Earl's Alibi Room.

Katie vividly described LeeAnn's terrifying encounter with 'Randy,' aka Briggs Bellerive, and how he strangled her with his hands and with garden string. Then she showed him the photos of the badly beaten woman.

He winced when he went through the gallery, spotlighting LeeAnn's wounds, the blood-streaked bed, and the bright purple bruises on her body.

'That poor woman,' he said. 'It hurts to look at her. She sure was smart to photograph herself inside his house before and after he beat her up.'

'She says a lot of working girls are using their cell phones for protection – and sometimes blackmail,' Katie said.

'Is there a name for what that slimewad did to LeeAnn? It's not auto-erotic strangulation, is it?'

'Not exactly,' Katie said. 'That's when people get off by strangling themselves. Mostly young men – teenagers – go in for that. "Auto-erotic" is a fancy word for jacking off alone. Some of those kids wind up accidentally killing themselves. We've had a case or two in the Forest. Most parents do everything they can to cover up why young Chumley was found hanging in his closet with a porn site on his iPhone, his pants undone, and his pecker out.'

Jace and I were both embarrassed by Katie's frank language. Jace stared down at his picked-clean steak bone as if studying it for secret messages. I looked around to make sure that Sandie, our server in the sweet pink frock, couldn't hear this conversation. Fortunately, she was ringing up a trucker's bill at the cash register near the door.

Katie didn't notice our unease. She was in full lecture mode.

'Auto-erotic strangulation is one version of EA, or erotic asphyxiation,' she said. 'It's also called breath play. Briggs is engaging in a warped version of it. Breath play is a kink that's getting popular. During sex, a person cuts off their partner's air by choking or suffocating them, even putting a bag over their head. It's damn risky.'

'Why would someone do that?' I asked.

'The people who do it say it heightens sexual arousal and makes their orgasms more intense.'

I must have blushed, and this time Katie noticed. 'Don't look so shocked, Angela,' she said. 'I saw a study – a legit one – that said one in five Americans were into some kind of kinky sex – spanking, tying each other up, breath play – to name a few. You'd be surprised how many people have tried something kinky and liked it. *Fifty Shades of Grey* has livened up a lot of suburban bedrooms. You can find all kinds of sex play tutorials and advice online, including a "Beginner's Guide to Kinky Sex, Health Benefits and Rules."'

'What health benefits?' I said.

'I'm not kidding,' Katie said. 'There are serious studies that say if your average Joe and Jane do some consensual kink, their psychological health is above average.'

'Yeah, LeeAnn can tell you all about those health benefits,' Jace said. He made a sour face and poured himself more coffee. If he kept drinking caffeine at that rate, he'd soon be buzzing like the neon beer sign at Earl's Alibi.

'You're missing the point, Jace. The key word is "consensual,"' Katie said. 'Briggs never asked LeeAnn for permission to strangle her, and he sure didn't care about her enjoyment. You're supposed to discuss each stage of breath play. Partners need a "safe word" or signal, if the action gets too scary. It's about trusting your partner.

'That douchebag Briggs got off on his power and LeeAnn's pain,' she said. 'What he did was damn dangerous, and he nearly killed her. She could have had brain damage, a heart attack and other complications.'

'I'll tell you one thing,' Jace said. 'I'll bet my next paycheck that Briggs never strangled his girlfriend, that big deal model.'

'Right,' I said. 'LeeAnn told us her bruises "really cut into my business." Desiree wouldn't stand for that.'

'Briggs uses poor country hookers like LeeAnn because they're disposable,' Jace said. 'If LeeAnn disappeared tomorrow, how many people would care? Would anyone go looking for her?'

We all knew the answer to that question.

Jace gave a quick report. 'My night was a total waste of time. I went to all three bars. In the first one, they spotted me as a cop and I didn't learn a thing. In the second, they said they'd never seen Briggs or anyone like him and I thought they were telling the truth. At the third, a bartender said that a hooker who hung around there might have been with Briggs. She came in at two-thirty and told me, "I never seen hide nor hair of anyone like that here," but she'd heard about some girls getting hurt bad by a freak. She gave me the name of a couple of bars, but it was three o'clock and you called.'

I poured more coffee and said, 'Back to LeeAnn. Can she file assault charges against Briggs?'

'The delay goes against her,' Jace said, 'but that can be easily explained. If it hadn't happened in the Forest, LeeAnn could go to the cops, and they would jump on it and turn her into a victim of assault so that we could arrest the bastard. Except I have orders to stay away from Briggs.'

'So what are you going to do?' Katie asked.

'I need a timeline, Katie. When are we supposed to get word on the bodies in the woods? I'm thinking those women might have been Briggs's failures. He strangled them for kicks and killed them.'

'We should know something by the end of this week,' Katie said.

'Then that's it. If there's no evidence that nails Briggs, I'll use LeeAnn to go after him.'

'That's very noble, but what about your job?' Katie said. 'Defy a direct order by the chief and you'll be fired. You have a family: a wife and a little boy.'

'I do, and he'll respect me more for doing the right thing.'

That was very true, and very brave, but I wasn't going to let Briggs claim another victim. Katie and I had to bring him down before a good cop was banished from the Forest.

THIRTY-FIVE

The Monday morning sun was streaking the dark sky when Katie dropped me back at home after our bar crawl. As soon as I opened my door, I kicked off those awful red heels – cheap shoes always gave my feet blisters and these were no exception. I climbed the stairs hanging on to the railing, pulled off my clothes and fell into bed. The two pots of coffee didn't keep me up. I slept away almost the whole day and woke up groggy and cotton-mouthed about six that night.

I wasn't as good at pulling all-nighters as I used to be, but at least I was one day closer to what I hoped would be more information on the skeletonized 'women in the woods.' If all went well, Dana Murdoch, the forensic archeologist, would have news for us by the end of the week.

I was on call as a death investigator for two of those days. On Tuesday, no one died, which was good news for the Forest and for me. The second day, Wednesday, I got a call at four-thirty in the afternoon: an eighty-six-year-old woman had died at home, and her teenage granddaughter Melanie had found her when she stopped after school to 'check on Grandma.'

At seventeen, the poor girl was too young and inexperienced to understand that her beloved Grandma had had a good death. That afternoon, Grandma Sarah Kenzie had walked a mile both ways to the neighborhood market, bought her groceries and trundled them home in her folding wire cart, put all the food away in the cupboard and the fridge, sat down at her kitchen table and died quickly, possibly from a stroke or a heart attack.

Judging by the time stamp on the grocery store receipt, her granddaughter Melanie found Sarah about three hours later. Sarah had, by all accounts, been a kind and generous woman, beloved by her family and friends. She would be much missed. Without sounding too morbid, it was the kind of death I hoped I'd have – no lingering illness and long, slow decline – though maybe I'd feel differently if I was lucky enough to get to be as old as Sarah.

Anyway, this death investigation was quick and uncomplicated. The police contacted Melanie's mother at her job, and once she recovered from the shock, she rushed to her weeping daughter's side at Grandma Sarah's house. We interviewed the women in the decedent's old-fashioned front parlor and got their statements. Melanie went home with her mother and Sarah went to her reward. It was a good ending for a life well-lived.

I rode American Hero every day for at least an hour. Time spent with him helped clear my head. At least once a day, Chris tried to call to see how I was. He was working double shifts and was tired, but happy for the overtime. I enjoyed talking to him and grew to miss his calls if for some reason he was too busy to phone.

Chris couldn't have devised a better method of courting me – slowly, simply and thoughtfully. Now I looked forward to our dinner together. I knew what would probably happen this Saturday when I had dinner at his house, but it was time I thought about love again. I was still relatively young, and I hoped my heart was big enough to love two men.

Meanwhile, Katie, Jace and I waited for news about the women in the woods.

At last I got the call from Katie that we'd all been waiting for. She phoned me at seven-thirty in the evening on Wednesday, when I was just back from riding Hero.

'Dana, the forensic archeologist, has finished. I have the report,' Katie said. 'You and Jace will meet at my office tomorrow morning. I want you there at eight o'clock.'

'No way we can meet tonight?' I asked.

'Nope,' Katie said. 'You'll have to wait until morning. I will tell you this: we caught a break. We were able to identify both women.'

'That is good news,' I said. 'Should I bring breakfast? I can defrost a coffee cake. It's homemade. I bought it at the school bake sale.'

'Good idea. Pick up a tray of fresh fruit at the supermarket while you're at it,' she said. 'I'll bring the coffee.'

Jace was already there when I arrived the next morning. Once again, Katie's desk was turned into a buffet. I poured myself some coffee in the I See Dead People mug, cut a slice of the cinnamon coffee cake, then added a few token pieces of fresh fruit to my plate.

When our plates and coffee cups were full, Katie began. 'Jace, we've found some physical evidence that supports your theory these two women might have been Briggs's earlier victims. And they might have died during rough sex. Again, I'm stressing *might*. There's no way to prove the victims even had sex, but one victim had a broken right arm, three broken ribs, and a broken neck. The other had more extensive injuries. They were definitely beaten.'

'Those sound like more severe versions of the injuries LeeAnn had,' Jace said.

'The bodies were skeletonized, so we have no idea what the soft tissue was like,' she said.

'The first woman was a nineteen-year-old who lived in Daltonville, Missouri.'

'That's a little town near Harland,' I told Jace. 'Was her name Paisley Parker? That was LeeAnn's missing friend. She was a working girl who got in a car with the wrong john.'

'No, this woman was Annabelle Futch. She had multiple arrests for prostitution and loitering. We know she had long blonde hair. She was about five feet five and had brown eyes, according to her rap sheet. Dana, the forensic archeologist, found the remnants of what look like black plastic boots, a short skirt made of some sort of synthetic material, and a fur-like jacket. The sizes were small, and so was Annabelle. She was young, blonde and thin.'

'Definitely Briggs's type,' Jace said.

'The killer tried to hide Annabelle's identity. He cut the labels out of her clothes, tossed her ID, even cut off her fingertips. But he forgot one thing: her implants.

'We were able to ID her because at age eighteen she had breast augmentation surgery, and went from an A cup to a double-D cup.'

'Ouch,' I said.

'Right,' Katie said. 'Boobs that big on such a small frame are a painful stretch, and I'm not making a joke.'

'Did anyone report her missing?' Jace asked.

'Sadly, no. Her mother died while Annabelle was missing and we haven't been able to find any other next of kin.'

We stopped for more coffee, and I briefly contemplated the short, sad life of Annabelle Futch.

'Who was our other victim?' Jace said

'The third was a seventeen-year-old girl, a runaway from Keokuk, Iowa, named Brittany Logan Richardson. Before Brittany ran away from home, she'd had very good dental care, and that's how we were able to trace her, through her dental records.

'Brittany disappeared nearly four years ago. She may or may not have been turning tricks to survive. She didn't have any arrest record.'

'Any idea why she took off from her home?' I asked.

'Best guess, according to local law enforcement,' Katie said, 'was that her mother's new boyfriend was way too interested in

Brittany. Mom divorced when the girl was fifteen. Her school
social worker reports Brittany was "acting out" before she left
home, but didn't say what that was.

'From her photos, Brittany was a pretty, almost ethereal-looking
young woman. We know she was about five feet six, slender – a
hundred pounds – with blue eyes and long blonde hair. Again,
Briggs's type.'

'What happened to her?' Jace said.

'Nothing good,' Katie said. She looked sad as she delivered the
grim news. 'Brittany was severely beaten at the time of her death.
She had multiple fractures around her eye sockets and nose. Both
arms and hands had more fractures. She may have held them up
to protect herself when she was beaten to death. She had two
broken ribs and a broken neck. The bones of her right foot and
right tibia were lost to scavengers.'

'Any belongings found with the body?' Jace asked.

'Parts of a plain gray hoodie, jeans and a gray T-shirt. No shoes
or socks.

'We found no connection to Briggs,' Katie said. 'Let me stress
that: nothing. That's it.' She put down her coffee cup.

'No, it's not!' Jace shouted.

I was so surprised I nearly dropped my coffee cup. Jace never
raised his voice, but now he sounded angry.

'That . . . that dirtbag is not getting away with this. I'm driving
out to Harland, and I'm going to find that young woman, that
LeeAnn Higgs. She's going to file a complaint against Briggs
today!'

'Jace,' Katie said, trying to soothe him. 'You know what will
happen if you defy the chief's order to stay away from Briggs.
You'll be fired.'

'I don't care! That dirtbag has hurt his last innocent woman!'

'Wait, Jace!' I said. 'Before you torch your career, let's exhaust
all our leads.'

'Leads? What leads?' He kicked Katie's desk. 'We can't wait
around for something to happen. How do we know that sicko isn't
going hunting tonight?'

'We don't,' I said. 'But I want to check in with Lisa McKim,
Rosanna's mother. I've heard through the grapevine she's hired a
private detective.'

'I can't go with you,' he said.

'I know that. And I can't be working on that case. But I can visit an old family friend and see how the search for her daughter is going. I'll go see her today. Meet you all here tomorrow.'

'Deal,' Jace said. 'I'll bring doughnuts.'

THIRTY-SIX

At ten-thirty that morning, I was at Lisa McKim's split-level. She'd aged ten years in the short time since Jace and I had last seen her. The Lisa I knew was always perfectly turned out from head to toe, with a neat figure. Now she'd gone from trim to scrawny and haggard. Her dark hair was unwashed and untidy and her sweatshirt had egg stains down the front. Lisa wore no make-up, not even lipstick, and her face was pale and lined. I tried hard to hide my shock.

Lisa greeted me at the front door with a tired smile and took me upstairs to the family room. Cozy and lived in, the room had comfortable couches and overstuffed chairs ranged around a working fireplace. Lisa turned off the TV over the mantel and said, 'Have a seat, Angela. What would you like to drink? Coffee, tea? Soda? Water?'

'Water's fine,' I said. I saw a man's shirt on the couch and a pair of men's running shoes on the floor.

'Sorry about those,' she said, whisking them away. 'They belong to Kevin.'

'Rosanna's boyfriend?' I said.

'Yes, that Kevin. He's given up his apartment and moved into my basement so we'd have more money to find Rosanna.'

She handed me a tall glass of ice water and a coaster for the coffee table. The philodendron on the table badly needed water and I was tempted to pour some on it, but feared the ice water would shock its little roots. My mother would have known what to do.

Lisa had poured herself a cup of coffee and sat down next to me on the couch. She held a red cell phone. 'Excuse the phone,' she said. 'I have a special number that people can call with information about Rosanna. It's always with me. When I sleep, it's next to me on my nightstand.'

'Do you get any calls?'

'Lots of them,' Lisa said. 'They're all cranks. Some of them say the nastiest things, calling Rosanna a slut and worse. They don't even know her. Kevin wanted to disconnect the number but I keep hoping someone will see something useful that can help us.'

I took a sip of ice water, then said, 'People can be mean.'

'They can, but there are good ones, too. My neighbors have been so nice. My church has a prayer circle. I believe in the power of prayer, don't you?'

'It can be a great comfort,' I said. Prayer was fine, but I believed God helped those who helped themselves. Turned out Lisa and Kevin were working that angle, too.

'Kevin and I have been doing everything we can to find Rosanna. The search is so expensive I sold my car.'

'Your new red Mustang convertible?' I'd seen Lisa tooling around the Forest on warm days with the top down and her curly hair blowing in the wind. 'That car is your pride and joy.'

'No,' Lisa said. 'My daughter is my pride and joy. I must find her. Kevin and I hired a St. Louis publicist to help us. You must have seen the stories in the newspapers.'

'A few,' I said.

'We've had more than a few.' Lisa handed me a thick stack of papers, including the *St. Louis City Gazette*, the St. Louis *Riverfront Times*, *The Chouteau Forest News*, and some of the bigger Missouri papers, including the *Kansas City Star*, the *Columbia Missourian*, the *Columbia Tribune*, and the *Jefferson City News Tribune*. 'We've spread out the ads to cover a big part of the state,' she said. 'The *KC Star* is on the other side of the state, the Columbia papers are in the middle, and Jeff City is up north.'

She handed me another fat stack. 'These are the Fort Lauderdale, Palm Beach and Miami papers.'

Some were tear sheets of ads with Rosanna's photo and the headline, 'Have You Seen This Woman?' They described Rosanna (five foot six, 124 pounds, dark hair, age twenty-nine) and the date she went missing, along with a phone number.

The rest were news and feature stories along these lines: 'Chouteau Forest Mother Searches for Missing Daughter' and 'Was This Young Woman Abducted Before Her Fort Lauderdale Cruise?' 'Boyfriend of Missing Housekeeper Vows to Keep Searching for "the Woman I Love."'

'We've had some TV interviews, too,' Lisa said. 'I can send you the links. We had these flyers distributed throughout Chouteau County, near the St. Louis airport, the Fort Lauderdale airport, Port Everglades and the cruise ship hotels.' The color flyers were similar to the 'Have You Seen This Woman?' ads.

'Those flyers must have cost a bundle to print and distribute,' I said.

'I sold my mother's silver to pay for them,' she said. 'I only brought it out on holidays, and there won't be any holidays in this house if Rosanna doesn't come home. Kevin sold his comic-book collection to help.

'We also hired a private detective to find Rosanna. We got Gussie Henderson from St. Louis. Do you know him?' She looked at me hopefully.

'I know *of* him,' I said. 'Gussie is supposed to be the best and I'm not just trying to make you feel better. The police detectives I know respect him. Gussie has a national reputation.'

'Thanks, that's a relief. Gussie certainly is thorough. Here in St. Louis, he interviewed people at the airport and with the airlines. He talked to taxi drivers, Uber drivers, even some of the airport sky caps. Nothing. Then he flew to Fort Lauderdale and interviewed the people at the cruise line, at the hotels that cater to cruise ship travelers, the airport, Uber drivers and taxi drivers. He has amazing sources, and he still had no luck.

'I made a copy of his report for you and that nice detective,' she said, and handed me a fat manila envelope.

'Jace Budewitz,' I said.

'That's him. Has he found anything?' Lisa asked.

I didn't have the heart to tell her that Jace had been ordered to leave Briggs alone, so I gave Lisa an edited version of the truth: 'He tracked down one of the young women that Briggs brought to his house. Her name was LeeAnn.'

'Amazing.'

'It was quite a feat, but Rosanna's diary was a big help,' I said.

'How was she, that young woman? Did he hurt her?'

I knew Lisa was looking for reassurance that her own daughter was safe.

'LeeAnn was having a drink at the local bar,' I said. Well, it was the truth.

'But you don't have any good leads?' she asked.

'We're still looking.' Hoping to change the subject quickly, I asked, 'What did Gussie the detective conclude?'

'That the trail started and stopped at Briggs's house. He thinks Rosanna never left the property – she's on it, dead—' Lisa's voice broke at that word, but she managed to pull herself together to gulp out, 'or alive.'

'And what do you think, Lisa?'

'She's alive. My girl's alive. I can feel it. She was part of me. I carried her in my body. We've always had a special connection. Please find her for me and bring her home.' Lisa gave me a tentative smile and my heart cracked in two.

THIRTY-SEVEN

After I left Lisa McKim's house, I couldn't wait to tell Katie and Jace about my visit. Too bad I had to wait almost a full day until we met again, on Friday morning. I was electric with restless energy. I paced my bedroom, and spotted a cobweb in the corner and another by the closet. The windows were streaked with winter dirt and the curtains were dingy.

In fact, the whole upstairs could use a good spring cleaning. I wore myself out washing windows, scrubbing floors, and dusting everything that didn't move – even the baseboards.

When I found myself scrubbing the pull-down stairs to my attic, I knew I'd gone clean out of my mind. I went up those stairs maybe once a year, at the most.

I shut the door to the upstairs hall closet that hid the stairs and cleaned one more thing – me. It was nine-thirty. Then I fixed myself a quick sandwich and fell into bed.

By eight o'clock the next morning, we were all in Katie's office.

Jace and I were petting Katie's pup, Cutter. Now eleven weeks old, the golden-lab mix looked like a fuzzy yellow toy. He was wearing a blue nylon harness and dragging a matching leash.

'I'm leash training him,' Katie said. 'He's catching on quickly. The training video says I'm supposed to let him drag the leash around so he gets used to both the feel of the leash and the harness.'

I picked up the pup and said, 'Whoa, Katie, he's a big boy. What does he weigh?'

'Twenty-two pounds,' she said. 'The vet thinks he'll be seventy pounds when he's full grown.'

Cutter slurped my nose.

'Don't let him get too close to your face,' she said. 'He has a bad habit of nipping noses. He nailed Monty after dinner yesterday and spent the night in his crate.' She stopped a minute and said, 'Cutter's crate, not Monty's.'

'We get it,' I said, and set the pup down. He raced back and forth across the small office, bursting with playful energy. Jace was on the floor growling at the pup when Katie called us to order.

'Enough with the puppy love,' she said. 'He's already spoiled.' At her command, Cutter reluctantly went back into his crate. Jace and I ate our breakfast of hot Krispy Kreme doughnuts and strong coffee, and we were ready to work.

I told them about my visit to Lisa McKim's house and her efforts to find Rosanna, even hiring a detective to fly down to Fort Lauderdale.

Jace raised an eyebrow. 'Rosanna's mom hired Gussie Henderson? The St. Louis PI? Impressive. He's a retired cop. Extremely thorough.'

I gave them copies of Gussie's report and they both read it.

'The detective concludes that the trail starts and stops at Briggs Bellerive's place,' Katie said. 'He thinks Rosanna never left the property, and she's there, either dead or alive.'

'Judging by when Terri the track star was kidnapped and when her body was found,' I said, 'the best guess is that Briggs stashed her somewhere on the property and kept her alive for several months before he killed her.'

'How long has Rosanna been missing, Jace?' Katie asked.

'Seven weeks,' Jace said. 'If that kidnap 'em and keep 'em alive theory is true, he could be tiring of Rosanna by now and kill her at any time.'

'Rosanna might be hidden in that vast mansion,' I said.

'Maybe,' Jace said. 'I was sure that's where he'd hide her. That's why I had two teams search that place with a fine-tooth comb. I even went over the architect's plans from St. Louis County – including the new kitchen addition. I checked for secret rooms and hidden passages. My team went through all eight-thousand square feet thoroughly.'

'What about the guesthouse?' I said. 'Briggs called it his "playhouse."'

'Couldn't find the plans for that place, but we searched it from top to bottom.'

'Including the attic?' I asked.

'There wasn't one,' he said.

'There has to be, Jace. Briggs told me his guesthouse is an exact copy of my home, which was originally built as a guesthouse on the Du Pres property. Both houses were built in the 1920s. Mine has a small attic. I can barely stand upright in it. It doesn't have any windows, just a little square air vent where the roof peaks.

'When you searched Briggs's guesthouse, did you check the upstairs hall closet?' I asked. 'My closet hides a set of pull-down stairs that lead to the attic.'

'Let me check my notes. I brought them with me.'

Jace had transferred the Briggs compound search files, photos and videos to a flash drive. He plugged it into his iPad and paged through the information. Finally, he said, 'Here it is! The upstairs closet was opened and searched. We found a water heater inside. A tall one, forty-gallon size.'

'A water heater?' I said. 'My water heater is in the basement. I'm sure that Briggs's guesthouse has a basement.'

Except I wasn't sure. Not any more. Briggs's upstairs water heater really threw me. 'Maybe the houses weren't exactly alike, after all,' I said.

That water heater in the upstairs hall nagged at me. I couldn't let it go. 'Do you have more photos of the upstairs water heater in Briggs's guesthouse?' I asked.

'Sure.' Jace opened another file folder on his computer and said,

'Here they are. A whole gallery devoted to the water heater: close-ups, medium shots and distance shots.'

There it was, an ordinary white water heater.

'Did you search the basement?' I asked.

'Of course,' Jace said. 'Here are those photos.'

The basement was just like mine and a thousand other older houses in the area – rough white limestone walls and a concrete floor. One side had wooden shelves for storage, stacked with dozens of cardboard boxes with labels like *pots and pans*, *Xmas decorations* and *canning jars*.

'We opened every box,' Jace said. 'They all held exactly what they were labeled.'

The other side of the basement held a washer and dryer, a big old furnace and next to the furnace a . . . water heater.

'Two water heaters?' I said. 'Why would a twenty-five-hundred square-foot house need two big hot water heaters?'

'It wouldn't,' Jace said. He looked crestfallen, and oh, so tired.

'Can you search that closet again?' I asked.

'No way. In fact, cops need to maintain a presence on the scene even overnight, if we had planned to come back the next day. I had a big enough team that we executed the warrant in one day. We can't get in that guesthouse without another warrant,' Jace said, 'and there's no way we'll get one now.'

'It's because Briggs lawyered up.' I felt bitter and angry. 'The rich have special privileges in the Forest.'

'No, not true,' Jace said. 'Money has nothing to do with that. Even the poorest house in the Forest would have the same protection against unreasonable search and seizure. This happened because I screwed up. The buck stops here.' I'd never seen Jace look so defeated.

'I just hope I don't have Rosanna's death on my conscience,' he said. 'I'll never forgive myself if something happens to that young woman.'

THIRTY-EIGHT

A discouraged, slump-shouldered Jace left for work. There was nothing Katie or I could say that would make him feel better. He was determined to blame himself for missing the water heater clue. But I had the germ of an idea. I thought I knew how to get into the guesthouse without getting all of us in trouble.

Jace was hardly out the door when I heard frantic yipping and scratching coming from Cutter's crate.

'What's wrong with the pup?' I asked.

'He needs to go for a walk,' Katie said. 'I ran out of puppy pee pads, so I'll have to take him outside.'

'I'll take him,' I said.

'Really? You won't mind?' She looked grateful. 'I have work to finish.'

'I'd love to,' I said. 'Is it OK to take him for a long walk?'

'It will be good for him,' Katie said. 'But he's going to drive you crazy sniffing every tree and peeing on every plant.'

'I can't be any crazier than I already am.'

'OK, you asked for it. If you have any problems, use these,' Katie said. She handed me a bag of puppy treats. I stuck them in my pocket.

'You use bribery to train him?' I asked.

'I prefer to call it positive reinforcement,' she said.

I opened the crate and Cutter romped out. I grabbed the fuzz ball's leash. The pup didn't walk. He had a swift, rolling waddle, like a teddy bear on the loose. I held the leash as Cutter led the way out of Katie's office and ran down the hall. I could hardly keep up with him.

Once outside, he slowed down, taking time to pee on every weed in our path in the parking lot. Really, SOS needed a better lawn service. It was too bad Cutter wasn't spraying weed killer.

I guided him to my car, and Cutter hopped into the passenger seat, paws on my dashboard. I scratched his ears and said, 'You,

Your Adorableness, are going to be my secret weapon to get me on Briggs's property and into that guesthouse.'

'Yip!' said the pup, wagging his tail.

And we were off. Like many Forest mansions, Briggs's home was guarded by impressive gates and stern security guards – in front. Most estates were not completely fenced where their land ran through the woodlands that linked the Forest mansions and gave the place its name.

I followed the system of trails that ran through the Forest behind the big mansions. I was pretty sure that Briggs's estate was either unfenced or fenced with something easy to get through. I stopped at a little park about a quarter-mile from Briggs's house. Cutter jumped out of the car, eager for a longer walk. I guided him though the park to the trail that led toward the Bellerive mansion.

As Katie had bragged, Cutter was surprisingly well leash-trained. He stopped once to bark at a butterfly. Another time he yapped at a squirrel and started after it with his rolling, roly-poly run. The smart squirrel zipped up a tree and taunted Cutter with loud chattering. I pulled the pup away and he was off again, peeing on every leaf, weed and sapling. I wasn't sure where he stored all that water. Finally, our comical walk was over. I recognized the ice-white chimneys of the Bellerive estate towering over the trees. As we got closer, I saw the back of the vast property was protected by three rusting strands of wire on equally decrepit poles. Sure enough, there was a hole in the fence. The bottom tier of wire had snapped.

Cutter easily waddled through the hole. I got down on the ground and checked that the green vine curling over the strands wasn't poison ivy.

'Leaves of three, let it be,' was the old warning chant, though it wasn't entirely reliable. These woods teemed with poison ivy, poison oak and poison sumac. I'd learned through bitter experience what all their leaves looked like. This vine turned out to be honeysuckle, and when summer came, its fragrance would be delicious.

I slid unharmed through the hole in the fence and shortened the leash to keep Cutter closer to me. If I encountered a security patrol, I could grab the pup and run back through the fence. We walked through the spring woods, following a small creek lined with ferns.

Cutter saw a frog, ran up and sniffed it, then froze when the frog hopped away. We followed a deer trail next to the creek until the trees parted and we came to the back of Briggs's guesthouse. It was eerie seeing a carbon copy of my home on the edge of the woods.

My heart was pounding, but not from fear. I was afraid that Rosanna might be in that house – and afraid she wasn't. I had the oddest feeling that time was running out for Briggs's missing housekeeper, and if I didn't find her here, we'd never find her. Not alive, anyway.

Cutter was tugging on the leash, dragging me toward the guesthouse. I gave him more slack and followed his lead. He went around to the side of the house, where the outside basement entrance was on my home. Same here, except Briggs's basement doorway was surrounded by pots of red and white petunias. Cutter lifted his leg to anoint the flowers, and I pulled him away. 'Cutter! No!' I hissed.

Now he was down the steps, pawing at the entrance to the basement. The door was painted white, like my basement door, and it had the same lock. It used an old-fashioned skeleton key.

I felt in my purse for my keys. Yep, I had my basement door key. It should fit this door. Cutter was pawing frantically at the door, yipping and scratching to get in. I could hear thumping and banging coming from somewhere inside. The sounds were faint, but they excited Cutter. Now he was throwing himself at the door with all his puppy might.

I tried to peer in through the basement windows, but they were boarded up. I had to get inside. What if Rosanna was in there? Were those her muffled screams?

Before I unlocked the door, I called Katie on my cell phone.

'Where the hell are you?' she said. 'Did you walk my freakin' dog to Kansas City?' She sounded more worried than angry.

'He's fine. Cutter does really well on the leash, too. I'm at Briggs's guesthouse. I'm about to open the basement door.'

'Are you out of your fuckin' mind?' Katie yelled into the phone. 'You broke into the Bellerive estate? If you're caught, you'll be fired. Fired! With no references! The whole Forest will come down on you! You'll be ruined!'

'I have to take the chance,' I said. 'I have no choice.'

'You have every choice,' she said, her voice low and slow. 'And going inside that guesthouse is the worst possible choice. You could be killed.'

'I'm going in anyway,' I said. 'Don't worry. I have my Swiss Army knife and pepper spray.'

'Pepper spray! Pepper spray won't do shit if that maniac's got a gun.'

Cutter was frantic to get inside, and so was I.

'Sorry, Katie. If you don't hear from in me in half an hour, call Jace.'

'Angela!' Katie shouted.

'What?'

'Be careful!'

'I will,' I said. I was touched.

'I mean be careful with my puppy. Don't let anything happen to him.'

I switched off the call, and reached in my purse for my pepper spray. I transferred it to my pocket where I could easily reach it.

As I expected, my skeleton key worked on Briggs's basement door. The old door swung open with a horror-movie creak. The pup let out a yelp of joy and ran into the dark basement. He'd pulled his leash out of my hand and disappeared into the shadows. Damn, I needed leash training, too.

'Cutter!' I whispered. 'Cutter! Get back here!'

I felt for a light switch near the door, but couldn't find one, so I waited on the threshold for my eyes to adjust to the darkness. I turned on my phone's flashlight app and the darkness swallowed it.

Cutter let out a terrified yelp.

Now I heard whimpers and puppy cries from the far end of the basement. Through the gloom, I could see Cutter cowering in a corner by the washer-dryer. I could hear him crying. A shadow loomed over him, almost as tall as I was. The puppy was frantically yelping and squealing. Upstairs, I heard pounding and screaming and a muffled cry. Was that someone shouting, 'Help! Help!'

I couldn't tell. But every nerve was alive, fizzing and alert.

I had to rescue Cutter first. Then I'd go upstairs.

'Screeeech! Yip! Yip! Yip!' said the frightened pup. 'Ow! Ow! Ow!'

THIRTY-NINE

Keeping my hand on the pepper spray in my pocket, I stepped over the threshold into the bottomless cave of a basement. I saw an old, dirty mop leaning by the door and grabbed it. It smelled like mildew, but I might be able to use it.

'Cutter!' I called. 'Cutter, I'm here. I'm coming, little dude.'

I followed the whimpers to the far corner of the room. Cutter was cowering behind the washer. His whimpers were heartbreaking.

'What's wrong, dude?' I asked.

His only answer was a frightened yip. I peered around the edge of the washer and saw the furry little pup rolled into a ball, being terrorized by . . . a mouse. A little gray field mouse. Standing its ground, teeth bared.

'Shoo!' I said, and prodded the ferocious mouse with the handle of the mop. It scurried behind the dryer.

Cutter's leash was tangled in the water pipes behind the washer and he couldn't get free. As I reached carefully around to free Cutter's tangled leash, I saw the mouse protectively shielding six babies in a nest of dryer fluff.

'Never underestimate the power of a mama, young pup,' I said, as I finally freed him. I picked him up and put him on top the dryer, where I brushed the cobwebs out of his fur and attached the leash. I couldn't keep him on the dryer for long. The pup was eager to go – and leave the site of his humiliation, no doubt.

Firmly grasping the leash this time, I followed the pup as he bounded up the basement steps. He stopped at the top of the steps and pawed at the door. I followed him, and saw a light switch at the top of the stairs.

'Let there be light,' I said to the pup, and suddenly, we were both blinking in the well-lit basement. Now I could see everything that Jace had seen during his search – the shelves of labeled boxes on one side and the washer, dryer and water heater on the other. He'd assured me there was no place to hide someone in the basement, and since I could hear muffled yelling and thumping from upstairs, I decided to move my search upward.

I tried the door.

Locked.

This door also needed a skeleton key. As the pup danced impatiently at my feet, I unlocked this door, too, and we were in the kitchen. As Cutter dragged me through the kitchen, I saw it was far more updated than mine. That breakfast bar was a nice touch, I thought, then focused back on where we were.

Whoa! What was that? I pulled on the leash and Cutter came tumbling to a stop. Someone had been using the coffee maker. There was at least a cup of dark sludge in the pot. Was the killer in here?

The muffled screams were louder now. Cutter tugged impatiently on his leash, and I followed his pudgy body through the dining room (clean but dusty) to the living room with the showcase furniture (tidy but dusty), to the hall with the guest bath (sparkling clean and unused), and up the stairs to the second floor.

Now the muffled cries were still louder. I could hear thumping overhead.

The pup frantically pawed the hall door.

I opened it and saw a hot water heater, just like Jace said. With no dust on the top. Odd. Water heaters were always dusty. The rest of the furniture was dusty, so who was dusting the hot water heater?

Stranger still, the water heater was not connected to anything.

Now the screams were sharper and more frantic. I looked up and saw the pull-down cord for the attic stairs. It was attached to a hook so it wouldn't dangle down.

I had to move the water heater. I tried to pull it toward me, but it wouldn't budge. It was not only heavy, it was awkward to grasp. The closet was so narrow, I couldn't get a good grip on it. I needed something to help me. Cutter was at my feet, dragging his leash. His leash! That was it.

I unhooked the leash, lassoed the bulky water heater, and dragged it out of the closet. I pulled down the steps. Unlike my attic steps, these had a retractable railing.

Now the cries were strident and the thumps were thunderous.

Before I could grab Cutter and put on his leash again, the pudgy puppy ran up ahead of me, barking and yipping.

As I ran up the steps, I was hit hard with a horrible odor. Someone in my business always recognized that stink.

Decomposition.

My stomach flip-flopped, and I tried not to gag. I held onto the stair rail to keep from vomiting.

Was I too late to the rescue?

If that's true, why was I hearing muffled screams, thumps, and cries for help? And why was Cutter barking so hard?

There was only one way to find out.

Pepper spray in hand, I cautiously climbed to the top of the stairs.

FORTY

Rosanna had both hands cuffed to a tarnished brass bed. At least, I thought this poor woman was the missing house-keeper. She was so thin, bloody and dirty, it was hard to tell. She was pulling on the cuffs and trying to scream. Her face was red and her mouth was covered with silver duct tape. Sweat gushed down her forehead.

The attic was hot, airless and windowless. The only light came from the louvered vent in the eaves. It had the same low ceiling as my attic.

I crab-walked over the dusty wooden floor to the bed, trying to soothe the frightened woman. 'It's OK, Rosanna, it's OK,' I said. 'Hold still while I get that tape off.'

I peeled off the tape and Rosanna was gasping for breath. 'Thank you. Thank you.' Her voice was a dry croak.

'It's OK,' I said. 'You're safe.'

'No!' she said, her eyes frantic with fear. 'He's coming back.'

Rosanna was badly bruised, especially around her neck – and bleeding from about four different areas – neck, upper arms, chest and legs. She was wearing a thin blue cotton nightgown, stiff with dried blood.

I called 911 and tried to make them understand this was an emergency. I had a hard time convincing the 911 operator, who must have lived in the Forest.

'Are you saying the victim is in the Bellerive guesthouse and Mr Bellerive doesn't know it?'

'Mr Bellerive is— Oh, just get here fast, OK? It's an emergency.'

'Please stay on the line, ma'am.'

'Can't!' I hung up and called Katie.

'I found her,' I said. 'Guesthouse attic. Get here as fast as you can. She's hurt and Briggs may come back and attack us both.'

'We're on our way,' Katie said. 'ETA ten minutes. Keep the phone on so we know what's happening.'

'Help is coming, Rosanna,' I said.

'Hurry!' she said. 'He could come up here any minute!'

In the attic's southwest corner was a faded red velvet camelback sofa with a tattered quilt on it. The quilt and the couch were covered with suspicious brown stains. The smell of decomposition seemed to be coming from both. The pup was pawing at them and rolling around on the quilt, possibly destroying evidence.

'Cutter!' I said. 'Come here.'

He ignored me until I said the magic words. 'Treat, Cutter, treat!' Then his little round body came bobbing over. I fed him a couple of treats.

'Sorry for the delay, Rosanna,' I said. 'Let me get you out of those handcuffs.'

Fortunately, they were cheap cuffs. I knew how to open those, thanks to a tip from an old cop. I opened my Swiss Army knife and used the screwdriver to pry away the two metal parts. The tiny screwdriver made my hands feel big and clumsy. It kept slipping before it finally worked. I twisted once more and Rosanna was free.

She was exhausted and weak. As I gently rubbed some circulation back into her raw, bruised wrists, I noticed the food stains down the front of her gown. Rosanna saw me looking at them.

'He wouldn't uncuff me so I could eat,' she said, her voice weak and tearful. 'He fed me my dinners. I'd spit the food back at him and he'd beat me.'

Suddenly, Cutter was raising a racket. He sprinted to the top of the stairs and barked frantically, bouncing up and down.

'It's Briggs!' Rosanna said. I heard the terror in her voice.

I also heard heavy footsteps on the stairs. Too late to pull them up. There was no railing or barrier around the stairs.

'He's bringing lunch,' Rosanna said.

Briggs wasn't bringing lunch – he was bringing trouble. I looked around desperately for some way to stop him. Damn! I'd left the mop downstairs.

'There's nothing up here to use as a weapon,' Rosanna said. 'Believe me, I've looked.'

I handed her the barking puppy. 'Take Cutter in the corner behind the sofa. Hide!'

Rosanna staggered across the attic with the squirming pup while I pushed the heavy brass bed across the room to the stair opening. It was hard going, since I had to crouch. One final push and the bed partly fell into the stairway and became a barrier.

Cutter was barking louder. Now I heard someone almost at the top of the steep stairs. 'Move that bed, or I'll kill you both,' commanded a cold voice. Briggs. 'Now!'

I didn't move from my spot on the side of the stair opening. Neither did the brass bed. It still covered the top of the stair opening.

Briggs fired a weapon – probably a shotgun – and the mattress exploded, tufts of stuffing flying everywhere. He fired again, and the bedstead shifted.

Now he could squeeze through. I brought out my Swiss Army knife, though I doubted it was any good in close combat, and my pepper spray.

Briggs would be up here in a moment. I could see Rosanna in the corner, struggling to hold the puppy. He was scratching her arms and nipping her fingers, trying to get free. Rosanna tried to hang on, but she was too weak to hold him.

I figured my pepper spray was the best bet and prayed it would subdue Briggs. But that stuff was tricky to use. I only had one shot.

Briggs's angry head popped over the top of the stairs, and I hit him with the spray. He ducked at the last second, and I got him, but mostly the top of his head. Some did get in his eyes and that infuriated him.

Briggs bellowed and fired his shotgun. The shot grazed my arm. He clubbed me in the head with the shotgun butt.

Now I was dazed and bleeding. And desperate. Briggs would kill Rosanna if help didn't arrive soon.

Cutter broke free from the kidnapped housekeeper, and launched himself at Briggs. The furry yellow missile landed on the killer's face. The pup clamped his teeth on Briggs's nose. Briggs screamed, but the pup wouldn't let go. He had the killer firmly by the beezer. Briggs howled – at least as loud as he could howl with a twenty-two-pound furball on his face.

Briggs dropped the shotgun during the struggle. He couldn't remove the pup without removing a big chunk of his nose. I grabbed the shotgun and clubbed him over the head with it, and managed to avoid the pup.

Briggs and the pup – who was still hanging onto the killer's face – tumbled down the stairs.

Now it was blessedly quiet. I heard sirens right outside.

'The police are here, Rosanna,' I said. 'Briggs can't hurt you any more.'

She was weeping quietly in the corner.

I peered down the stairs. Far below, Briggs was unconscious on the floor, his leg twisted at an awkward angle. Cutter was still clinging to his nose, chewing it like an old shoe.

'Briggs is out cold, Rosanna,' I said. 'I think his leg may be broken. All we have to do now is hang on as well as Cutter did.'

FORTY-ONE

'Cutter! Let go!'

I could hear Katie at the foot of the stairs, trying to get the pup to stop chewing on the unconscious Briggs's nose. He did, but not before a four-by-three-inch piece of skin was missing.

Yep, Cutter had gulped it down, but none of us said that out loud. Katie wiped the blood off her pup's mouth and sent the schnozz-swallowing pup upstairs, where I fed him treats and praised him. The official report would say that Briggs's nose was 'damaged during the fracas.'

Jace dragged Briggs out of the entrance to the staircase and he and Katie raced upstairs. Katie checked Rosanna first, and made sure that the paramedics carried her out of the attic to the hospital.

Then she checked me. 'Looks like you've caught part of a shotgun blast to the shoulder. You'll have to go to the ER to get the pellets removed. You may need arthroscopic surgery. Don't worry, that's not as serious as it sounds. You also got clubbed in the head. Maybe it will knock some sense into you.'

'Katie!'

'OK, I'm pissed that you let my dog off the leash and he chomped Briggs's nose.'

'I needed his leash to move the water heater,' I said. 'And I saved Rosanna. And so did Cutter.'

'OK, we'll talk about this later. You've got a nasty wound on your hairline from the shotgun butt. You're going to need plastic surgery. You'll probably get antibiotics and a tetanus booster shot. You'll be out of the hospital in a day.'

In time for my date with Chris, I thought.

That's almost what happened, except the hospital kept me in for two days. I had a concussion and there was dirt or something on the shotgun butt, so I was stuck in the hospital while the docs dealt with the concussion, did surgery on my arm to remove three shotgun pellets, plastic surgery on my hairline, and IV antibiotics for the whole mess. Part of my hair was shaved for the plastic surgery, but I knew it would grow back. I was groggy from the painkillers. I had my date in bed with Chris that Saturday night. Too bad it was a hospital bed.

On Saturday afternoon, Katie had brought my good pink robe, so Chris didn't see me in that ugly hospital gown, and she wrapped my bandaged head in a pink-and-blue scarf.

At dinner time, I was happy to pass on the hospital's mystery meat, stewed green beans and apple sauce.

Chris arrived with flowers – a bright spring bouquet with a pink ribbon around the vase and a dinner he'd cooked himself. He pulled the curtain around my bed for privacy. We dined on cold lobster salad with crusty French bread and had chocolate mousse for dessert.

Chris looked so strong and handsome in his dark sports coat and gray pants.

'How are you feeling?' he asked. 'They wouldn't let me see you yesterday. They said you had two surgeries.'

'I did, and I slept most of the day.'

'You're the bravest woman I've ever known,' he said.

I laughed. 'The pup is the real hero.'

'Don't underrate yourself,' he said. 'And you're avoiding my question. How do you feel?'

'Much better since you're here,' I said.

Then he kissed me – a deep, yearning kiss that took away all my pain.

EPILOGUE

We blamed the dog.

It wasn't fair, but it worked. I claimed that I was walking the pup when Cutter got loose and ran through the hole in the fence at the Bellerive estate. I chased him to the guesthouse. The basement door was open and the pup ran in and up the steps. By that time, I could hear Rosanna's muffled screams. I tracked the pup upstairs to the hall closet, pulled out the water heater, ran upstairs and found Rosanna. I called 911, and then, worried the operator didn't understand the urgency, I called Katie. Jace just happened to be consulting with Katie, and the two of them rushed to the estate.

This story had more holes than a lace curtain, but it allowed the bosses to save face. After all, they'd told Jace to stay away from Briggs, the killer, calling him 'one of our finest citizens.' But Jace had ignored their orders and saved Rosanna. Greiman had sense enough to keep quiet about getting everything wrong, and the powers that be appreciated his tact – and his silence. Like Jace said, the man was a cockroach and, as usual, he survived. Jace was given a letter of commendation in his file. It was done quietly, of course. Like I said, the Forest knew how to keep its secrets.

Besides, we were heroes. Especially Cutter. The mayor gave him a special ceremony at Chouteau Forest City Hall, where the adorable pup got a medal. The mayor clutched the fuzzy photo op as if his (political) life depended on it. Rosanna presented Cutter with a raw steak. I couldn't watch the dog eat it.

As for Briggs Bellerive, he was taken to SOS hospital with a concussion, a broken right leg – that left him with a permanent limp – and of course, the gnawed nose. Briggs was no longer the Forest's most eligible bachelor. Thanks to Cutter, he was now as ugly outside as he was inside.

Briggs's mutilated nose needed what's called a 'full-thickness graft.' The surgeon removed a piece of skin from his groin to graft over Briggs's mauled nose.

Too bad SOS's best plastic surgeon was on vacation. The man on duty could be called competent, on a good day. The surgeon told Briggs he was 'lucky' the graft had taken. When Briggs finally healed, his nose still looked like a dog had chewed it. In prison, the nicest name he was called was Dog Face.

And Briggs did go to prison – forever. The evidence against him was overwhelming. In addition to Rosanna's testimony, the police found fingerprints, hair and DNA for all three dead women. Missouri was a death penalty state, and Briggs, whose cruelty knew no bounds, was terrified he'd be executed. The DNA for the flower in Terri's pocket was a Salmon Baby nasturtium, which matched Briggs's prized plants.

The Chouteau County prosecuting attorney made a deal: Briggs could get life in prison with no possibility of parole. But only if he talked.

And Briggs did. He confessed that he enjoyed killing his best friend, way back in high school. Strangling the boy during sex was a thrill that Briggs wanted to relive. When he was packed off to the UK to go to school, he kept himself under strict control. But once he returned home, he felt bolder. He began to allow himself 'celebrations' – his word for kidnaping a victim and committing erotic strangling. Briggs kept a 'special few' of the women alive in the attic and had sex with them, strangling them with garden string. Sometimes he'd go too far and kill his victim. Then he'd move their bodies to the couch, until it was safe to move them without being caught. At that point, he would drive the bodies in his Range Rover to the edge of the woods, then use his wheelbarrow to take them deeper into the forest and bury them. He murdered his high school friend and three women, including Terri.

Briggs saw Terri on her run, and was struck by her blonde beauty. He began stalking her. She was different from his other victims – she was from the Forest, and she wasn't a lost waif like so many of them. He admired her strength. He read about her success and her scholarships and wanted her. He saw her running one afternoon, identified himself and said he wanted to talk about sponsoring her career. Briggs said he knew she'd need the best trainers and those were expensive. He asked her not to say anything, not even to her mother. They could bat some ideas around and when they had a deal, she'd be free to tell everyone. Terri knew his reputation as a philanthropist and thought it would be safe to visit him. She agreed to meet him the next day.

He drove Terri to his home on Rosanna's day off. Instead of offering the young track star sponsorship, he tried to seduce her over tea. Terri wanted nothing to do with him. To someone her age, Briggs was an old man. Briggs said he understood. He offered her more tea and roofied her drink. Terri woke up in the attic, handcuffed to the bed, her mouth duct-taped. Briggs told Rosanna to keep the staff out of the guesthouse. That was fine with the housekeeper. She had enough to do. Briggs found Terri a 'disappointment' after a while and killed her. He went back to his old pattern of picking up young women who wouldn't fight back.

After Briggs buried the track star, his housekeeper wondered why he'd bought a new wheelbarrow and thrown away a perfectly good one. Rosanna's curiosity may have saved lives. Briggs avoided killing more young women after Terri the track star. But he grew restless. Briggs knew he had to get rid of Rosanna 'if he was ever going to have some fun.'

He also knew the speculation about how Casey Anthony had avoided a murder conviction. Briggs let the barbecue meat rot in his Range Rover, then bought more meat for the real barbecue and blamed Rosanna. He couldn't let her leave his compound. He was sure she knew he'd killed those women. Briggs terrorized his housekeeper and planned to kill her on Saturday – the day after Cutter found him.

Rosanna spent a week in the hospital, and many months in counseling. Lisa, her mother, and the faithful Kevin were there to help her through the worst. Six months after her ordeal, Kevin asked Rosanna to marry him. She said yes.

Monty represented Rosanna in a civil suit against Briggs. They settled out of court for an undisclosed amount. Rosanna and Kevin were able to buy a new house and Lisa got a new red convertible for Mother's Day. Rosanna is going back to college for a degree in hospitality management.

Monty also represented LeeAnn Higgs in a civil suit against Briggs. Her dramatic photos convinced Briggs's lawyers to also settle out of court. LeeAnn retired from the oldest profession and went to college. Three more of her colleagues also sued and got a good payday. The Uber driver testified that the women were badly beaten when he drove them home.

Oh, and after Monty made a phone call to Evarts Evans, the letter of reprimand was removed from my file.

There was one other case settled during the Briggs brouhaha. Remember Shirley, the woman who mutilated her sick old mother's finger to get her diamond ring? The autopsy revealed that the mother had been poisoned by the eye drops in her tea. Shirley pleaded guilty to first-degree murder and is serving life without parole. Her sister, Ellen, got the ring.

As for Melissa DeMille, the pretty fourth wife of the obscenely rich hedge funder, there was no way to pin Dr Robert Scott's death on her, but his widow, Samantha, and her Forest society friends meted out their own punishment. They made sure that Melissa's husband, Joe DeMille, found out all about Melissa's adventure with Dr Bob, including their champagne-fueled romp at the St. Louis hotel. He filed for divorce. Melissa had signed a prenup, but thanks to her adultery, Joe cut her off without a dime. She now lives in low-rent Toonerville and works as a checker at a Walmart.

A month after I got out of the hospital, I was healed enough to have that dinner with Chris at his house. Mario fixed my hair to cover the plastic surgery scars at my hairline, then treated me to a manicure and facial.

It was a warm night, and Chris served dinner by candlelight on his back deck. Surrounded by pots of fragrant flowers, we had a spring salad with pomegranate dressing, chicken and asparagus in white wine, and lots of crisp, dry wine. For dessert, he brought out warm chocolate sauce and strawberries. We began feeding each other chocolate-drenched strawberries, and then we were kissing, and then we were in Chris's big bed. A bed that held no memories for me, good or bad.

I won't give you the details, but I will say this: some things are worth waiting for.

THE INSIDER'S GUIDE TO CHOUTEAU COUNTY PRONUNCIATION

Missourians have their own way of pronouncing words and names. We're called the Show Me State, and you don't tell us how to say something. The French were among the first settlers, but we resist Frenchifying words.

Chouteau is SHOW-toe.

Du Pres is Duh-PRAY.

Gravois is GRAH-voy.

Detective Ray Greiman is GRI-mun. His name is mispronounced German.

So is my name. It's pronounced VEETS, and rhymes with Beets.

Missouri can't even decide how to pronounce its own name. The eastern part, which includes St. Louis, calls itself Missour-ee. That's how Angela pronounces the state's name. In the west, which has Kansas City, it's called Missour-uh. Politicians have mastered the fine art of adjusting their pronunciation to please whichever part of the state they're in.

Elaine Viets